DAVID DONACHIE was born in Edinburgh in 1944. He has always had an abiding interest in the naval history of the eighteenth and nineteenth centuries as well as the Roman Republic, and under the pen-name of Jack Ludlow, has published a number of historical adventure novels. David lives in Deal with his partner, the novelist Sarah Grazebrook.

Enemies at Every Turn

DAVID DONACHIE

Allison & Busby Limited
12 Fitzroy Mews
London W1T 6DW
www.allisonandbusby.com

First published in Great Britain by Allison & Busby in 2011.
This paperback edition published by Allison & Busby in 2012.

Copyright © 2011 by DAVID DONACHIE

A CIP catalogue record for this book is available from
the British Library.

10 9 8 7 6 5 4 3 2 1

ISBN 978-0-7490-1149-9

Typeset in 12.75/16 pt Adobe Garamond Pro by
Allison & Busby Ltd.

The paper used for this Allison & Busby publication
has been produced from trees that have been legally sourced
from well-managed and credibly certified forests.

Printed and bound by
CPI Group (UK) Ltd, Croydon, CR0 4YY

This book is dedicated to my elder brother
Victor Donachie
who died after a short illness while it was being written.
Not many people are lucky enough to have
such a person in their life:
a generous friend, a wise advisor
and, most of all, great company.
Every book I write has a hero;
in the book of my life he was and still is mine!

CHAPTER ONE

Set free by the Justices of Sandwich, John Pearce was strongly tempted to stop off in Deal or nearby St Margaret's Bay in the search for those who had got him into trouble in the first place, a pit so deep it had very nearly seen him incarcerated for a decade or transported to the recently established penal colony at Botany Bay.

That had to be set aside; he had pressing business in Dover and not just to ensure the welfare of the two companions who had saved him from such a fate by freely volunteering to serve in the King's Navy. He also needed to intercept a letter, the contents of which were no longer accurate, that by force of time being his primary task.

Some relief was afforded when he learnt that the mail coach which would carry his letter to London would not depart until the following day, yet it was a misfortune that he found in the person of the Dover postmaster a fellow who, for sheer inflexibility, deserved to have his ears boxed, for he would not hear that the passage of the mail should be interfered with in any way.

'The letter is addressed to a Mrs Barclay at 18 Jockey's Fields in Holborn,' Pearce insisted. 'I know that because I not only wrote it, but paid for it to be sent. If you dig it out you will see upon it the superscription with my name.'

A portly fellow, full of his own importance, the postmaster's hands went to grasp the blue facings on his bright-red coat while on his face there appeared an expression that attested to a forthcoming refusal based on sound practice and fixed rules.

'So you say, sir, so you say, but you must know that by recent statute once stamped it becomes the property of the person to whom it is addressed. It's more'n my position be worth to interfere with that.'

Holding a walking stick, necessary to support him in his temporary invalidity – he had sliced open the sole of his foot on broken glass a week previously and it was still heavily bandaged – Pearce was tempted to lift it and crown the man, but having just that morning been released from certain conviction as a caught-in-the-act smuggler, he was not inclined to risk further arrest for an assault upon a public official.

Standing behind him was Michael O'Hagan, the third of his companions who made up a quartet collectively known as the Pelicans. A man of such height and girth as to near fill the room, he was certainly one to draw the eye, as he had done several times from the corpulent postmaster, who clearly knew a bruiser when he saw one. Not that Michael was in any way threatening in his manner.

He habitually wore a kindly expression on his broad ruddy face, with a twinkle in his eye, more amused by his fellows than disturbed by them; it was his mere size and what he might accomplish with his ham-like fists that made folk careful with the Irishman, that and the steady look with which he was now favouring the fellow.

Then he spoke and his obvious brogue, judging by the startled reaction, added to the impression in the postmaster's mind that he might be subject to violent assault if he did not do something to mollify this supplicant of a naval lieutenant; it was all very well to say it would be a crime to do so, that the law would have them up for the offence, but by the time such an accusation could be laid – the post house was a long way from that of the local watch – he might well be suffering a broken skull.

'Sure, it's a simple enough request that you seek out the thing and see if Mr Pearce here is telling you the truth.'

'Lieutenant, I—'

'Simple, as I say,' Michael added, seeing no need to change the even tenor of his speech. 'And the act of a kindly man, a Christian soul, who could look his maker in the eye come Judgement Day.'

The implication that he might be making that acquaintance soon had no need to be openly expressed. With a sigh the postmaster went to the bags brought in from around the local area, rummaging around the one from Sandwich, not by any means full, yet with enough letters to require a search. Eventually he located the required missive and checked the address before turning it over, his eyes, much as he tried to disguise it, registering his astonishment at the address from which it had been sent, made doubly obvious by the device on the wax seal.

'It was written in Sandwich gaol,' Pearce acknowledged, 'and at a time I fully expected I would never again see a morning without chains. It is, in its nature, a plea to a woman to free herself of any thoughts of me, but now, sir, as you can plainly see, I am a free man.'

'It is also true,' Michael added, in a slightly edgier tone, 'that we have pressing business elsewhere.'

Where, the postmaster was thinking, *is a mail coach guard when you need him?* One of that fraternity, with their two regulation pistols and a blunderbuss, would soon see off this pair! But the London coach was yet to arrive and today's Dover conveyance had already left. In thinking on that his expression had hardened, leaving Pearce with the impression that he would not achieve that which he desired, a return of the letter so he could destroy it. Only then did it occur that there was another way.

'I appreciate, sir, that your duty forbids you to pass over the letter and I would not ask you to risk your position to oblige me, but I would beg that you allow me to append a short message on the cover, to say the contents no longer hold true.'

'The seal stays unbroken, sir?'

'Yes.'

It was with some relief the postmaster answered. 'Then I fail to see the harm.'

Given a quill and ink John Pearce merely wrote on the cover that Emily Barclay should ignore the contents as he was now a free man, which, when it was handed over, caused the postmaster to ask for what crime he had been arraigned.

'Smuggling, sir.'

The man threw back his head in what was close to disgust, proving that on this coast his thinking lay with the majority.

'Well, sir, if that be a crime, and I fail to see it as such, then they had best feel the collar of half the folk of Kent, many of whom would starve if they could not avoid the duties levied by our greedy government!'

As Pearce was penning his superscription, the gaoler at Sandwich was wondering, as had been the postmaster moments before, if he might get his head broken before anyone could come to his aid. Before him stood four real ruffians, the leader of whom, a man of high colour and temper, as well as a gruff cracked voice and pockmarked skin, had gone bright red with fury when he heard that Lieutenant John Pearce was no longer his prisoner.

'Set free afore ten of the clock this very morning, sir.'

'So he paid the fine, the thief?'

'No, he couldn't run to that.'

'How so he was freed then, when it was told to me he was caught in the very act?'

The gaoler stepped back; that red and furious face had come too close for comfort, so close he could see clearly where the pox had marked it deeply, as well as the fact

11

that the man's light-brown eyes seemed to be flecked with gold, more catlike than human.

'Two fellows turned up in court and said they had volunteered to join the King's Navy at Mr Pearce's request. Now they did not say they were in the contraband game but it stands to reason that will be the case. I daresay you know the navy loves a smuggler for their skills, as well as the statute that says a man may set off his penalty for the crime of avoiding customs dues if he offers up a pair of volunteers to the King's service.'

'So where has he gone, this Pearce?'

The gaoler shrugged. 'None of my concern, sir, so I did not enquire.'

The hands that grabbed him by his shirt were too quick to avoid and the way he was picked up and slammed violently against the bare brick of the town gaol wall took his breath out of his body, the shock of the attack, as well as two fists pressing on his ears, making him only dimly aware of the string of invective to which he was being subjected.

'You stinking cur, I'll rip out your gizzard with my teeth.'

'Steady, Jahleel, let the man down.'

One voice had come to the gaoler's aid, but several hands were required to drag this Jahleel backwards at the same time as separating his hands from his victim's body, given he was like a man possessed. Two of his companions restrained him while the third, a calmer fellow by far, fair of skin but with a similarity of countenance, straightened the gaoler's shirt and sought to mollify him.

'Do you have any notion of to where this Pearce might have gone?'

'I think he might have headed to Dover.'

'And how would you describe him?'

'You don't know him?' the gaoler said, surprised.

'That is none of your concern, now is it?'

For all the voice was soft there was no kindness in it – quite the reverse; it was cold and carried undertones of as much threat as his more physical companion.

'A tall fellow and straight-backed, a fair phizog, unmarked, a ready smile, handsome, many would say, dark hair and dressed in his naval coat and hat.' It suddenly occurred to the gaoler that Dover might have a few naval officers wandering about, so he added, 'But right now he has a bandaged foot and a limp, needs a stick to walk where he says he cut his foot on broken glass.'

What made Jahleel roar then the gaoler did not know, only that it required an increased effort to restrain him, while spittle flecked his mouth when he spoke. 'It'll be his damned throat that gets cut, Franklin, not his damned foot.'

'Will you be quiet, brother, I am sure our friend here has more to tell us.'

When Franklin turned back, the gaoler saw where the likeness lay most – in and around those eyes, which were of the same colour and shape. This one, for all his quiet manner, was just as dangerous as his fiery kin; best aid them as much as he could.

'He wrote a letter afore he was taken to court this morning.'

'Where to?'

'London, a lady called Barclay, resides in a place called Jockey's Fields.'

'You read and write?'

'Have to for the job I has. Got in a strop about that and wanted to get it back afore the lady received it, but I had to tell him a coach had already come through to lift the mailbag. That's why he's gone to Dover, to catch it before it's put aboard for London.'

'And will he?'

'I'd say he had scant hope of catching it before it departed this day.'

'We've got to get after him, Franklin,' Jahleel growled.

'Dover first, I reckon,' Franklin replied, still looking at the gaoler, 'but before we depart, you will tell no one we came, will you, not a name or a description?'

'Now why would I?' the gaoler replied, his gullet suddenly dry, sure as he was that to say otherwise was to risk it being sliced open.

'No reason to, has you, friend? Happen if you did we might have to come back this way and set you to rights.'

The man who ran Sandwich gaol was still standing with his back to the cold brick wall when he heard the sound of departing hooves. He did not move until they had faded away completely, though he did wonder at the level of noise they made given there seemed many more than four mounts.

The wagon in which sat Charlie Taverner and Rufus Dommet, the two other Pelicans, was not designed for comfort; unsprung, it knew the name and depth of every pothole on the cross-county road that would lead eventually to the Medway ports. The floor provided the seating, the walls the back support, while at one end the straw was supposed to act as a place of rest. Right now that was occupied by a couple of filthy creatures, stinking of stale drink, whose movements tended to be towards scratching themselves frequently, evidence of their infested state.

Taken straight from the Sandwich courthouse by a court bailiff to the home of the captain who controlled the Dover Impress Service, the two men who had saved John Pearce spent no more time there than it took to enter their names. The closed wagon was waiting to go and they were put straight aboard without so much as a cup of water to sustain them, their request for some vittles scoffed at with the response that such comforts cost money, which had to be paid for out of their bounty.

'God save us if we have to spend a night in this thing,' Rufus moaned.

Charlie Taverner just sighed; normally a man to vehemently curse his lot if he felt discomfort, he now seemed resigned to whatever fate might hold. 'We've suffered worse than this, lad, when times were hard. How many nights were we reduced to hot-bedding, eh?'

'Aye, but we've had better since our life in the Liberties. A ship's hammock might not be comfort, but—'

Charlie laid a reassuring hand on young Rufus's arm. 'Just hope we has better goin' forrad.'

'D'ye think Pearce can get us out of this, Charlie?'

'Can't see how; we volunteered, so those protections he got us are not of any use.'

'He will try, though, will he not?'

'Course he will. We're fellow Pelicans, he is bound by honour to save us as we saved him.'

Pearce was seeking to do that very thing, with little hope of success. He was sat at a table in the White Lion Inn, which overlooked the long strand of pebble beach that, enclosed as it was by a double mole, formed the safe anchorage of Dover Harbour. The man he was seeking to persuade was more interested in his dinner than any plea from his fellow naval officer, though as a courtesy he had listened with polite concern.

Captain Tobias, in appearance and manner, seemed ill fitted to his occupation; most officers of the Impress Service were not men of much refinement – it could not be said to be a task that attracted ambitious types and certainly not gentlemanly ones. Tobias was the exception.

'You really should have a beefsteak, Lieutenant. Today it is particularly fine and, of course, the mackerel they are serving is fresh caught this very morning from the end of the harbour mole.'

Looking at him, Pearce wondered how he had come to this place and this occupation. The man had very cultured features to go with his fastidious manner, a sharp slightly upturned nose, a pale thin face and somewhat lazy hooded eyes under his wig. Likewise his consumption of food was fussy, his meat carefully cut into morsels for slow mastication. Had he been partaking of a temporary assignment it would have made sense – many a captain would take any posting rather than seek to exist on half pay; that he was permanent in the position and content with his lot seemed odd.

'The two men of whom I speak were caught this morning too.'

That produced a chuckle. 'Not caught, sir, they cast themselves onto the hook, what?'

'To save me, as I have told you.'

The elegant features closed up. 'You did the King's Navy no service, sir, for being apprehended in the act of smuggling.'

There was a temptation then to tell this Tobias he was, if not innocent, more of a dupe than a villain, but he doubted he would be believed. In truth, he was not sure an admission of the facts, exposing his own gullibility, would do anything to bring about a more elevated opinion.

'I have shown you their protections.'

'From impressment!'

'Would men with such scarce documents really volunteer?'

That Pearce was clutching at straws he knew; just as obvious was the plain fact that Tobias knew it too.

'It would seem so, and if it is unusual, which I admit is the case, there is a first time for every event and God moves in mysterious ways his wonders to perform, don't ye know.'

'So the protections would not provide sufficient grounds for their release?'

'They signed on as volunteers and will remain in the service till we have peace.'

'You do, I believe, receive a bounty for each man you provide to the navy.'

That saw the eating implements put down with a sharp clatter. 'I hope you are not suggesting, sir, I perform my duty for purely financial gain?'

Pearce had a good mind to say yes, for what other reason would a man like Tobias carry out such a task? But such an admission would not aid his cause. 'No, but I am prepared to offer more than that bounty for their release.'

The eyes were not hooded now. 'No doubt so you and they can go back to your nefarious and highly profitable trade?'

Pearce was in a quandary here; as well as protections, both Charlie and Rufus Dommet had long-standing warrants for arrest against their names, therefore he could not press too hard. Also, having offered themselves up in the circumstances in which they did, as well as the place in which it occurred, it took no great leap of the imagination to see them as smugglers on a coast riddled with people pursuing that as an occupation and him as their leader.

'Is that an offer you would be prepared to consider?'

If anything, Tobias, having gone back to his dinner, was now eating even more slowly, as though he was considering it. 'I doubt you have the means, sir.'

'Surely we cannot be talking of such a superior sum to cover the cost of two bounties?'

That got Pearce another direct look. 'Oh, but we are talking of a very superior sum, sir, for you are asking me to risk my present commission as the impress officer for

Dover, given to do what you request, if discovered, would open me up to a court martial and possible dismissal.'

It was only a toe in the water when Pearce responded, given he was unsure of his true financial state; it might be healthy, it might be dire. 'I may go to a high payment, sir, for I value these men. I have a deal of prize money owing to me.'

'You'd need a Spanish Plate ship, sir, for I doubt you have the faintest idea how lucrative my position is, given the men I command hunt the narrow neck of the English Channel, where pressing men is akin to netting sprats. Do you think I would consider such a post if it was not one that provided a healthy income?'

Tobias leant forward, more animated than previously. 'My command provides more men for the King's Navy than any other in creation and I enjoy the rewards while never having to set foot on a heaving deck, or risk my neck on the vile ocean that regularly renders me nauseous.'

He actually snorted then, through that slightly upturned nose. 'No, sir, I would not accept payment in lieu of my bounty even if you could run to the sum, quite apart from the very simple fact that the men you mention are out of my hands, they are on their way at this very moment to the Nore.'

'Already!'

'I collect so many and have so little room to accommodate them, sir, that I am obliged to ship them out daily. If I did not, I would also be obligated to feed them at my own expense.'

'John-boy, a word.'

Tobias looked over Pearce's shoulder to where stood Michael O'Hagan, the captain's face a picture of offence that anyone dressed in common garb should address an officer by his Christian name. Turning to look, Pearce saw real alarm in his friend's face, and with a murmured excuse he stood and limped over to where they could speak without being overheard.

'I was in the High Street and there's a rate of people going around asking after you by name and rank, even describing your bandaged foot. It's only by the grace of Jesus that you were not seen coming into this place.'

'Who are they?'

'From what I see they look like those rough coves we saw in that tavern in Gravelines a week past.' That occasioned a sudden and unpleasant memory of a bunch of real hard bargains carousing in the Flanders port, professional smugglers to his mind, as well as the unfriendly glares they got as they entered the place. 'Strikes me it might be the same fellows whose boat we pinched and if it is . . .'

There was no need to finish that; to run in with such a crew would be painful, even deadly, quite apart from which they would ask him questions to which he did not have the answers, like where was their cargo of valuable contraband.

'How many?'

'Too many to take on. I counted half a dozen and armed with swords, too, which we are not. I say we have got to get out of here and sharp.'

'Maybe best if you go, for I can't run with this foot.'

'I have not been tempted to land my fist on you since

the night we met, and that I do not recall for I was in drink, but I am minded to do so now. Go back to the table, talk to that captain, while I see if I can find a litter.'

'We can't go very far in that.'

'We don't need to go far, John-boy, sure we only need to get clear of the town limit.'

'And then?'

'We make for the first change of horses on the London road, I will find out where, and then we take the mail coach or any other passing on the morrow that gets us clear of this coast.'

'Charlie and Rufus are already on the way to the receiving hulk. Can we just abandon them?'

'Holy Mary, Mother of God, we're no good to them as dead men.'

'You're right,' Pearce replied, looking back at Tobias clearing his plate. 'But God only knows what I can say to this sod now, for I hate to leave them to stew.'

'As of now they are safer than we are.'

Pearce limped back to the table, looking at the ditty bag he had, resting against his chair, which contained his few possessions, one of them being his unused shoe. Then he looked at his foot and he knew that the only way to get it on was to remove his bandage. Yet even if he did that, he wondered if he would be able to walk on the stitched cut without it reopening. Given the circumstances it had to be tried but it was not something to do in public.

'Can you tell me, Captain Tobias, does this inn run to a place of easement?'

'There is a privy out to the rear, sir,' Tobias sniffed as if he was on the inside of the thing, 'but it is not a standard I would be inclined to use.'

'When one is caught by necessity, sir, standards are of the least concern.'

The look Pearce got then, from the very refined Captain Tobias, was one of utter disagreement.

CHAPTER TWO

At the same moment as Pearce tossed aside his bandage and gingerly eased his foot into first his stocking, then his shoe, Emily Barclay, to whom the letter he had so desired to intercept was addressed, was sitting in the office of her solicitor, waiting while he rummaged in his strongroom to fetch out the papers she had left in his care.

These consisted of a fair copy of the statements made in evidence at a court martial the previous year for illegal impressment, which had taken place in the great cabin of HMS *Britannia*, the 100-gun flagship of Admiral Sir William Hotham, anchored off the besieged city of Toulon, the person accused being her husband, Captain Ralph Barclay.

How long ago that seemed and how much had happened since, yet that paled when she considered what had come to pass since she had first clapped eyes on those pressed men from the Pelican Tavern, John Pearce being only one amongst many. He had come aboard her husband's ship, HMS *Brilliant,* on a cold grey morning as the frigate lay off Sheerness.

Not long married – Emily Barclay herself had only just arrived on the deck – she did not know that to look with sympathy at the poor creatures, miserable and bearing the marks of their forced impressment, was the wrong thing to do. That she did so with sincerity was compounded by the way Pearce had then returned the look.

Neither meek nor defiant, his response had been openly admiring, quite ignoring both his circumstances and his surroundings, which had sent Ralph Barclay into a paroxysm of rage that his young wife should be so slighted. This saw the offender struck a heavy blow, and in a sense that had sealed the relationship; it seemed as if Pearce and her husband had been at loggerheads ever since.

'Here you are, Mrs Barclay,' said Studdert, emerging from the deep cupboard secured by a heavy door, a thick bundle in his hand. 'Your papers.'

There was hesitation as he handed them to her, for to take them was to cross a sort of Rubicon, to nail her colours to the mast, as she had so nautically imagined it. The act would go a long way to seal her decision never to live again under the same roof as her husband, not for that first struck blow to a man with whom she now thought herself in love, but for all his subsequent actions, including those cruelties he had also visited upon her.

A man she had once seen as a person to admire – he was, after all, a thirty-seven-year-old post captain in the

King's Navy, she a mere seventeen and innocent – Emily now knew him to be a beast. He claimed his behaviour was brought on by his harsh upbringing and brutal naval apprenticeship, but it was in fact nothing less than his true nature.

Perhaps he could be forgiven for flogging the seamen under his command; that, cruel as it was to anyone with an ounce of Christianity, was within the tenets of the service of which he was a part, maybe he could even be excused for his lies and evasions. But the way he had violently exercised what he insisted were his rights as a husband she could not abide.

The package was in her hand now, feeling heavy, and Studdert had been speaking, only she had not heard what he said, being so lost in reverie.

'I was saying, Mrs Barclay, that my sole duty to you was to store and keep safe the papers you now hold. Unless you have some other duty for me to perform that will, if you wish, conclude our business.'

'No!' The lawyer's head dipped to one side and it was clear by his look he was posing a question. 'I may have other requirements, so I would be grateful if you would consent to be still retained.'

'To undertake what, precisely?'

'As of this moment I am not sure, but . . .' She had to hesitate, there being nothing she could think of to say, only then to take refuge in the too obvious. 'However, if you have a bill that requires to be satisfied . . .'

Studdert smiled, which did much to make more attractive his long, angular, rather anxious face. 'It amounts to a trifle, Mrs Barclay, a modicum of time including this. It is not something I would press you for.'

Emily stuffed the thick bundle of papers into a bag she had brought along for the purpose. 'I would not, however, want to be indebted to you a moment longer than necessary. Please send an account to my rooms at Jockey's Fields.'

'Very well,' Studdert said, standing as she did, with, she thought, an odd look on his face. 'Until we meet again.'

It was only when she was outside that Emily made some sense of that strange expression. Mr Studdert had surmised a great deal more than he was prepared to say about her relationship with John Pearce, a man he had met and declined so recently to represent because he acted for her.

The lawyer might have been surprised to know that he and his client had been, that very morning, the subject of discussion elsewhere. It had taken place in Brown's Hotel, in the rooms of Captain Ralph Barclay, and had involved the necessity of getting back those very same papers which his wife had just stuffed into her bag, this discussed by her husband with Cornelius Gherson, the man he employed as his clerk.

A fortnight had passed since the confrontation, in the same hotel, between Emily and her much older spouse, in which she had informed him of her decision that they should lead separate lives, albeit that for the sake of propriety it should appear they were still man and wife. Society would not be fooled, but as long as certain decencies were observed they would not suffer condemnation for what was seen as a social crime.

Up until that moment when he had faced her, expecting to command her obedience as a husband had a right to do, Ralph Barclay had been in ignorance of the existence of those damning documents. Made aware, he had been presented with an ultimatum: if he did not agree to a separation, as well as provide the support Emily required to live a comfortable life, she would use them to dish him professionally and quite possibly bring upon his head a capital charge of perjury.

The tissue of lies he had caused to be uttered at his travesty of a court martial had come back to haunt him. He had persuaded others to lie; in the case of his wife's nephew, the weasel Midshipman Toby Burns, he had employed coercion, all to prove that the charge against him, of illegally pressing men out of the Liberties of the Savoy, was false.

A place of refuge for those under threat of arrest, to enter the Liberties for that purpose was expressly forbidden by statute; that he had done so, he might claim, had been forced on him by his shortage of men to man his new frigate, a vessel already ordered to sea. Nevertheless it was, even to a naval court, a crime and it must be established that he was innocent.

With the contrivance of the second in command of the Mediterranean Fleet, Admiral Sir William Hotham, he had had sent on detached service anyone who could counter his claims of blamelessness, the likes of John Pearce in particular, as well as a Lieutenant Digby and a midshipman called Farmiloe. The admiral had also ensured the court did not see the depositions which the other pressed men, the so-called Pelicans, had made, condemning him.

Emily had claimed to have a fair copy of that cooked-up evidence in her possession and, when challenged that all she had was in her own hand, she had proved the opposite to be the case. Only when he saw the original handwriting did Ralph Barclay realise that it was that of John Pearce, a man who would certainly use it to destroy him, threatening everything he had strived for; nothing could be allowed to stand in the way of retrieval.

'Well,' he demanded of Gherson, as soon as his clerk entered the room.

The slight smile he received in response led to him angrily waving the stump of his missing left arm, that lost at Toulon, for there were many things about the man that annoyed him, his assurance being one, as well as, to a man of dark countenance and bellicose nature, his absurdly good looks.

Gherson had curly fair hair which he took good care to keep barbered and a face that was close to girlish, so smooth was the skin, so full were the lips and so long were his eyelashes. Offended, he was wont to pout as well, but that which was really irritating now and had been for some time was that Barclay needed something done and he could not do it himself.

The Admiralty would have the original court martial record by now but it would take Holy Writ to get them to disclose it, they being always protective of their serving officers, so he was secure on that flank. That fair copy represented the threat and the solution to his problem;

the only way he could feel protected was to get hold of it and destroy every page.

This required they be extracted from the lawyer's office, which they were close to certain was where his wife had deposited them – not something the fellow was likely to agree to. That left only an illegal entry and theft, a felony which Gherson, in possession of the right contacts, had undertaken to arrange.

'I have made enquiries to establish that certain parties whom I know of are still active, sir,' Gherson said, 'whilst it is also necessary to seek to find out how exposed they are to scrutiny. We must choose the right fellows to ensure that nothing comes back to endanger us.'

'You've taken your damn sweet time about it, man!'

Accustomed to Ralph Barclay's brusque manner, Gherson was not in the least offended, yet the time had arrived to proceed with an act he had drawn out for as long as he could, doing so for the very simple reason that it made his employer dependent on him. Not that Gherson thought he was ever otherwise; to his mind, and in an opinion shaped by a great deal of vanity, Ralph Barclay was a bit of a dud when it came to anything requiring brains or subterfuge.

True, he was a good sailor, a very competent seaman according to those who knew of such things – Gherson was glad to remain in ignorance – but once ashore, like so many naval officers, he was somewhat adrift. He was, however, destined to prosper, having just been given command of a new and powerful ship by the Admiralty, the 74-gun HMS *Semele*, entirely refitted down to her keel and presently sitting off Chatham Dockyard taking on both her stores and a crew.

The stores were not a problem; the entire needs of the ship, if they had not been pilfered, were sitting in a Chatham warehouse. A crew, with the war over a year old, might be more of a problem. Barclay, with Admiralty approval, had selected and written to those men he wanted as officers, telling them not to turn up for duty without they brought along a body of volunteers, and there was a receiving hulk in the Medway filling up with men, mostly pressed.

Somehow the vessel would be manned and got to sea, where opportunity was waiting for an enterprising commander interested in profit, which Barclay had proved to be. And as he rose in the service, to larger vessels and beyond, so would increase the opportunities to profit for his clerk, there being much room for peculation in the King's Navy, more in a line-of-battle ship than in the lowly frigate his employer had originally commanded and in which Gherson had first encountered him.

In time, if he lived and there were dead men's shoes to fill as well as the right level of political patronage, Barclay would get his admiral's flag and perhaps a command on a profitable station like the West Indies. Within such an office lay the route to a fortune for a sharp mind, and if his man fell by the wayside, either to death or disgrace, by that time Gherson, like the parasite he was, would be well enough connected in the service to move to another promising host.

'I have identified the fellow I think can carry out the deed.' Barclay's head jerked then; it was as if he was about to enquire of the name, but no words emerged – best he did not know, and anyway, Gherson would not tell him. 'Having done so, I feel, sir, I can now proceed to an approach, but I am anxious that you understand those points I raised with you originally.'

'Damn it, Gherson, that lawyer has those papers and they must be got hold of, by fair means or foul, which I seem to recall you agreed to see done.'

Papers, Gherson thought, *the location of which you would have had no idea, if I had not discerned that what your wife showed you was a copy in her own hand, inadmissible as evidence, no spouse being able to testify against her husband. You would not have known about the solicitor or seen Pearce's handwriting had I not set your bully-boy servant to trailing her.*

Even then it was a guess, not a certainty, that she had stored the originals with the solicitor. You seem to have forgotten that there was any doubt! Simple-minded as you are, you see a problem, then a solution and drive on by impatience rather than by any exercise of intellect.

He could think such thoughts, but he dare not utter them. 'As long as you accept that payment will be stiff, sir?' That got him a jaundiced look; his employer did not trust him, but then he worked for a man who did not really trust anyone. 'As I have pointed out to you before, there is no profit in stealing papers. Whoever breaks into those offices will require that their efforts be rewarded, and handsomely, from your purse.'

'Find out the figure, man, then I can decide.'

About to grin, Gherson had to fight to control his features; Ralph Barclay would pay whatever was demanded and in that would include a decent reward for his own efforts, more now than if he had acted, as he could have done, straight away. He would employ the thieves and Barclay would never meet them, so would never know the true cost of the transaction.

'Then, sir,' he said, 'if we are fully agreed on what must be done, I will be on my way.'

It was hard for John Pearce not to favour his foot by walking gingerly; just as difficult was to walk with an air of insouciance and not catch the eye of anyone, for if those people Michael had mentioned were looking for a bandaged foot, they knew his rank and would be bound to give an extra examination to anyone dressed in a blue uniform coat and the distinctive naval headgear of his fore and aft scraper.

The port and town of Dover sat in a deep coomb that ran down to the sea, with steep wooded slopes on either side fronted by the dirty white cliffs, so the way out was a long trudge uphill along the valley floor, which seemed designed to put extra pressure on his wound. As soon as they cleared the town gates and were out of sight, Michael offered to carry Pearce by piggyback, a piece of generosity immediately refused.

Luck gave them both a lift on the tail of a hay cart which was going as far as the hamlet of Kearnsey, by which time Pearce felt he could favour the injury even if it affected his gait, yet it was still a long walk and it was with stiffening muscles that they made to the village which was their destination, the first stop of the London road.

Given the slope and a heavy carriage, horses exiting

Dover soon became exhausted, too much so to cover the customary ten miles between stops. Michael had found that the first change for coaches after Dover was only just over five miles distant at a place called Lydden and it was there, if there was room, they would catch it on the morrow and proceed to Canterbury and eventually to London.

It was a tired and grateful pair who, after a filling stew of local mutton and root vegetables, sat themselves in front of a fire at the Bell Inn in the late afternoon, having bespoken accommodation, not much of the remains of a pot of porter in hand. Pearce, once the proprietor departed, had removed his shoe, pleased to see there was, on his stocking, no trace of blood, which showed the stitches holding the angry red weal together were intact.

Propped on the copper fire surround, the sole was being nicely warmed by the blazing logs; it might be springtime, but the evenings were still chilly, the nights cold. It was then they heard the sound of a large party of riders and instinct fed by fear had Pearce leap up, grabbing his hat and his ditty bag, signalling to Michael that they should get out of the parlour and into the passage that led to the rear and the stables. Stopping just inside the door, he pushed it to so it was open a fraction, putting his ear to the crack to listen.

The Irishman went out the rear door and came back in without his ale jug, carrying two long firewood logs to use as weapons, one silently put in Pearce's hand. From being quiet in that parlour it was suddenly very noisy as the large party of riders came in and loudly demanded to

33

be served, the boots thudding on the bare floorboards.

'You're too soft, Franklin,' said a gruff, distinctively cracked voice. 'I would have stuck a knife in that postmaster's gut and he would have told all of what he knew.'

'He affirmed what we needed to know, Jahleel; our man was there with a big bugger at his back, seeking that which that gaoler told us of. Besides, that's all we need, the law on our tail an' to what purpose, when we already know where Pearce is headed.'

'How long we goin' to ride, Jahleel?' said another voice. 'I got sores on my arse as it is.'

'You'll have a sore damned head if you ask that one more time.'

'We can't ride all the way to London without we stop, not on them plodding mounts you gave us, especial when we ain't accustomed.'

'Give me a ship any time,' said another of the group.

''Cepting we ain't got one, numbskull, it was seized by the excise. London's where Pearce has gone, man, and if we are to lay the bastard by the heels so must we. God damn his luck, if we'd heard a mite earlier of him being had up we would have caught him afore he got away.'

'I've no mind to carry on in the dark, Jahleel,' insisted the voice that went by the name of Franklin. 'I reckon we must stop at Canterbury an' I doubt we'll make that before the light goes complete.'

'I expect more of you, brother.'

'I am not so daft as to push our horses till they drop, especially our fine racing mares. It be madness to break a good horse even for such a prize, so let us rest them overnight and we will happen make London on the day after the morrow if we start out at first light.'

'We've got to catch the sod, Franklin, afore he disappears, and get back what he has stolen from us.'

'All sold now, Jahleel, I reckon, given it took a week to reach us that he was the villain and there was little trace of our stuff.'

'Then we'll have the coin he got for the cargo, or his skin in place of it.'

'Gentlemen.'

That got a hoot from someone, the owner of the Bell Inn addressing them so, a sound taken up by others, mixed with exchanged ribbing not short on the odd cuss word.

'Some food,' the gruff voice said, loud enough to command silence.

'With such a number, sir, it will be a while if'n you want it hot.'

'Bread and cheese will suffice,' said the calmer Franklin voice, 'and ale for eight thirsty souls.'

If there had ever been any doubt about who was in pursuit, it had been laid to rest, nor any question of what was in store if they were caught. Easing away from the door and putting his ale pot on the floor, Pearce indicated that Michael should precede him out of the rear door. If any one of those sods asked if a man with a bandaged foot had happened by, it would not be too much of a leap for the innkeeper to admit to who had.

All he had to do was tell them there had been a naval officer and his well-built friend sat by the fire not five minutes before for those fellows to be made curious enough to come searching. He had not only looked at these men who now filled the parlour in that Gravelines tavern, he had also seen their faces from the deck of their ship a week previously; they would have seen his likewise and it was quite possible it would register.

'Is it who we reckon?' Michael whispered.

Pearce nodded and once outside he slipped back on his buckled shoe, then, with Michael bringing up his rear, he made his way unseen past the door to the kitchen, then around the corner and along the side wall till he could look at the front courtyard, filled with tethered horses, eight in number, with a lad watering them from a leather bucket. Still fully harnessed and saddled, they were waiting to be ridden on.

Dropping his makeshift club and bag, slipping off his coat and handing both that and his hat to Michael, Pearce walked out into the open, aware that the courtyard could be seen through the windows and thus keeping as much as possible his back to the front of the inn. The horses he saw were, in the main, broad of back and sturdy of flank, animals that might be put to haul a cart and maybe even a plough, slow lumbering cuddies that would never be speedy.

But two were different creatures, as was their livery. Instead of scuffed saddles and rope-made head collars and reins, these two had harness of high quality: good leather and polished metal. While no equine expert, he knew enough to see these for what they were, the property of men who could afford to ride for pleasure. Getting close he ran a hand down the leg of the nearest mare; when he stood up the stable lad looked at him and smiled, which was returned.

'Fine mounts, wouldn't you say?'

'Handsome they are, sir.'

Now at the horse's head he was stroking its nose and it was responding; clearly it was accustomed to being much cosseted. He stretched out a hand to include the other mare, made jealous by not getting the same attention, recalling the words Franklin had employed.

'You could race this pair.'

'Aye.'

'Michael, come and have a look.'

Pearce registered that his companion had loaded his coat into the bag, though he had to carry the hat, yet more pressing was that he was in a quandary. Pearce did not want to harm this boy but he was stroking the means by which they could escape. Michael could ride like every Irishman country raised and if they could get away on this pair nothing left behind would have the speed to catch them. Yet he could hardly just mount them without the lad crying out and that would require him to be silenced.

'It would please me to feed them an apple each,' he said, more in hope than expectation.

'I was told not to feed them, Your Honour, and to go easy on the water, given they are soon to be moving on.'

Pearce laughed, which he hoped sounded sincere because it certainly was not. 'I doubt an apple will slow them, and would they struggle to keep pace with the others even if they had a bucket of oats?'

'Never,' the stable lad grinned. 'There's a tub of

windfalls in the stables, which we keep for the mail coach horses.'

'For which I will happily part with a sixpence – these two ladies deserve a treat.'

If the lad had a wage it would not run to that much in a month of stable-cleaning and horse-minding; probably he worked for his food and board and was grateful. As he ran off, Pearce was still dithering; the boy could find himself without his job and maybe even with a birch rod on his back for negligence. It was Michael, well aware of the way Pearce's mind was working, who settled matters.

'The lad they won't kill, John-boy, and they might not even touch him.'

Michael's hands were cupped and the decision was made. Unlooping the reins from the hitching post, Pearce allowed himself to be lifted aboard by his good foot, slipping easily into the stirrups. As Michael followed suit – he was big enough to get himself astride with a leap – a face peering out of the window of the inn saw what they were about and his shout was loud enough to penetrate the small panes of glass.

Hauling hard, Pearce brought the mare's head round then he kicked with his heels and set her in motion, just as the door burst open and the men who were after them poured out. If there was one fact he knew about horses, they were ever ready to run and, even more spooked by the ballyhoo to their rear than his thrusting knees and insistent hands, his mare was soon in full flight, the second one right behind.

They tried to catch them, they even had swords out and were waving them but, thank the Lord, they had no pistols. Also, they were wearing thigh-high riding boots, with heavy coats, and that made even harder what was in any case impossible – to catch a galloping horse. Soon their angry voices faded into nothing and Pearce could tug on the reins to slow his mount's pace to a fast canter.

'The bill those creatures want from us just got longer, John-boy,' Michael called, 'and we are thieves of horseflesh as well, which is a hanging offence where I was born.'

'Whatever else, I do not think they will report us for that. They do not strike me as men who use the law to settle their scores.'

'They will follow us, for sure.'

'To London, Michael, which is the biggest city in the known world. I wish them joy of ever finding us there and we will not go by Canterbury.' He looked at the sky, clear, but now no longer bright as the sun had dropped. 'If there is one thing I have learnt, it is where the North Star resides in the firmament. So we will make for the road from Ramsgate to the Medway and we will not, even in the dead of night, get lost.'

CHAPTER THREE

Cornelius Gherson stood on the borders of a world he hated, the rookeries to the east of the city, where stinking poverty was the norm, sometimes little more than a hundred yards away from the fabulous riches of London's better coffee houses, a rising tumble of stinking, crowded, crime-ridden dwellings so close to places where millions were traded daily.

Of decent Huguenot stock, the son of an upright father in a good and profitable trade, Gherson *père* being a highly regarded manufacturer and repairer of superior-quality carriage lamps, it was to the coffee houses his son should have progressed. Precocious and with a quick mind, well educated in letters and good at numbers, he had been first driven to these rookeries after falling out of grace with his own family, who took objection to his constant petty theft in a household where trust was essential, given the valuable materials used in the business.

His mother had protected him from parental wrath for a long time but when she had passed away his father had cast his continually errant young son out of his house, his trade and his prospects. Forced to make his own way in an unsympathetic world, Cornelius Gherson had used his angelic looks, ready tongue and quick mind to find good employment, but from time to time things had gone against him.

This was usually the discovery of some peculation or other: a bookkeeping error that could not be explained away, some missing item of value or a too close proximity to the lady of the house that broke the bounds of prudence, age and looks being no bar to the young man's endeavours to gain access to the household monies. Shown the door each time, it was to these rookeries he had returned, to recover his purpose and seek out new avenues to pursue among the dregs of humanity, who by their bearing and manner were the very spur he needed to force him to escape.

The last time he had been caught in the wrong bed had nearly proved fatal, for he had cuckolded a very powerful and vengeful man called Denby Carruthers, middle-aged, rich and successful, an alderman of the City of London, who had made two glaring errors. The first was to marry, just like Ralph Barclay, a woman much younger than himself, whom he had no idea how to treat properly. The second was to employ a good-looking clerk of near the same age called Cornelius Gherson.

Caught out, Carruthers had hired a pair of real toughs to exact revenge, but instead of the beating he anticipated, these fellows, having stripped him of the clothing bought for him by the alderman's wife, had tipped him over the parapet of London Bridge into the roaring Thames as it came through the supporting arches.

Had a naval cutter not been passing right where he entered the water, had a hand not grabbed him, he would have drowned. Instead he ended up aboard HMS *Brilliant* as a pressed man among many, those fetched out of the Liberties of the Savoy by a gang under the command of the man who now employed him.

It had taken much effort and not a little chicanery to get him to where he was now, but he had never doubted his ability to rise like a phoenix from any setback. There were others, who when his name came up saw it differently, responding with the well-known expression that 'Shit ever did float!'

As he entered this dark world, he first ensured his purse was so placed that it could not be stolen by slick hands, then wrapped his cloak tight to hide his good clothing – high-quality apparel he had acquired for a pittance from the distressed and needy refugees of Toulon – while ignoring the filth that stuck to the hem as he walked, this being no place for sweepers.

To raise it would expose his silver shoe buckles and that, in this location, could get his throat slit. Next he made sure to meet the curiosity of the seemingly idle with a steady eye, to let those who would seek to rob him know that he could smell their game as much as their grime-covered bodies.

There were places Gherson knew that he wished

he did not, low dens where a whore was as cheap as a thimble of rotten gin and just as foul, and the price of a stolen linen handkerchief enough to allow a man to drink himself insensible; places where, in the past, he had sought information about those in the city who possessed the wealth he so craved – if anyone knew where the household chests were bulging it was those desirous of stealing them.

These dens were much frequented by those who robbed for a living and it was in such pits they met with even more dubious creatures: the men who fenced their valuable goods, usually selling them back to the original owners for a reward. There was little market for outright money exchange as well as too much risk attached to it, and when it came to pieces made of silver or gold, melting them down led to a loss of value.

The fellow he sought was known by the single name of Codge – no one ever used his given name of Jonathan. The man was a liar, thief and cheat of epic scale, a fellow of such low morals as to make the common shit-eating dung beetle look virtuous, his other trait the certainty, which he took no pains to hide, that he was far superior in brainpower to any other man alive.

To deal with him it was necessary to flatter his vanity, as well as listen to his endless boasting of imagined feats of brilliance – acts that usually left some other soul paying a very high price, not excluding the rope. Gherson found him at a table with a quartet of idiots who fawned on his every utterance, men who were content to listen to his endless droning self-regard, which he seemed to be able to pursue without the need to draw breath; I this and I that – Codge was a man addicted to the first-person singular.

That he could provide what Gherson needed was not in doubt, but care was required to be taken, for once he had been paid his fee for whatever service he provided, Codge was as likely to pass on what he knew to the Bow Street Runners as to keep any promise he made to remain silent, this to ensure that his own crimes were never brought to his door and his nefarious ways could continue, the thief-takers turning a blind eye for an easy catch.

It was a mystery to more than Cornelius Gherson as to why anyone trusted him but there were fools who did, men so stupid or desperate that they did not see, when he turned on one of his grovelling coterie to protect himself, that the proper reaction was not to praise him for his foresight but to get well away from his orbit, for they were in danger of being the next victim.

There was no need to attract his attention; Codge, quite apart from his habit of keeping an eye on the door, was a man who could smell the possibility of an ill-earned coin, and besides, when a non-habitué of his favourite burrow came through the low portal, even in a fug of thick tobacco smoke, with a hat pulled well forward to hide his face, it caused those who frequented the place to drop their voices, cease to puff their pipes and wonder at the visitor's purpose.

The square head jerked as Codge reacted to his entry and Gherson caught a glimpse of his bead-like blue eyes under lowered lids, added to that look he generally wore on his face, one of outright arrogance. Taking a seat in an ill-lit corner and ordering a pot of gin he had no intention of imbibing, for the brew in this place might rip out your gut, Gherson waited until Codge sent one of his minions over to manufacture a false and insincere greeting. He gave him no chance to speak.

'Tell Codge I want a word.' The head jerked to where the man sat. 'Not at his table and other ears.'

'He reckons he might know you.'

'He does, but he has not enjoyed my company for a while.' Gherson nearly added he had never taken pleasure in the reverse, but such truth would be wasted on the dense specimen to whom he was talking. 'Just say I'm here on business.'

There was no rush to compliance; Codge took his time, making a show of downing his ale to underline his own importance. Everyone was watching, all curious, for there is nothing so nosy as a felon when it comes to another rogue's affairs.

Just as slow as his drinking was his walk to stand over Gherson, making sure his height and build were established, for he was a well-built tough as well as a double-dealer. The man he was seeking to overawe was not brave – in fact, he feared Codge physically – so it took some effort for him to keep a tremor out of his voice, to ask him to sit and then, when he did so, to make a very quick proposal.

'I have a job needs doing, and I have a man willing to pay handsomely for the service.'

Codge smiled, trying to look sincere, yet managing, with his foreign-hinting features, to do a fair impersonation of a well-fed rat. 'Handsomely to some is poverty to another.'

With the large frame of Codge between him and the rest of the room, Gherson lifted his hat enough to show his full face and his curly fair hair, before pulling it down again, just long enough to register the look which Codge could not fail to disguise.

'It is you. I was told you was a goner.'

'Nine lives, Codge, but you know me, so you know that when I say "handsomely" it is just that.'

The head came closer to Gherson's own and in a voice near to a whisper the need was outlined, with Codge nodding and the man he was talking to wondering what thoughts he was harbouring about doubling his bets.

'Whatever the lawyer has locked away we need to examine, so we can select what we are seeking.'

'You don't know what it looks like?'

'It's a bundle of papers and the man being in the law, he will have a rate of such things. Mortgage deeds, wills and the like.'

'Then there's only one way to play it, to get you in and let you take what you want.' The jerk Gherson gave to that suggestion had Codge continuing. 'Stands to reason we can't carry out his strongbox, for it might be more'n a couple of jemmy-men can bear. No, you needs to be along to take what you want, while my lads clear out anything they think might turn them a coin.'

That was a worry, for Gherson would be putting himself at risk, something to which he was habitually averse, but a moment's consideration told him there was a way to deflect any notion of him being caught in the lawyer's office with Codge.

'You'd have to be there as well, then. I pay you, you pay them.'

'You must have come up the Thames in a spice boat to think I will be anywhere near the place.'

'I never thought you would, Codge, you're far too clever.'

Silhouetted against what little light came in through the doorway, Gherson could see the shoulders square with the conceit he had witnessed so many times before; flattery was a speciality of his, the trait which had seen him prosper in many of his situations, both carnal and commercial.

'But I am not far behind in that regard. It's papers I want, not a metal box, and they can be borne in a sack. Let your men do the thieving and we will meet just after, you and I, at a place I shall choose where I can search for what I want and I will pass over your price in golden guineas the minute I find it. Then we can go our separate ways, for I will choose with care where we meet.'

That set those same shoulders, so recently squaring with pride, twitching with offence; Gherson was saying there would be no reliance on good faith, and no man reacted to an accusation of untrustworthiness more than one who had that as the core of his being.

'I'll need to know that afore any break-in.'

'You shall, for if you do not, you will decline to do what is required.'

'I'll set a few eyes around this day to see what's what. Where can I get you?'

'I shall come again tomorrow,' Gherson responded; there was no way he was going to let this bastard know where he was residing or the other thing he would want to know, who was the true paymaster.

'The fee?' Codge asked.

'To be negotiated, when we meet to agree it can be done and to set the thing in motion.'

'How long before that happens?'

'As soon as the matter is finally decided and I have the means to pay you, I will give you the nod.'

'With you doubling the figure I charge for your principal, happen?'

'As long as you get yours, Codge, allow that I get mine.'

Gherson stood and went straight out the door. He knew without looking back that Codge would put someone to tail him, but he had one advantage given to few who dealt with the viper. It was not a matter he was proud of but he knew the rookeries inside out through past necessity, so losing Codge's man was easy.

It was the second instruction Codge gave to one of his knuckle-dragging supporters that would have been more worrying. 'I can't recall who it was who wanted to do for a fellow called Gherson a year or more back. Find out an' be quick about it.'

The main gate of Chatham Dockyard, surmounted by the royal coat of arms, was well guarded, the whole surrounded by a high brick wall – not surprising given that within its confines at any one time were stored and stacked goods that amounted to a fortune in money. Here were built many of the great ships that provided England's wooden walls, and for sheer acreage Chatham would not bow the knee to Portsmouth, even if the Solent dockyard was now of greater import than hitherto.

At the time of the Dutch Wars, Chatham had been supreme, with its satellite at Sheerness and the Nore anchorage resting on the silt at the mouth of the River Medway. But the main naval enemy was now France and other ports were better placed to contain her ambitions, not just Pompey but Plymouth as well. Still home to the North Sea Fleet it was also a place into which poured those men needed to man the ships wherever they anchored, many at the outbreak of war, volunteers with experience of the sea, although there were fewer of those as time passed.

Now they tended to be landsmen tempted by tales of untold riches in prize money, bored youths and the odd disposed-of burden on the parish, or men so drunk when offered the King's shilling they knew not what they were doing. Plus, of course, there were pressed men, some from homecoming merchant vessels caught in the Channel, others taken up by roving gangs who ignored the law that only men of the sea should be at risk of impressment; a bounty was a bounty.

It was through those gates that the wagon came, having stopped the night at Reculver, carrying Charlie Taverner, Rufus Dommet and men from Ramsgate as well as Dover. They were taken out to a slop

49

ship; conscious of the risk of disease from the newly recruited – gaol fever and the like spread quickly in the crowded confines of a man-o'-war – the new arrivals were stripped, washed and issued with new and appropriate clothing. They were then passed over to the receiving hulk to await the vessel into which they would be required to serve.

'Well now, Rufus, this is a rum do.'

Charlie said this while looking at the crowded main deck of a ship long past serving in the line, one with its masts removed, anchored head and stern in the shallows of the river, a hulk that sat in its own filth and never moved, relying on the strong flow of the Medway after heavy rainfall to take out to the wider Thames the detritus of those who lived aboard.

It was temporary home to hundreds of men, and looking at them it seemed that every type was represented – long, short and fat – except that none of them appeared even remotely like sailors, for all they had been issued with the proper slops. Each had been entered and paid their due, less the cost of what they wore and the tobacco they were now puffing away at, as had Charlie and Rufus.

'You could not swing a cat on this deck, that's for certain.'

The air of the place, certainly from the bottom of the companionway on which they stood, was listless, with men sitting around below hammocks that had been rolled and tied, given they were not in use. The problem was the number; there did not seem an overhead deck beam with space to sling another. The only saving grace was that, with the redundant gun ports open, there was a breeze to carry away the smell of too many bodies, though not that of the bilge water, which rose from the decks lacking daylight below.

'We might need sharp elbows to get us the space for a hammock.'

'This is where Michael would come in handy,' said Rufus.

'Aye, but we don't have our Irish bruiser to aid us now, do we?'

That made both of them think; they could claim now to be proper sailors for all they had at one time been illegally pressed out of the Pelican Tavern, and it was plain now, if it had not been before, how much they had relied on each other. When it came to dreams of release it was John Pearce; to ensuring they could claim their due, Michael O'Hagan could secure that merely by his presence; Charlie, being the sly clever one, was good on comfort, while Rufus was the innocent step-and-fetch-it.

'We have to make our own way now, Rufus, but at least we can thank the Lord we are no longer ignorant of how.'

'Can you hear that fiddle, Charlie?'

For all there was no great animation in those they could see, there was enough conversation to set up a low hum, which made hearing anything above it difficult. Charlie had to cock a hand to his ear and listen hard to pick up the faint scraping of the instrument, but eventually he heard a high note and nodded.

'Get a move on you two.'

The voice was harsh and the face from which it came when they turned to look did nothing to soften the effect. The scully that spoke, as broad as he was high, took the notion of ugliness to new depths. He had a forehead that was near to half the size of his head which hung over his eyes, a tiny nose and a great lantern jaw. In his hand he carried a knotted rope, a starter, and that swung a fraction as if to tell them he was about to use it.

'We're a'looking for a place to sling a hammock,' Rufus said.

'There be room a'plenty two decks below this one.'

'And I hazard full of stink, they bein' below the waterline.'

Ugly looked at Charlie, with his hammock slung over one shoulder, his lip curling slightly. 'So what is it to you?'

'I fancy a sight of the day and night, friend.'

The starter swung more menacingly. 'What you fancy and what you get ain't the same in the King's Navy, so move on.'

There had been a time when both Charlie and Rufus would have been in terror of that rope as well as the authority of the man who seemed prepared to wield it, clearly a fellow permanently attached to the receiving hulk. That was what it had been like the day they had been taken aboard HMS *Brilliant* not too far from where they now stood, in that case the swinger a rat-faced sod called Kemp.

But time at sea, for all its tribulations, had taught them much, even if they were not always aware of what they had imbibed. The one thing that had taken root was that a Jack tar had rights and he was not to be shoved from pillar to post by any Tom, Dick or Harry. Sure, care had to be taken with proper authority, but a stand was needed too when that was arbitrary. Odd that Rufus, still looking younger than his years, with his freckled face and faraway expression, was the one who spoke up and he was serious.

'Don't reckon this barky sits with much water under its keel, mate, but you look short-arsed enough to me to drown in what's there. Might be best if you was to sling your hook and let my mate and I find our own place to berth.'

The message was as plain as the daylight outside the gun ports: use that starter if you want, but have a care after, for you are looking at a pair who might just seek you out in the dark night and give you what you seem ready to hand out, maybe even toss you over the side. That it was taken as the threat intended could not be doubted, even if Ugly did not blink or step backwards.

'Then be quick about it,' he growled.

'Why, brother,' Charlie said, 'we've got all the time in creation. Come on, Rufus, let's see who is on that fiddle you heard, for they are as like as not to be as we are, blue-water men.' That sent another message to Ugly: we know what we are about. 'And I have no mind to go and slumber among the rats on the decks below.'

As they eased through the crowded deck, eyed with a mixture of hope and suspicion by those that occupied it, Charlie praised his friend. 'You put that bugger in the right, Rufus.'

'Won't be talked to like that, Charlie, 'cepting maybe from a blue coat, and even then it has to be right.'

Charlie nearly said that Rufus, who had always deferred to him and had always seemed a bit gormless, was finally growing up; but it was not necessary – the lad knew that already and had just shown it plain.

They found what they were looking for where the wardroom would have been at one time, had the hulk had bulkheads to cut off accommodation for officers. A group of fellows with long pigtails had messed around the housing that still covered the rudder on which stood the fellow with the fiddle, with the blessing also of the casement windows that not only admitted much light but that could be opened a fraction to admit fresh air, though there was a batten across them to ensure they did not provide a means of escape – nobody, not even a nipper, could squeeze through the tiny gap.

As well as that there was some space, certainly enough for two more, although the eye contact Charlie and Rufus received when they appeared was not friendly. Yet they had a way of communicating without too many words that told those already there that these new arrivals were men who would know how to behave. Besides, they only had to look at their tar-ingrained hands to know these were a pair of proper seamen.

'Space for two more, brothers?' asked Charlie.

Those present looked at each other to check their assessment, until one fellow nodded.

'Then,' said Rufus, putting a hand into his bag and producing a packet of baccy, 'it be time to share a pipe.'

'And a penny for the entertainment,' said one of the group.

With that, Charlie slipped a coin from his palm, one he had extracted as they approached, a sure indication they knew the ropes. 'As required by custom.' Then he slapped it on the rudder housing.

CHAPTER FOUR

Having stolen a pair of fine horses, the question was now what to do with them; Pearce had no intention of riding all the way to London and stabling them, they did after all have brand marks and he could not be sure those owners would not report their loss, while just abandoning them was not fair to animals who were accustomed to good treatment. In the end it was a problem solved by Michael O'Hagan, who knew they were strapped for money and scoffed at his friend's sensibilities.

'Have we not stolen enough of their goods, John-boy? What difference is it going to make if we sell their horses?'

'It's not something I am accustomed to.'

Michael grinned. 'Are you after saying I am?'

'No, but who will buy horses that are not ours?'

That made the Irishman laugh out loud, his shoulders shaking as he walked his mare.

'Sure, you don't know much about those who trade in

horseflesh, do you? If there is a bunch of more dishonest folk then I have yet to encounter them. If they suspect the animals are not ours they will not do other than offer us a poor price. For certain they will not ask from whence they came.'

If it was not a trade John Pearce knew much about, the reputation of horse dealers preceded them, for if they appeared in public entertainments they were always shifty seedy-looking characters, even in their dress, which tended towards loud checks and misshapen hats, added to a habit of talking out of the sides of their mouths, while always looking to cheat whoever they were dealing with.

'I'm not sure it is something I could bring off, even if I could find the right person to sell to.'

'Then it is best left to me, John-boy.'

The place to sell was in the Medway towns of Chatham and Rochester, where there was a lively trade in many things due to the arrival and departure of men going to and coming from the sea, including goods of dubious provenance that often bore the marks of being government property: ropes with a red identifying thread; copper, it was rumoured but never proved, coming from the middle parts of bolts that were used to hold the keel timbers of a warship together, the two ends slotted in at each side to mask the theft.

Anything that could be lifted was fair game to the men who entered and left the Royal Dockyards of Chatham and Sheerness. Those who were supposed to check they were not hiding stolen property under the clothing, being as poorly rewarded as those they were set to search, could easily be bought off with rum tapped from the barrels in the spirit store, and what could not be carried out could be thrown over the long brick walls to waiting companions.

Lead, canvas, nails, turpentine, good timber, the aforesaid spirits, barrel staves and the metal hoops to make them whole, clothing, blocks of tar, even, it was said, the great cables made to secure the anchors of line-of-battle ships could go a'walking. The Medway towns had, for a hundred years, received so much in the way of purloined property it was no longer considered a crime to own any.

Hardly surprising then that the local horse-traders were as unscrupulous as their neighbours, people who, having no honesty themselves, reposed no trust in others. In a world where the animals they bought and sold were ubiquitous – nothing of weight could travel by road that did not require one or more horses – the space for underhand dealing was rife. When sold, mounts were doped, dyed a different colour, had any defects covered up by a variety of low tricks, all to extract an extra guinea or two.

'Now you must understand, John-boy, that even a sailor off to sea would never sell his livery – his horse yes, but the harness no.' Michael patted the saddle. 'But this here is as fine a piece of leather as ever I've been sat on, as is your own, and the rest of the harness is the same.'

'I do not know what you are driving at.'

'We will come up against sharp practice. These be fine horses but be prepared to be told they are spavined and useless, to hear a list of faults as long as your arm. I will wager we will be offered a sum so low as to make an honest man laugh, and what will happen then? Our man will give a loud sniff and say if we throw in the livery he might consider a better price.'

'You seem to know a great deal about the trade for all you say you do not.'

'Have you any idea of how many men of that occupation are Irish and have I not been to the weekly markets at home and watched how they go about the business? If you can play the fool, I can play a part too.'

'Which will be?'

'Unreliable servant.'

'The norm, then,' Pearce opined.

That led to a long discussion of how they should act; Pearce had to pretend to be a Kentish officer going to a new ship, Michael his less than wholly trusted servant. The need to dispose of these fine mounts for a fellow off to sea for a voyage of unknown duration was, it was hoped, enough to close off too many questions, and if they came too thick then they could just walk away. The Irishman made it sound so easy, Pearce was less sanguine.

'Shall we not invade France, just you and I, Michael, for I am sure it would be easier?'

In the end it was ridiculously easy and as simple as Michael said, for as luck would have it the Rochester market was in full weekly ferment. Mostly cattle and sheep, it was noisy with the sounds of livestock, lowing cows and bleating sheep, fowls of every description including cackling geese, and that was before you included the babble of trading humanity, buying and selling, with every transaction a shouted exchange and a slapping of spat-on hands; as a place to do an underhand trade it could not be bettered.

Horse dealers too were gathered in enough numbers to hope that one, sensing a trade as the pair led the horses slowly through the crowd, would approach them rather than the other way round. The man who obliged was a short fellow who appeared from seemingly nowhere out of a jostling mass, and if they had taken him to the playhouse at Sadler's Wells he would have been on the stage in a flash, so much of a caricature was he, button-brown eyes, a snub nose and clothes so loud they were close to screaming.

'Now there be a pair of true beauties,' he said, his mouth under one ear, his brogue strong Irish. 'By the Lord God in heaven, if you was lookin' to sell, you'd find an honest buyer in Fergal Keegan.'

'One of your fellow countrymen, Michael, I hazard,' Pearce said, in a foppish tone, which would have been perfect if he had not blushed so.

'Is that so?' Keegan cried.

'Sure, I am that, from near Ennis in Galway.'

The switch to Erse was immediate, and even if he was pretending to be vague John Pearce could not miss the look on the horse dealer's face as he conversed with Michael in a tongue only these two Paddies understood; being from Lowland Scottish stock and never having ventured north of Perth, the language of the Gaels was a mystery to him.

His friend played his part, using his height and build to cut out Pearce from even a sight of what they were transacting, this while the horse dealer edged them away from where they had met to a corner where the angle of a warehouse partly cut them off from view, no doubt out of sight of any competition.

'Why, Your Honour,' Michael cried, 'this fellow seems in a fair way to be an honest trader, who will give you a good price he tells me.'

'He is supposed to tell me.'

'I am curious, sir, as to your name and from where you come?'

'Franklin is the name, my man,' Pearce said, quickly, 'and I hail from the manor of Lydden.'

'Why I'm sure that is as fine a place as any in Kent County and the Franklins a fine upstanding family.'

Pearce replied, unsure if he was being guyed, 'I am not here to discuss my antecedents.'

That got another exchange in the Erse between the two Irishmen, the tone of which told Pearce he was being tagged as a cussed stuck-up sod, albeit both men were smiling at him as if he was a paragon.

'Your man here, Michael is it now, has told me of your predicament, about you being overdue aboard and is it not the work of the angels that had brought you to me.' With that Keegan crossed himself. 'Let me have a good look at what it is you want to sell.'

Given the man's opening remark, what followed was pure comedy, so much so it was hard not to laugh. Fergal Keegan had a glum way of sucking in breath through his teeth, and an awkward cast of the eye when he looked up, which was supposed to allude to any number of faults in the two mares. The ribs were showing a mite too much for a truly fit animal, the fetlock and shanks hot to the touch, indeed there did not seem a part of the mares from poll to hoof that was not in some way slightly imperfect.

'Well now, it just goes to show that a look is not enough,' he said eventually. 'What seems perfect from afar shows its faults by close inspection. I expect I could run, maybe, to twenty guineas.'

'Each?' Pearce snapped.

'Lord no, twenty guineas the pair. Now I will grant that they look fine to an unpractised eye, sir, but if I was to list what was not right, sure we would be here all of the day.'

Ignorance only extended so far; to John Pearce's reckoning they were forty-guinea horses in anyone's money and possibly, if they did race well, worth a great deal more than that and the truth of the thoughts showed on his face.

'Now I am a fair man, Lieutenant Franklin, and I will not say you could not do better, if you had the time, so it may be I can stretch to an extra five guineas since you are a kindly master I am told by one of my fellow countrymen.'

'I will not be robbed, sir. Come, Michael, there will be other dealers here on market day.'

'Hold, sir,' Keegan cried, his hands up and near to actually pressing on Pearce's breast, 'you are too hasty.'

A burst of Erse from Michael resulted in a theatrical ponder from his countryman, leg thrust out, eyes cast down, finger on chin. 'Would twenty guineas a mare be acceptable, sir?'

'I would consider it.'

'That would, of course, include the livery.' Keegan,

pushing for a conclusion, spat on his hand and held it out. Michael nodded and Pearce took it and shook on the deal. 'If we can move close to, sir, I would not want the exchange witnessed.'

They were in a huddle for a whole minute of counting, as coins were carefully laid in Pearce's hand. The sum paid, Keegan spoke to Michael again in the island tongue, nodded to Pearce and led the mares away into the crowd.

'Do you think he knows they're stolen?'

'Sure, John-boy, it's not a question of what he knows, but what he cares about.'

'What did he say to you last?'

'How to collect my fee of five guineas for telling him you were easy to dupe, which I am supposed to collect this night at a place called the Rose Tavern.'

'And are you going to?'

'Why would I bother, when I doubt he would be there?'

Heinrich Lutyens, the one-time surgeon of HMS *Brilliant* and John Pearce's good friend, stared at the papers in his hand, for in doing so he avoided looking at Emily Barclay, which served to hide his disappointment. The last time he had seen them had been aboard the ship bringing him and Emily, as well as many wounded seamen, home from the Mediterranean.

John Pearce, also aboard, had asked him to keep the papers safe by hiding them in his instrument chest; he felt they were unsafe in the tiny wardroom cabin he had been allotted, especially since the wounded Ralph

Barclay was travelling home in the same vessel, albeit he had just lost an arm and was housed in different, better accommodation. Emily, refusing to share that with him, had berthed next to Lutyens on the orlop deck, acting, as she had on many occasions for him, as a nurse to the wounded for whom he was caring.

HMS *Grampus*, a vessel in serious need of a refit, had mysteriously caught fire, a nightmare to every man who sailed in wooden ships. In the mayhem that followed, while his personal possessions had been saved, that heavy instrument chest had required to be abandoned, as had the *Grampus* itself; they had watched her burn to the waterline before sinking beneath the waves, John Pearce being convinced that his valuable evidence had gone down with it.

That Emily should have taken them was surprising enough; that she had kept secret from John Pearce she had possession of them bordered on a level of artifice he thought her incapable of, yet it was understandable. The real hurt, which he was reluctant to admit, was that she had taken them from his own chest and had not seen fit to put them back into his hands, an act that could only have occurred because she knew they were there and what they contained.

'Why give them to me now?'

'I do not trust my husband not to send someone to rob me, which he would if he knew I had them in my rooms.'

He looked at her now, his fish-like face showing real distress. 'And how am I going to explain their sudden reappearance to John?'

Emily was shocked. 'You misunderstand, Heinrich, I will tell him how and why I have them.'

'He may well suspect I colluded in your act, he may well wonder if I showed them to you after they were entrusted to me.'

'Then if he does, I will inform him of his error, which was always the case from the first.'

'Such calculation.'

Unused to his disapproval, Emily was wounded by it now. 'That is not a word I expected to hear from your lips.'

Lutyens waved the loose sheaf of papers, which flapped, creating a draught of air that touched Emily's face. 'You must have read these prior to . . .' There being no need to finish that statement, Emily nodded. 'Which means you eavesdropped on the conversation John and I had about his leaving them with me and why.'

'It was impossible not to, all that lay between our two berths was a canvas screen.'

The response was terse. 'It is always possible not to eavesdrop.'

Such an admonition induced a long period of silence; he was clearly angry and Emily had little in her defence to deflect it. She was far from ashamed, though she knew she ought to be. Yet what she had done, an act that flew in the face of the way she had been raised, was just, to her, another indication of her desperation, though at the time it had been instinct which had informed her actions.

'I admit it was wrong, Heinrich, and I beg your forgiveness, but I would like you to consider what feelings

I had when I heard what was said. I acted on impulse not, as you seem to suspect, from calculation . . .'

'And since?'

Her response was a whisper. 'I kept them to protect myself as well as my position. I used them to persuade my husband to agree to that which I demanded of him.'

'Which is somewhat less than admirable, given how important they are to a man you profess to care for.'

'You are being cruel, which I did not think was in your nature.'

'It is not, but I cannot keep these. You must take them away from here, for I want no part of what you have done.'

'And where do you suggest I take them?'

'Back to Studdert.'

'Which would make me look foolish indeed.'

'John has engaged a special pleader to prepare his case against Captain Barclay, take them to him.'

'Who is he?'

'That I do not know, but his prize agent, a fellow called Davidson, does. Ask him.'

'Do you know where John has gone?'

'He did not tell you?'

She shook her head. 'All he said was that he was engaged upon an enterprise that would bring in such profit that I would not need any support from my husband.'

'Then it seems,' Lutyens snapped, 'he reposes in me even less trust than do you, for he did not even bother to tell me he was going anywhere at all.'

It took great effort to hold back her tears, for she saw this man as a dear friend, but Emily was also determined not to let him see how much he had upset her. Part of her reasons for coming to him had been that faith, but there had also been the chance to talk, to ask advice, to seek to map out part of that future about which John Pearce appeared so confident and she so dreaded.

They were in the very room where, encouraged by Lutyens, they had finally admitted what he knew and they had sought to suppress, that they were deeply attracted to each other. How swiftly that had moved to a notion that they could live as a couple! The word 'mistress' terrified her, yet Pearce seemed so convinced that they could enjoy that estate, or live abroad as man and wife without anyone knowing of the deception. She wanted to test that with the only friend who might understand and give her untainted advice on how she should proceed.

'Heinrich, you are the person I have most trust in.'

'Not John?'

'I will not hide from you, I cannot hide from you, that I have feelings for him, but I am not sure the kind of faith I have in you is something I can extend to him, he is too impetuous for that.'

'He is certainly that.' Lutyens threw up his hands and sighed. 'You say he has gone off on some errand that fills him with elation, which leads me to suspect, given his nature, that it is not without risk.'

'He implied to me that was not the case.'

'John would.'

Alexander Davidson lived and carried out his business in Harpur Street, not far from her rooms in Jockey's Fields, and was happy to take an unannounced visit from her; as a prize agent who lived above the shop, it was something to which he was accustomed from time-pressed naval officers. He had no idea where John Pearce was either, nor, it seemed, was he aware that he was sitting opposite the wife of the man against whom he was hoping to bring a case.

The name of Barclay had never been mentioned to him, only that Pearce required legal assistance, so he had happily named the special pleader who had been engaged to prepare a case against Emily's husband, a fellow called Lucknor, to whom his client had gone as a recommendation from him.

'But how,' she asked, somewhat disingenuously, 'can he proceed without evidence, which he has given me to understand he does not have?'

'Lucknor tells me he has written some letters on Mr Pearce's behalf to be sent out to the Mediterranean, asking for evidence. To a Lieutenant Digby Mr Pearce served under and a couple of midshipmen.'

'Midshipmen?'

'Yes. Both apparently served aboard HMS *Brilliant*.' Davidson thought for a moment, seeking to recall the names. 'Yes, one is called Farmiloe and the other Burns, Toby Burns; do you know of them?'

'Only too well, Mr Davidson, the last named is my nephew.'

The dejected way she said that induced silence, but it did not last long.

'Mr Davidson, I wonder if you would be prepared to hold on to some papers for Lieutenant Pearce? He left them with me but I reckon them to be better placed here.'

'I can see no reason why not, but are they valuable?'

'Not in any terms of money, but I'm sure they have a value to your client.'

'Then,' Davidson smiled, 'he will have the use of my safe.'

When she left, Emily Barclay was thinking about Toby Burns; if she did not know the contents of the letter that had been sent, she could guess at the questions it might pose. And she knew him only too well; would her nephew tell the truth or continue to lie?

CHAPTER FIVE

'How's the arm, Mr Burns?' demanded Admiral Sir William Hotham.

He had just arrived by the entry port of his flagship, HMS *Britannia*, anchored in the bay called San Fiorenzo after the town at its base. Outside the entry port the sea was a sparkling blue, reflecting a sky of the same colour, while coming in off the land was a warm and pine-scented breeze; it was, after all, the springtime and the whole rugged island of Corsica was in bloom.

Hierarchy ensured the admiral had first to enquire after the commissioned officer on this particular duty and also he had been obliged to acknowledge the file of marines that always attended the departure or arrival of the second in command of the Mediterranean Fleet. But that done, no one could mistake the extra air of benign interest he took in the welfare of Toby Burns.

Much to the chagrin of his fellow midshipmen, all of whom sought the favour of so powerful a man, Hotham talked to the boy in the manner of a favourite uncle; the only person failing to see him in that way was the being so addressed. The question related to a slight wound Toby Burns had received while helping to haul a brace of naval cannon over the high mountainous Pass of Teghime to besiege Bastia in the company of a regiment of redcoats; the whole thing had been a fiasco, a short engagement leading to a hurried retreat.

'Healing, sir,' Toby Burns replied, careful to add as he touched the sling, 'yet it still pains me somewhat.'

'Then, young fellow, I require you to see the surgeon and, once he has examined you, tell him I want a full report on your condition, but that can wait until this tedious errand is complete, can it not?'

'Aye, aye, sir.'

'You are about to dine with the great and the good, young fellow, and perhaps relate your adventures. We cannot leave it to the bullocks to tell the navy how they fared, or should we say failed, outside Bastia. You will not struggle to make my barge?'

The article in question was bobbing up and down several feet below at the end of a stepped gangway, fully manned with smartly dressed oarsmen, those sticks rigidly upright and dressed. Hotham was a stickler for his dignity and before he descended in the wake of both Burns and his flag lieutenant he paused to ensure that nothing was out of place. Particular anyway, he was off to sup with a man he equated to the devil and nothing must be untoward enough to invite comment.

The major part of the fleet commanded by Samuel, Lord Hood was anchored in the deep bay, but only once they got close to *Victory* was it possible to observe that HMS *Agamemnon*, Commodore Nelson's flagship, lay to seaward, his blue pennant still on the mizzenmast. Being in the presence of several senior officers and only holding his own rank as a courtesy, that pennant should have been struck – a fact alluded to and not with much joy by the admiral, albeit *sotto voce* so that only the lieutenant and Toby Burns could hear.

'Fellow's a schemer of the worst sort, you know. All Nelson's projections somehow end up with him chasing after the laurels and damn anyone else. I daresay our foolish C.-in-C. has indulged him in allowing the pennant, but I'm damned if I would.'

Hotham was piped aboard with all the ceremony due to his rank and having carried out the required inspection of the marine guard he made his way to Hood's cabin, the flag lieutenant at his heels; prior to dinner there was to be a conference on how to proceed in throwing the French off the island, basically by taking both the only places they still held, the heavily fortified towns of Bastia and Calvi.

This left his midshipman at something of a loss, so he made his way down to the berth in which he had at one time been accommodated to seek a familiar face, shocked to find that of the twenty-four souls who had been occupants all were now serving in other vessels, so rapid was the turnover of souls in a fleet at war. Instead of receiving a greeting he was met by those present with blank stares.

Not wishing to linger with strangers he made his way

back up to the main deck, seeking to look inconspicuous in amongst an international knot of officers, both British services in red and blue, green-coated Spaniards and some very swarthy coves who seemed to dress as they pleased, whom he took to be Corsicans. Drifting through the throng, he picked up hints of what was afoot: an attack on Bastia from the sea.

'Well I wish you joy of it,' he said softly to himself, his free hand going to his wounded arm, as if that was a talisman that would keep him away from such a hare-brained escapade.

'Burns?'

The use of his name stopped Toby in his tracks and he peered at the fellow who had addressed him, for there was nought but lantern light on this deck, the voice identifying the speaker as much as the face. Taller than Toby Burns and a bit older, it was a fellow mid from HMS *Brilliant*.

'Farmiloe?'

'What are you doing aboard?'

'I could ask you the same question, could I not?'

'I came with Commodore Nelson in command of his barge.'

There was a hint of boast in the reply from Toby Burns. 'I am here at the express command of Admiral Hotham. It seems I am to dine in the great cabin.'

That such a lowly mid was to take a place in the commanding admiral's cabin evoked no curiosity; it was habit in the service to include the odd minnow in such gatherings, in order to teach them some proper manners, as well as being a sign of favour.

'Still in Hotham's flagship, then?' Burns nodded. 'What's with the sling?'

'Took a musket ball in the hills outside Bastia.'

'Did you, by damn?' The why and the how explained, Farmiloe added. 'That is where we have just come from.'

'Are you still in *Brilliant*?'

'No, though she is part of the squadron. I shifted to *Agamemnon* as acting sixth.'

Farmiloe grinned, showing very white teeth in what was now a face made brown by the Mediterranean sun, his voice full of good-humoured self-deprecation. He was a good-looking youth, fair-haired, taller than Toby Burns and it was obvious that he had matured somewhat since they had first met at Sheerness under the command of Ralph Barclay.

'Which just goes to show, Toby, how short is the fleet of commissioned lieutenants.'

'It does, Dick.'

Burns gave that reply in a flat inappropriate tone, taking at face value Farmiloe's jocular modesty, which sent a confused flicker across the speaker's face, though only for a moment.

'Mind you, we are short of everything; *Agamemnon* is so high in the water for want of stores she can barely hold to her wind, but you cannot get our commodore away from action to re-victual. The man is a proper terrier and insists that the mountain must come to us.'

The interjection after the word 'terrier' – 'So I have heard' – reflected what Hotham had said in his barge, which was in stark contrast to the enthusiasm evident in

Farmiloe's bright-blue eyes, his manner as animated as his countenance.

'Not a day goes by that we are not at some task or other, taking merchant vessels, raiding ashore. We went in and had a bash at bombarding the port, which we reckoned did no damage at all to the walls of the citadel and left us with half a dozen forty-two-pound balls lodged in our scantlings, not that they threatened the ship in any way. It was only when a Dane came out next day that we learnt we had dismounted three cannon.'

'How splendid.'

'You should get yourself out of an admiral's ship, Toby.'

There was a note of real pique in the reply. 'I get out too damned often, Dick. I went in with the army's boats at San Fiorenzo yonder only to see my lieutenant take a ball that crippled him, while I nearly got my head blown off. No sooner was the town captured than I was sent off over the mountains under a mad marine who managed to get himself killed in a mad charge on an enemy battery.'

Toby Burns checked himself then; he had been about to add that he thought Hotham had it in for him but that was not a wise thing to say to anyone.

'Damn it, Toby, I wouldn't miss it for the world.'

'Servants are gathering,' Toby said, nodding to the line of men in clean checked shirts and red bandanas; not quite a deliberate change of subject, it was close.

'I'm invited to the wardroom for dinner, which I hazard will be a damn sight more relaxed affair than what

75

you are going to attend.' Farmiloe began to walk away, calling over his shoulder. 'Don't disgrace yourself.'

Which left his one-time shipmate wondering what he meant.

There was a great deal of glitter in the admiral's great cabin and not just from the crystal and silverware. Toby Burns was surrounded by senior officers of both services, all loud in their conversation, most of which went over his head. Like most midshipmen – even he conformed to the description of a growing lad – he was in a state of permanent unrequited hunger and what he was being served was not only fresh from the shore, but of a much higher quality than he was accustomed to, while it was pleasing to have one of the servants, on spotting his sling, cut up his food for him.

At the head of the table sat Lord Hood and on his right an elderly man he knew to be General Pasquale Paoli, the hero of Corsican independence, a man he had been told had once been much lionised by London society, while the next seat was taken by Sir Gilbert Elliot, a civilian diplomat type who seemed to have Paoli's ear.

On Hood's left sat Hotham, eating with a refinement lacking in most of the guests, careful with his napkin to ensure that no food remained visible on his face or clothing after consumption. It took no great discernment to observe that Hood's conversation was entirely to his right, to Paoli and Elliot; in terms of inclusion in what had to be the prime conversation, Hotham was being ignored.

Nelson was a couple of places away from the admiral, in strict order of rank, and he was clearly in the kind of high spirits that so impressed Farmiloe. Given the arrangement of the tables, his voice was loud enough to carry over the hubbub of other conversations to what could be considered below the salt. The man was an object of curiosity, for Toby had heard him described as a combative sort by fellows other than his one-time shipmate, which was amazing given he was so short in the leg and no great shakes in the chest either, obvious even if he was sitting down.

As well as that he was a conversational arm-waver, emphasising what he was saying with sweeping gestures that went with the nature of his piping high-pitched voice. He had just finished relating an action at sea, involving some French war vessel called *Melpomene*, which sounded like a sharp engagement, and had moved on to the subject of Bastia, around which, backing up what Farmiloe had said, he had made several excursions ashore to burn whatever he could find.

'Population's about four thousand in all, we reckon, with a garrison that cannot number more than a quarter of that number.'

'Cannon?' asked another post captain, a fellow unknown to Toby Burns.

'Forty-two-pounders and well worked, for you can trust John Crapaud to handle his guns well.'

'As we found to our cost at Toulon,' Nelson's companion replied.

'They have stripped out a frigate called *La Flèche* and landed her guns,' Nelson said, adding a bit of a glass-rattling slap to the mahogany tabletop. 'But I mean to have her, sir, and damn me if we don't take the town with her.'

'You do not anticipate, Captain Nelson, that Bastia might be a harder nut to crack than you stated at the conference?' Those words came from Hotham and in his expression it was plain he had reservations. 'After all, if our army friends decline to support you, then they must have sound reasons.'

That stopped whatever words Hood was saying to Pasquale Paoli and had him turn his head to glare at Hotham, heavy grey eyebrows lowered above that very prominent nose added to a look he took care to soften, given the number of people present, even if it was no secret that they despised each other.

'Sir William, the matter has been decided. While I respect the soldiers' right to decline to take part in the investiture of Bastia, I have the troops at my disposal to undertake the task without their involvement.'

The reply was as smooth as the man making it, this while some of the soldiers growled and looked along the table; Hood was making them sound shy instead of prudent for their insistence that they lacked the numbers to be effective.

'I know, Milord, but I cannot help but think that Captain Nelson, whose plan it is, might have underestimated the difficulties.'

'Which we have discussed.'

'I only seek a fuller picture.'

'Sir,' Nelson interjected, 'the garrison is locked in to landward by the very excellent troops of General Paoli.' That got an appreciative nod from the Corsican, who having spent so much time exiled in London spoke good English. 'They cannot be reinforced except by sea and I will bar that . . .'

'With my aid,' Hood added.

'Of course, Milord,' Nelson nodded, so emphatically that several locks of his abundant corn-coloured hair slipped from his queue. 'Despair is as much a weapon as cannon fire, Sir William, and I cannot but feel that the men of the garrison will be disinclined to lay down their lives for a revolution which cannot support them.'

'Especially when I announce what I was going to leave till our dinner was over!' Hood barked that statement and stood looking to the Corsican leader. 'But now will do as well as any. General Paoli has asked that he be allowed to petition His Majesty, King George, to accept the island the general has fought so long and hard for as a territory owing allegiance to the British crown.'

Hood let the buzz of conversation carry on for a few seconds before picking up his goblet of wine, an act immediately copied by everyone else, Toby included, albeit he was a bit tardy.

'When Bastia falls, gentlemen, as I am sure it will' – that came with a sideways flick to Hotham – 'then two flags will fly above its citadel, that of our Corsican allies alongside the standard of King George. So, a toast to a long and happy association with the free people of this island, under the benign sovereignty of John Bull.'

Everyone stood to toast that and it came with three times three in cheers; even Hotham was driven to a few muted hurrahs! When things had died down and everyone went back to their previous conversations, Hotham caught Nelson's attention once more.

'Captain Nelson, may I point out to you that midshipman

well down the board?' Toby Burns found himself under more eyes than those of the admiral and the commodore, so much so that his neck disappeared. 'He carries a wound, for he took a ball graze in the arm outside Bastia in support of our gallant soldiers.'

That got some hard looks from the redcoats present; they could sniff an insult however well disguised and they had barely tried to invest Bastia. They had claimed it was too well defended with the troops they had at their disposal and still was.

'But I expect Mr Burns' arm to be fully healed within a day or two.'

'Brave fellow,' said Nelson, with a look that seemed as if he meant it.

'He is that, Captain,' Hotham continued, 'and I can assure you he will liven your table with stories of his exploits, young as he is.' Toby Burns knew what was coming, just as he knew he could do nothing about it. 'Given his love, nay his addiction to risk, it would be tragic for him to languish aboard my flagship with action in the offing.'

'You wish me, sir, to take him to Bastia, sir?' Nelson asked, grinning inanely in the direction of Toby Burns, who was thinking maybe he had drunk too much.

'I do, Captain, as long as you promise me that he will be given further opportunity to distinguish himself. I would not wish to spare him for no purpose.'

'I weigh as soon as we complete our dinner, sir.'

Hotham was looking directly at Toby then, his pale-blue eyes as bland as his habitual facial expression, until he leant back to signal to one of the servants. 'Then I suggest you must take him aboard immediately. I will send my barge for his dunnage this very instant and have it aboard *Agamemnon* before you set foot in her.'

'Well, young fellow,' Nelson cried, his voice full of hearty good cheer. 'What can you say to that, except to most humbly thank Sir William for such favour?'

There was no one to talk to, not a single soul he could confide in, and it was hard enough to get some peace to think aboard Nelson's ship as it prepared to weigh. Hotham was deliberately putting him in the way of danger again and all because he had been the chief witness at his Uncle Ralph's court martial. Typical of Toby Burns he would not, in his misery, admit to being the chief liar as well; to his mind coercion – and Ralph Barclay had applied that in bucketloads – absolved him of any blame for the untruths he had uttered.

The only person he knew even vaguely was Richard Farmiloe, yet he constituted the last person who could provide a confessional ear. Farmiloe had been with Barclay the night he had deliberately raided the Liberties and was such a threat to the captain that he, like Pearce and his stupidly named Pelicans, had been sent off on an errand to La Rochelle, allowing the trial to take place when they were well out of the way.

And now it was apparent Hotham felt threatened, for if lowly Toby Burns ever told the truth and denied the testimony he had entered to the court off Toulon, that he had been with his uncle when he had not, that it was not, and could not be, his fault they had entered the Liberties by his navigational mistake, for the very simple reason he was not present at all, the repercussions could ripple out to engulf even an admiral as well connected politically as Hotham.

It would have cheered miserable Toby Burns immeasurably to know that the admiral was harbouring the same thoughts. He had taken Barclay under his wing as a client – every captain needed a flag officer on his side – partly for the favours he had done on the way out to the Mediterranean, but another reason was that Hood disliked him. This meant while the man owed a duty to him, Hotham owed a reciprocal obligation, as he did to any of the captains who supported his flag and backed him against the C.-in-C.

Thus he had set up that sympathetic court, chosen as judges officers he could trust, suppressed the written depositions damning Barclay and sent away the witnesses who could do him harm. Yet like an itch he could not scratch there was that little toad Burns, whom he had taken into *Britannia* to hold him close; Barclay would never betray him, for to do so would incriminate himself, – but Toby Burns? He had the backbone of an eel and would not withstand any pressure if questioned.

'Let us hope,' he said out loud, 'that Nelson gets the little bugger's head blown off.'

Truly there was no joy in being second in command to the likes of Hood, a man who had made a fatal error at Toulon by not only accepting the rebellious French officers as allies, but also by occupying the port as a bastion against the Revolution. The fleet should have sailed in, sunk every ship in the harbour and burnt those tied up on the quays, but he had not and what was the result now?

Not only had they been evicted from the main French base in the Mediterranean, with significant loss of life, but he now had to take a squadron of line-of-battle ships and blockade those very same ships Hood had failed to destroy in that very same harbour. It was not long before pen and paper were in use as he composed another complaint to his political patron, the Duke of Portland, the subject being the same as many others – that he, William Hotham, was better suited to command the fleet than Samuel Hood.

CHAPTER SIX

The party that arrived on the main deck of the receiving hulk was strong enough to handle any trouble, a clutch of hard-case impress men, quite a few with the look in their eye that hoped for a bit of a scrap. Their presence, where they could not be seen, was announced by the way the babble of talk fell abruptly silent. Charlie Taverner knew there to be upwards of five hundred souls accommodated on the decks, this told to him by those he and Rufus had joined by the casements; he also knew how few were seamen, which meant many would have been taken up by violence.

These hard bargains were led by an officer, a scarred lieutenant who looked as if he might relish his job. As he walked down the deck he counted off parties of a dozen at a time and told them brusquely to gather up what they possessed and make their way to the boats waiting to take them to their new home; it was not long into this task that one man protested to his being on board as a crime and the result was swift.

The lieutenant stepped forward and grabbed him by the hair, half lifting his squealing body and shaking it; what followed was a spittle-filled diatribe that told this unfortunate if he thought he had once had rights, they were now no longer his. He was subject to the disciplines of the navy and the Articles of War, so he had a choice: move his arse or face a rope at the yardarm.

'He's a real beauty,' said Rufus. 'Happen we should go forrard and tell the fellow he's tugging that the blue coat is talking shite.'

'I'd hold my wind, boyo, and stay close to us if I was you.'

These words were uttered by a burly Welshman the Pelicans had come to know as Davy; they had yet to find out if that was a first name or last, not that it mattered.

'You don't know about hulks, look you? They're not like rated ships and there are folk that have died from being battered on this barky and nought will be said about it. If you look you will see them buggers are carrying clubs, not just starters, and by Christ they like to employ them.'

That was followed by a loud sniff through substantial nostrils. 'There's safety in numbers, mind, which I might take leave to show you should they come our way.'

The near-scalped individual having been hauled away, the lieutenant, judging by the expression on his face, was now looking for another victim but there was no one willing to oblige. Slowly the impress party made their way towards the stern, groups of men being taken away by the scruff of their necks or a boot in the rear if they showed any hint of dawdling, and finally the lieutenant came face-to-face with the body of proper seamen, some thirty in number, silhouetted against the light from the casements.

'On your feet to a man,' he barked. 'You're shifting.'

'So where are we off to, Your Honour?' asked Davy, winking at Charlie and Rufus.

'Does it matter?'

Davy stood up very slowly, followed by all the others. 'It would be a kindness to be told.'

'Kindness,' the lieutenant scoffed, half turning to share what had to be a jest with his men, not one of whom so much as smiled.

'You bein' the soul of that commodity, look you.'

'Don't you josh me, Taff.'

'Now would I do that to you, a man in a blue coat? And the name is Davy.'

'As if I care.'

Charlie nudged Rufus and gave him a look, while a clasping of his fists told him to be prepared to fight; for all Davy had said about remaining quiet it was clear he wanted to challenge these men, just as it was obvious by the way his companions had gathered they were prepared to back him up.

'The name of the ship an' who is to command her . . .' The pause was too long and that showed in the lieutenant's face, which did not soften as Davy eventually added, 'Sir.'

'You'll go aboard her, regardless.'

The way Davy slowly shook his head had Charlie on his toes – these men with whom he had messed were ready for this; pressed sailors or volunteers, they had come aboard with what every Jack tar carried in their ditty bag, which would include a knife and a folding razor. Hands were in duck pockets and it took no great imagination to think what they were holding in a place where violence could occur at any moment.

'We are not, look you, like those poor buggers who have been pressed from backstreets or lied to when in drink. We're worth a kindness, as I say.'

It was interesting to watch the officer's eyes and the calculation going on behind them; with the look of a fighter himself he was backed up by half a dozen men of the same ilk, but it was a case of games and candles – was the bloodshed worth the refusal to answer a simple question, or was his authority so central to his being that he was prepared for a brawl?

Maybe it was good sense, maybe it was that he and his men were well outnumbered, that eventually made him speak after a substantial tense and long pause. 'HMS *Semele*, Captain Barclay.'

'Jesus,' whispered Rufus. 'I ain't going.'

'You are,' Charlie replied in a soft voice as, satisfied to have won a small victory, Davy picked up his ditty bag prior to moving, that followed by the rest. 'We are only two.'

Low as they were, Davy had overheard Charlie's words and he very quietly hissed a response. 'Numbers, boyos – never act against the powers that be without you are backed up by numbers.'

The boats had not long gone to where their new home was berthed, wallowing midstream out in the Medway, when a hired wherry pulled up at the gangway of the hulk, John Pearce seeking permission to come aboard, which was granted. Having asked for the commander he was led to a hutch on the upper deck, leaving Michael behind.

The man's accommodation was a housing constructed where the wheel and binnacle might have been. Knocking and entering he introduced himself, thinking the scarred fellow looked more of the article than the man Tobias he had encountered in Dover; this fellow was a proper ruffian who would likely not be suited to the manners of a normal wardroom. The question was, would he fall for a downright lie?

'I am, sir, in search of a couple of men who were my followers, wrongly taken up at Dover.'

There was, unsurprisingly, a pause, while the request was filtered through layers of probability, but the methods of recruiting, the law notwithstanding, did not often lead to a prior interrogation of a man's status. Still, an officer's close followers being pressed men was unusual, they either having tickets of leave or being too well versed in avoidance to be collared. Yet it was also a courtesy, adhered to by long custom, that any fellow officer seeking his own men should be obliged where possible.

'Names?'

'Taverner and Dommet.' That saw the opening of a thick ledger and a request as to when they might have arrived. 'Yesterday, possibly today.'

The finger moved up the list of names. 'They are entered as volunteers.'

The rehearsed reply was smooth. 'An error, admitted to by Captain Tobias.'

The man was not quick of mind, or perhaps he knew Tobias well and doubted the statement. 'Well you've missed them, I'm afraid, Lieutenant Pearce, they have not long been taken aboard HMS *Semele*, indeed within the last hour.'

The 'damn' was inadvertent but loudly expressed.

'So I fear you must take up their status with the man slated to command her and see if he will consent to give them over to you, though I should be quick, for she is already ordered to sea and subject to the admiral's impatience.'

'And that commander is?'

'Captain Barclay is to captain her.'

'Ralph Barclay!'

'I believe that is his given name. Do you know him?'

It was an ill-tempered John Pearce who rejoined Michael O'Hagan – the term 'spitting blood' would not have been exaggeration – but there was nothing he could do in Chatham about an act of fate so hard on his friends. By the time he could stamp his foot on terra firma it was getting dark, so they made for the Angel Inn, the Medway end of the London post-chaise service, to eat a gloomy dinner and spend the night.

In the morning, prior to catching the coach from London, Pearce insisted they visit an emporium dealing in naval supplies. There he bought himself a new sword and a pistol, as well as a holster that went over his shoulder under his blue coat.

'We were lucky with those horses, Michael, and I do

not intend to be caught out again. Now what will you take as a weapon?'

'Not a long sword, John-boy, for I would look like a fool bearing one of those, as most men do.' The look he got from Pearce then produced a laugh. 'I will not have a sissy weapon but a proper hanger will do nicely.'

Short, curved and heavy of blade, when Michael stuck the sword in his waistband belt it seemed to disappear, wholly so when he closed his jacket.

'There's upwards of four hundred souls coming aboard with us, and more to come, I reckon,' Charlie insisted, as they approached the side of the 74-gunner, 'an' I don't reckon Barclay to know us from Adam, so we keeps our head down, our noses clean and our arses out of his path.'

'It ain't him that worries me, Charlie, an' you know it. What if Devenow is still with him?'

That did give Charlie pause and he looked at the dark waters over the gunnels, barely disturbed by those rowing them to their destination, Devenow being a drunken bully whose only passion in life seemed to be to serve with Ralph Barclay. He was nearly as big as Michael O'Hagan and a total bastard.

His favourite trick was to 'persuade' his shipmates to give up their ration of grog, which he would hoard until he had enough to get insensibly drunk. That this often led to a flogging, handed down to him many times by Barclay, neither bothered him, deterred him or affected the regard he had for a captain he had followed from ship to ship.

'If we was missing Michael,' Rufus added, 'we miss him double now.'

'He could handle Devenow, all right,' Charlie acknowledged, recalling the bare-knuckle fight they had engaged in aboard *Brilliant*, 'so let's hope he is still acting as Barclay's servant, as he was aboard *Grampus*, though Christ knows he must be the worst in creation.'

'There might be others who pick us out, that little shit Burns for one.'

'No, Barclay got rid of him off Toulon; now let's get ourselves set and pick the right mess.'

'Davy might be a good bet.'

'You have the right of it there. Stay close to him as we get aboard and see if we can share his table.'

'Be a lot of folk seeking that, Charlie.'

'Then sharp elbows are needed, Rufus, and you being a skinny bugger, yours is sharper than most. An' when we is set, let us find a man who can write and get a message off to John Pearce to tell him where we are.'

HMS *Agamemnon*, of sixty-four guns and reputedly the fastest line-of-battle ship in the fleet, having raided the rest of the fleet for enough stores to remain at sea and accompanied by transports carrying a thousand troops in her wake, had weathered Cape Corse and was now beating down the east of the island to rejoin the squadron of frigates off Bastia, while on the upper deck, under the supervision of Acting Sixth Lieutenant Richard Farmiloe, were assembled a line of midshipmen newly arrived from home.

Some were barely able to see over the bulwarks they

were so young and stunted. With their sextants in hand, they were shooting the sun and the horizon to establish local noon – and giving several conflicting answers – while looking out upon a sea that was the same azure blue as the clear sky, with the tiny island outcrop of Monte Cristo a smudge in the distance, while not far beyond that lay Elba and the Italian coast.

'Which I am told you can see from the mountain tops on a day like this, Toby.'

'Really, Dick?' Toby Burns responded, his knees giving to try and compensate for the excessive roll of a ship lacking the ballast provided by a proper quantity of stores. 'I saw nothing but cold mist from up there myself.'

The sling was gone and with it his excuse for being left alone for, as soon as he had boarded, Nelson had done what Hotham had clearly required of him. *Agamemnon's* surgeon, a Scotsman called Roxburgh, had examined his wound and then, clearly quite mad, had suggested that fresh sea air might be efficacious in further healing the angry scar left by the musket ball, his advice that Toby should appear on the deck in nought but his shirtsleeves and that with one rolled up, for which the surgeon would seek permission.

The only good reason to be on deck was to get dry, this being a vessel in serious need of a refit. Her seams were moving alarmingly, even in what was a fairly benign swell, and the working of the pumps was a constant background to the whistle of the wind through rigging that, even to an untutored eye, was looking very worn indeed, while the deck planking had been scrubbed and sanded for so long there was a wonder if the boards would support the weight of the cannon.

'Nelson won't hear of the dockyard when there's a fight in the offing,' was the reply Toby Burns got from Farmiloe when he alluded to the state of the ship. 'But when we have Bastia, I think it is not a task that can be much delayed.'

He had stuck close to Farmiloe, he being the only fellow he knew, and on hand to explain to Toby the difference between serving on this ship and any other, which was, of course, that the man in charge was Horatio Nelson. Toby saw a fellow not much bigger than himself, who for all his smiles and bonhomie was an odd creature, and he wondered at what everyone was on about, for his old shipmate was not in any way an exception when it came to regard for the pint-sized commodore.

To Toby's mind he lacked *gravitas*. 'But he talks to the crew as if he is one of them, I have seen him do it.'

'He feels he is,' Farmiloe had replied, 'because he once sailed as a lad before the mast on the triangular passage and he knows the 'tween decks as well as he does the great cabin. We are all one to Nelson, whatever our rank.'

Fodder to his pride and ambition, Toby had thought, but he did not say anything of the sort; that would be most unwise.

The cry of 'sail ho' and the news that they had sighted the squadron was enough to make even Toby strain to see, for HMS *Brilliant*, at one time his Uncle Ralph's ship and the vessel in which he had first gone to sea, was one of those Nelson commanded. The cry also brought the man in question on deck.

His immediate enquiry was to the lookout atop the main, this as to the presence of other transports, these being the ships he had hoped were come from Naples with the larger ordnance he needed to invest Bastia. The affirmative reply took some time to be relayed and had the commodore pacing the windward side of the quarterdeck in obvious impatience, his mood changing immediately on receipt of the good news.

'Gentlemen,' he cried, his bright-blue eyes alight. 'Write your letters home this night, for on the morrow we will begin to set a fox amongst our French geese and get them a'cackling.'

The hurrahs swept along the deck, making Toby wonder if he was the only one aboard who was not a mad fool – something driven home with even more force when, later in the day, he joined a mass of red coats and blue, the captains and premiers of the remainder of the squadron and the army men from the transports, all crowded into Nelson's cabin, to hear from his own lips his plans.

This time, Toby noticed, Nelson was abstemious in the article of drink, which he had not been at Hood's dinner. While he had not returned to *Agamemnon* drunk, he had been exceedingly merry, so much so that his man, a dour cove called Lepée, had been required to help him make his cot. You did not have to be aboard *Agamemnon* very long to realise that if Nelson had an Achilles heel – that is apart from his lack of height, his high-pitched voice and being lightweight in the article of drink – it was in his inability to control his own cabin.

Lepée was a nuisance, at constant loggerheads with his master, a disrespectful drunk, a poor servitor and a man not in the least loved by the crew. Listening to Nelson now, and also seeing crab-faced Lepée moving about to fill various tankards, Toby had to wonder how a man who could not control his own servant could control a squadron of fighting ships.

Yet when he looked at those listening to their commodore to question that opinion, he saw the light of enthusiasm in their eyes, picked up by the glowing sunlight streaming through the casements, each admonition from Nelson to be bold, to seize every opportunity, to be brave and see obstacles as opportunities, received as Holy Writ.

'And remember,' Nelson piped, 'France is not loved hereabouts. They can expect no aid from the natives of the old town and must remain shut up in their citadel, nor, I hazard, will they sally forth in strength enough to dislodge us if we can get our men and guns ashore, while our Corsican allies will keep busy the northern enemy outposts.'

He had already identified the place they would land – a bay about a mile and a quarter south of the citadel walls – and it was only when first light came that Toby Burns, like everyone else aboard examining that prospect, realised that it was no more than a tiny strand of narrow beach enclosed by high crags, while between base and the top lay the same kind of dense pungent scrub that he had encountered crossing the island previously, so thick as to make progress near impossible.

Someone must have alluded to it being difficult, only to get from Nelson what Toby was to learn was a typical reply. 'Think of General Wolfe, man. Yonder are our own Heights of Abraham and like him we shall scale them. He took Quebec, we will take Bastia.'

'And he,' Toby said *sotto voce*, 'died in the attempt.'

The cutters of the squadron were soon in the water, each with a cannon in the bow and the appropriate shot with which to load them, this to suppress any attempt by the defenders to oppose the landing. The first parties ashore were the redcoats of Colonel Vilette's 69th Regiment, Lord Hood's bullocks to do with as he wished, given they had been sent out to the Mediterranean as marines. They were tasked with clearing paths through that undergrowth, while over their heads grapeshot from the cutters ensured they were not impeded.

On board *Agamemnon* it was all bustle. They were required to get out from the lower deck through the gun ports, on a cat's cradle of ropes and pulleys, the twenty-four-pounders that would be used to bombard the walls, while from one of the Neapolitan transports they were lowering over the side onto rafts the thirteen-inch mortars which would send their balls over the defences to wreak havoc to the rear.

Not a man aboard was without a task and Toby found himself once more plying back and forth to an opposed shore in charge of a boat full of redcoats, as he had done off San Fiorenzo only weeks before. Nelson was already ashore with Colonel Vilette on what was now a packed strand, watching pathways being cut to the top, and when the commodore spotted him he called out to give him instructions.

'Mr Burns, I want you to go back aboard *Agamemnon*, fetch ashore Sir Gilbert Elliot and I want you to take care of him. Damn me, if he takes a ball I will have to deal with the Corsicans myself, and that would never do, for I am no politico.'

Mistaking the crestfallen look on the youngster's face, Nelson was emollient.

'It is not, I grant, a duty in which a lad may distinguish himself, Mr Burns, but from what I have heard you have garnered enough to be going on with and regardless of my promise to Sir William I must give opportunity to my own youngsters first.'

As the import of those words sunk in, really a statement that Nelson was not going to push him into deadly combat to please Hotham, Toby smiled and was forced to shout his reply over the sound of cannon and musket fire.

'I am happy to be of any service you require, sir.'

'Well said, Mr Burns,' Nelson cried. 'My God, you are an example.'

By the time Toby got Sir Gilbert ashore most of the ordnance had been landed, paths had been widened, skirmishers had ascended to protect the landing area and there were sailors above their heads lashing great leather straps and single-block pulleys round the most prominent rocks.

'Would you look at these crags,' Sir Gilbert cried, his Scottish accent very pronounced. 'They're steeper than Minto.'

The shout, which left Toby Burns wondering where in the name of creation Minto might be, made an officer standing right in front of them turn. As he did so, he lifted his hat, which revealed the thin sandy hair and skeletal face of Lieutenant Glaister, who had been premier of HMS *Brilliant* under Ralph Barclay. For Toby it was not a happy moment – the Highlander was not a man who loved him, evident in the cold glare. What followed, and it did not include him, was an exchange of names and Caledonian courtesies.

'How will you get these damn things up those crags, Mr Glaister?'

'With great ease, Sir Gilbert.'

Which proved the case, despite the look of doubt on the diplomat's face; the tars, having set up their pulleys, gathered ropes to their hands and, on a command, proceeded to run down the precipitous rock. The cannon, the slings that encased them lashed to other ropes, went up smoothly, never once touching stone, as the collective bodies of the sailors acted as counterweights to their metal.

Other paths, into which narrow steps had been hacked out, provided a means of ascent for the main body of redcoats and before the day was out the whole panoply of Nelson's force was above the escarpment, with Corsican skirmishers well forward so that the next stage, the construction of battery positions within range of the walls, could be carried out.

That night was spent ashore, under a mass of stars, with hundreds of fires burning that pungent undergrowth, scenting the air with arbutus, myrtle and thyme. Out at sea, the squadron, HMS *Agamemnon* and five frigates, were lit from bow to stern, while to the north and west other pinpricks of light showed where the Corsicans were encamped, so that the defenders of Bastia could be in no doubt as to how parlous was their condition when it came to the prospects of resistance.

Back on board, taking an example from the great cabin, everyone who could write was penning an addition to their serial letters, a near-daily account of their life afloat – missives that would, when the chance presented itself, be put aboard one of the regular packets that sailed to and from home carrying despatches.

Toby Burns, who had not written home for a long time, joined in, though he struggled to think of what to say to his family once he had composed a less than flattering pen portrait of the commodore, also adding the strange nature of the adulation Nelson seemed to be able to inspire.

He did describe the recent events in his life: the struggle over the snowbound Pass of Teghime, a mere dozen miles from San Fiorenzo to Bastia but seeming so much longer, the death of the marine officer called Driffield in the fiasco of a land battle and the receipt of his wound while retreating, which he pleasingly managed to make sound much more serious than it had truly been.

Words of affection he found more difficult and he could not put in to a letter what he really wanted to impart, that as of this moment, he would rather be anywhere else in the world than sat off the Corsican coast, sure in the knowledge that battle would be joined on the morrow and that he would be required to participate.

Later, as he lay awake, listening to the snoring all around him, he conjured up any number of scenarios in which he was killed or maimed, until, with a vision in his mind of the rolling sheep-filled fields of home, of wooded copses and burbling streams, the whole more sylvan than it was in truth, he drifted off to sleep.

CHAPTER SEVEN

Codge was not the sort of person with whom Alderman Denby Carruthers normally dealt and the initial request for an interview, based on a description of the supplicant provided by his clerk, had been rebuffed. But the city worthy was dealing with a man who, if he was a veritable snake in the grass, was also very shrewd and well versed in the ways of manipulating people, and not just the gullible.

He sent in a slip of paper with the simple inscription 'Gherson' written on it. Looking at the name nearly stopped the alderman's heart; though it was one that occurred to him from time to time, always with pangs of several different emotions, none of them pleasant, it was not one he had ever expected to see written down. He sat looking at it for some time, wondering what it portended.

That it was like a ghost in his household he knew; his

relationship with his wife had been strained ever since he had disposed of the man who had cuckolded him. Firstly because he had disappeared, this after a confrontation in which all the sordid details of what had been going on had been aired, with he in a towering rage and she in tears. Secondly because later that same night, without explanation and in silence, he had burnt in front of her the fine coat he had had removed from Gherson just before the creature had been tossed over the parapet of London Bridge.

The garment had been bought for him by Catherine Carruthers from her household monies; it was his way of telling her he was gone for good, though he would never admit to how it had come about, or say he was dead. Had someone talked? Had what he had ordered done, and actually overseen, been witnessed? What was the meaning of this slip of paper and who was this fellow in his outer chambers, this early in the day, with the single name of Codge?

He did not want to see the man but he knew he would be forced to, for to send him away would leave him wondering about the nature of the call, though he suspected blackmail, which had him running through his mind to see to whom he could turn if it was the case. Then he realised his clerk, Lavery, the man who had replaced Gherson, long in years, jug-eared and unprepossessing with it, was still before his desk.

'This fellow, you say he is of the lower orders?'

'Very much so, judging by his clothing, sir.'

'Is there anything else about him?'

'He seems very sure of himself – cocky, I would say.'

Denby Carruthers made a great play of taking out his watch from his waistcoat and looking at it, really giving himself time to think, that was until he had an uncomfortable reflection, which had him waving the slip of paper, now refolded.

'Did you look at this?'

'No, sir, I was expressly told not to. It was for your eyes alone.'

'It refers to a piece of business I am unsure of, Lavery.'

'Do you wish for my opinion, sir?'

The 'no' was too sharp, too revealing. 'Send the creature in.'

That Codge had swagger was evident as soon as Carruthers clapped eyes on him, taking in the large frame, the pale skin and lidded narrow eyes that hinted perhaps at a foreign bloodline. But it was the assurance in the gaze which was most telling, steady blue pupils and no hint of obsequiousness, while the voice with which he introduced himself was a deep confident timbre that made the accompanying expression, 'At your service', seem risible.

To a man who, on a daily basis, made instant trades, high-value investments and disbursements, very much concluded on snap judgements, this Codge reeked of menace.

'I wonder at the meaning of this.'

Codge looked at the slip of paper, still in the alderman's hand, and shrugged. 'I can see the name registered.'

'It is the name of a fellow I once employed.'

'And a fellow who, at one time, you wanted seen to in a certain way.'

'I do not follow,' Carruthers snapped, but he did.

His sister's husband was a prize agent called Druce and very successful he was, with his partner Ommanney operating out of a fine set of offices in the Strand. As well as sea officers, some of their clients served with the impress service and it was that connection which had provided the men to do the necessary to Gherson, Druce willing to oblige with contacts so as to keep the whole matter discreet and thus avoid any disgrace to the wider family – by which really he meant himself.

Prior to approaching Druce – and he had not told his brother-in-law of this – Carruthers had put out feelers to see if anyone knew of the kind of men who would do what was required before the folly of so open an indication of his intentions struck him. Somehow that request must have reached the ears of this Codge, but why wait so long to bring it up?

'I heard you was willing to pay handsome for the service, too.'

'Then, fellow, you heard wrong.'

The steady look was still there and the reply had a harder edge than what had been said previously. 'It's not often Codge is wrong, as any with a sharp mind will attest to.'

'He is on this occasion, which I think concludes our business.'

'Happen I might tell Gherson, then, that he is safe from your desire to settle.'

'Tell him!'

Carruthers should have kept the surprise in check, but he could not do so. It was more than just the words, which came out as an exclamation, it was also in the expression on his face, arched eyebrows and stretched fearful skin, to which Codge responded with a slow smile.

'I heard he had been done in proper, and then what occurs? He walks into where I take my leisure, as bold as brass, to makes a lie out of that notion.'

The words 'He's alive' died in the alderman's throat, for to use them was tantamount to admitting he had sought his death.

'It strikes me, as I am sitting taking a brew with Gherson, that the piece of work being touted long past might still be sought and that it would yet pay handsome.'

Denby Carruthers had recovered himself somewhat, his years of experience in business, where the need to conceal his true position was often required, now coming to his aid. He managed to get a degree of doubt into his tone of voice.

'You're sure it was the Gherson I used to employ?'

'It's your man all right; corn-coloured hair, girlish lookin', an easy manner and the values of a sewer rat. There ain't too many like him.'

'For which the Lord be praised.'

If the alderman expected a response to that expression he did not get one; what he got was silence, an unblinking stare and a slight smile around Codge's lips that was close to a sneer. He knew the tactic: say nothing, force the person you are dealing with to keep talking and they will betray something they would rather keep hidden.

But there was another way to respond, to move matters on. If this Codge was right, and Gherson had somehow survived, he was a greater menace now than hitherto, in a position to threaten the alderman's life and position, not just his marriage.

'I suspect you came here with some purpose in mind?'

Codge looked slowly around the well-appointed room, as if to convince himself the walls had no ears, only speaking when his eyes came back to stare at Carruthers. 'My purpose is usually profit and given I can hand to you som'at that you was once willing to pay substantial to get . . .' The voice trailed off, there being no need to elaborate.

'You are offering me your services?'

'Gherson came to me with a proposal. He wants something taken care of which is outside the law – a "commission" you might term it. Now I has a choice, for I am an honest fellow at heart and that might oblige me to hand him over to certain folk, for which, it being the way they work, I would profit by.'

'Would this be before or after you have executed his commission?'

'Now that depends.'

'What would happen to Gherson if it is after?'

'Who knows, Mr Carruthers, but if he was caught in felony it could be the rope or it could be Botany Bay. That would depend on how bloody things get.'

The delicious thrill that ran through the alderman's mind then, of Gherson rotting and going to seed in an Australasian penal colony, had to be suppressed, for this matter required careful consideration. Gherson was a threat to his position as long as he was alive but there was little point in removing that hazard only to replace it with the potentially greater one of putting himself in the hands of this fellow before him. Revenge might be sweet but common sense came before that. He was tempted to ask what it was Gherson required of this Codge but he doubted he would be told, for, positions reversed, he would stay silent.

'And you would want from me what?'

'I reckon him to be worth fifty guineas of any decent soul's money to be got rid of.'

'How long do I have?'

'A day at most would be my guess.'

'It will not surprise you that I need to think on this.' That got a look, which said 'It is up to you'. 'Is there somewhere I can get hold of you?'

'Best I keep in touch, Mr Carruthers, not the other way round. I'll send a man round tomorrow, early doors, to find out how you want to work it.'

'Very well.'

With Codge gone Alderman Denby Carruthers sat thinking for quite some time. He then penned a quick note, which once sanded and sealed was handed over to his clerk. 'Take this to Sir Richard Ford at Bow Street, Lavery, and await his reply.'

Lavery's employer was a clever man, rich and successful, but he was not infallible and he was not of the kind to be loved by those who saw to his needs, being peremptory in his manner and unforgiving of minor error. In hiring the man to replace Gherson he had reasoned the last thing he wanted in his house-cum-place of business was another young and handsome rogue, quite failing to realise that an older and less comely fellow might be just as soft on a sweet young lady of a considerate and kindly nature as a fellow her own age.

Nor did a man, as he grew in years, even one whose ears were like windsails and whose nose was bulbous and purple, ever accept that all hope of romance was lost for, in his breast and imagination, as long as he avoided the mirror, he was still the eager aspirant he had been in his youth.

Despite Codge's strict admonition not to, Lavery had looked at the folded but unsealed note and seen Gherson's name. Having been in position for over a year he had picked up from the other servants the tale of what had gone on before.

So while Codge was closeted with his employer he had taken the chance to inform Catherine Carruthers of the visit and its purpose, without being able to enlighten her any further. Lavery saw no harm in telling her and he received in return a heart-swelling smile of gratitude, which encouraged him to also inform her, at a subsequent meeting, of where he was now headed.

'What can my husband possibly want with the Bow Street magistrate?'

'Perhaps I may be able to discover that in his reply.'

The soft hand touched the back of his own, sending a shiver through his bones. 'You are so kind, Lavery, I do not know what I would do without your support.'

Well beyond the age to skip, Lavery nevertheless felt he was doing so as he headed east from the City to Westminster, quite unaware as he passed through the City gate, for he had never met the fellow, of passing Cornelius Gherson going in the opposite direction to make his rendezvous with Codge.

* * *

As soon as he entered the drinking den, Codge stood and indicated they should go back outside; he was a stickler for never letting anyone overhear his intentions. He walked quite a way, looking backwards continually, Gherson trailing him until they came to the long low mudbank that sided the sluggish Thames. Codge took a seat on a berthing post.

'My lads had a look over the place and it is as simple as kiss my hand. Ground floor, single barred window at the back, though it ain't a box he's got but a strongroom behind his desk, which argues at much to keep safe.'

Gherson just nodded and did not ask how he came by such information – that was his business. He must have sent someone to see the solicitor on a false errand using a made-up name and purpose, that being the usual method. Sufficient it was that the deed had been done.

'The price?' he asked.

'Twenty guineas.'

'That's steep.'

'Is it, Gherson? I had to slake a strong thirst to get my lady friend to give the place a look-see, inside an' out, and the boys to do the deed need paying, just as I am not acting for free.'

Gherson nodded; he had no intention of arguing, given it was not his money. From his pocket he pulled a note, which had on it details of the meeting place.

'You're a reading man, Codge, this is where and at what time we will rendezvous.' Codge read the note then scrunched it up and threw it into the mud; some time that day the tide would come back in and wash it away, but he did not speak for a while, Gherson unaware of his thoughts, which had more to do with increasing his fee than accepting either it or the rendezvous.

'Tonight then, at the White Swan, nine of the clock.'

'That quick?'

'What needs done is best done soonest.'

'I don't like them words, Gherson, for to rush, well that is the way to Tyburn.'

'But you're too clever for that, Codge.'

'Happen we both are, mate.'

Charing Cross was its usual bustling midday self; the place where coaches left and arrived from all over the country, even the mail ones prior to going on to a central clearing house. If John Pearce had been silent on the journey, he was obliged to shout loud to get him and Michael a hack that would take them to Nerot's Hotel, where he had retained a room.

Even if he could bring himself to request anything of Ralph Barclay, which was near to impossible, he knew the bugger would take great delight in refusing. He had been gnawing at it, thinking of one scheme after another, overnight and on the journey, only to discard them as useless.

The only one that had any chance of success was if he could come up with a swap in numbers of seamen so favourable that even Barclay would be a fool to refuse. Yet that required him to have a ship and a crew, something in which he was singularly lacking and also unlikely to attain. His low hopes were raised on arrival at Nerot's, where he was handed a request from William Pitt that he call at Downing Street at his earliest convenience.

'He's got a damn cheek, Michael,' Pearce asserted, as once in his room he read it out loud. 'The last time I spoke with him it was as if I was some long-lost son, he was going to do so much for me and he had business of a very pressing nature. Then what? – nothing; time and again, you recall, I knocked at his door only to be told he had no desire to see me and now, at my earliest convenience, by damn!'

'So you will refuse him?'

'God no, he's the King's first minister, you do not refuse someone like him however arrogantly he behaves. Besides, the matter discussed before hinted at a return to the Mediterranean, which I was interested in, given I might be able to get another copy of Barclay's court martial record. But now the case is altered – if he wants a favour so do I, and that would be that Charlie and Rufus are shifted out from under Barclay's thumb.'

'And you think he will oblige you?'

'He will, if he wants something badly enough, Michael.' He started to strap on his sword, but not his pistol holster – he could not take that into Pitt's presence without being taken for an assassin. 'I shall go to see him, but I wonder if you would do me a favour and go to Jockey's Fields and tell Mrs Barclay I am back in town. Discreetly, mind, for her landlady is much given to nosiness.'

Progress for Jahleel and Franklin Tolland had been slow indeed, riding as they had been two to a horse, with numerous changes and even more frequent rests and walks. Being in a strange place, they hardly knew

London, Franklin having only visited it occasionally to seek funding with which to purchase contraband. It was necessary for them to ask for directions, requests in which they found just how disinclined the locals were to aid a stranger; Jahleel was left frothing often, on more than one occasion needing to be restrained from doing violence.

Their route took them through the heart of the City, a place of such bustle that no man could be anything other than overawed by the size and the activity, not to mention the prosperity, which sat so close to stinking poverty – there were beggars everywhere, it seemed, as well as people lying dead or drunk in the streets. Not that making a way was easy, for Londoners were no more inclined to yield a passage to anyone than they were to give friendly directions.

If the scales of justice atop the Old Bailey registered as they passed it, no one in what was a crew of long-practising criminals voiced any thoughts. Finally sure they were close to the destination of Pearce's letter, it was time to find a place with stabling as well as the means to eat and drink, both available at the Cittie of Yorke, where underneath its dark oak beams, even though it had been endlessly discussed, time had to be taken as to how the matter was to be approached.

'Bargin' in won't do, Jahleel,' Franklin insisted, 'for he be like a fox, this Pearce, and if we start him who knows where the chase will take us in a place this size.'

'Might make for the docks and cross the water,' opined one of the gang.

Jahleel Tolland was a bad-tempered man, who often

let that get the better of his judgement, but he was not a complete fool, and tankard to his mouth he nodded slowly before dropping it and speaking.

'That letter we were told of was sent to a lady and she was married and of a different name, while it seems he is sweet on her, which tells me it might not be where he lays his own head.'

'Pity we could not have seen what was wrote inside,' Franklin replied.

'I would have got to see it if you'd let me,' Jahleel growled, his eyes ranging round the men assembled, who concentrated on their ale or food rather than contest the assertion; their leader was not a man to dispute with.

'Not without violence and that would have had us running from a hue and cry, brother. You can't touch the mail without the law will be on you.'

'So,' Jahleel said after a think. 'We keep an eye on the place an' wait for him to show, is that what you reckon?'

'Either that or we enter the house of this Barclay woman and hole up there, which I don't fancy, us not knowing the person or the way things lay.'

'Then we'd best go an' have a look-see at what's what,' Jahleel said with a grimace of anticipation, the eyes ranging around his men again. 'Eat up, an' be quick. We'll get our horses proper stabled and then go a'hunting.'

CHAPTER EIGHT

'You took your damn time in responding, Pearce,' cried Henry Dundas, William Pitt's staunch political ally and, many said, the man who fixed his votes in Parliament and kept him in power.

'I believe I came here to see the First Lord of the Treasury.'

'Had you turned up as you were requested to you might have done so, but you have missed him, he has gone down to Walmer Castle.'

'When?'

'Three days past, as if it matters.'

Pearce was not stupid enough to blurt out what he was thinking; he had read the maps and studied the charts of the East Kent coast – Walmer was hard by Deal and in the same judicial jurisdiction as Sandwich. Not only had he passed him on the way to Dover, but also he had missed a chance to engage with a man who was very strong against smuggling and might know something of what he needed to find the locals who had helped to humbug him.

'Then perhaps I should proceed there and talk with him.'

'It was I who generated that note, you will deal with me.'

Eyes locked, the pair stared at each other, for if they shared a nationality they shared little else. As the man who controlled the Scottish vote in the House of Commons, Henry Dundas was a real power in the land and, if Pearce's late father Adam was to be believed, also one of the most corrupt men ever to enter government.

That Dundas had hated Adam Pearce was a given; a radical speaker and pamphleteer known as the Edinburgh Ranter, he and Dundas had known each other well and never once agreed about anything, both part of that enlightened and well-educated class of Scots who had benefited from a good education at Kirk school and a university not dedicated, as were Oxford and Cambridge, to producing pompous clerics.

Dundas had applied his education to becoming an advocate, then to naked self-aggrandisement and the acquisition of wealth; Adam Pearce to pointing out how fraudulent was a system in which a few had so much while the great majority of folk possessed so little.

Travelling the country with son John in tow – Adam Pearce was a widower – he had stopped wherever a crowd would gather to listen in order to harangue them about the injustices of the world in which they lived: a gimcrack monarchy mired in scandal, rotten borough elections to Parliament, votes for forty-shilling freeholders easily bribed or coerced by landed magnates, none for the ordinary citizen and especially the fairer sex.

A thorn before the French Revolution, that cataclysmic monarchical overthrow had raised Adam Pearce to national prominence. Now his speeches drew crowds in the several hundreds, his pamphlets which excoriated the rich and powerful sold in their thousands. He had become a menace and it was Dundas who had moved to have him and his son jailed for inciting public disorder.

A short stay in the Fleet Prison had followed, until Adam's radical friends got them free. Unabashed, the Edinburgh Ranter had redoubled his attacks on the state and those who ran it and that body reacted with a writ for sedition, a potential death sentence if brought before a corrupt judge and there were any number of those. Adam and John Pearce had been obliged to flee to revolutionary France, where a well-known radical was initially welcome.

'I would prefer not to deal with you,' Pearce said, making no effort to keep his dislike either out of his voice or his gaze.

'You have not heard what is proposed.'

'Anything put forward by you is not likely to be to my benefit.'

'You are as stupid as your father, boy.'

'Which tempts me to ask what you would prefer to meet me with, Dundas, swords or pistols?'

'Would it mollify your overweening pride, Pearce, if I said I was speaking for William?' About to say no, he was given no chance, Dundas just kept talking. 'We need

116

to know what is happening in the Vendée, so we require someone to take a vessel to that area, get ashore and find out.'

'A vessel?'

The uncertain way Pearce responded brought forth a truly sarcastic response, typical of a politician like Dundas. 'Yes, you know, a ship, one of those things that travels on water, as your father thought he could do on foot.'

Dundas could not know what Pearce was thinking of: with a ship and a crew he might be able to do something about Charlie and Rufus.

'I thought you wanted me to go back out to Lord Hood?' he asked, more to prevaricate and give himself time to think than for any real purpose.

'That will very likely follow, though his position and actions have become mired in politics. But you speak French like a native, you know about the Revolution and, though it pains me to say this given your parentage, you know how to keep your mouth shut.'

'And why would I need to do that?'

Dundas did not speak; a man who played his cards close to his chest by habit, he was not the kind to freely give away information – indeed, the fact that the fate of Lord Hood was even mentioned to be mired was unusually open. That was all to do with Hotham and his political support from the Duke of Portland, of course, the latter commanding a bloc of votes in Parliament, which was needed by Pitt to keep the war going.

'Let us just say it is an investigation that I would not want talked about in any old coffee house or tavern. I have been pressed by some very vocal French émigrés to

117

support the rebels there and if they are still fighting it might be a good place to offer assistance.'

'Toulon was better.'

Pearce said that, unsure if it was true, but it riled Dundas and that was enough. He had sent what soldiers Britain had available to the West Indies when Lord Hood had begged for them to be sent to support him at Toulon; there was a lively debate still in the navy as to whether one was better than the other, given that to do both was impossible for a country without a standing army.

'That is by the by, I have this commission for you if you wish to accept it.'

He needed to say yes; even if it was a very long shot the fate of Charlie and Rufus demanded it, but Pearce was damned if he was just going to acquiesce to this man right away, his pride would not permit it.

'What kind of ship?'

'I do not know, I would have to ask the Admiralty what is available.'

'And who is to command it?'

'Again—'

Pearce did not let him finish and it was with some pleasure, though he knew he could not push too far, that he could push at all.

'I will assume we are not talking about a frigate, but more of a lieutenant's command, so I have to be given both the ship and the authority. I will not have what I must do subject to the approval of another.'

'You have some damned effrontery, Pearce.'

Had Dundas insisted, he would have backed off,

118

but what he had, which the man wanted, was his discretion; John Pearce was not loved in the King's Navy – the way he had been promoted to his present rank by the express command of King George had created deep resentment amongst many officers and to that was added his disdain for their conventions. He was therefore unlikely to gossip, as another given the commission might do.

There were, too, deep waters here; Dundas, and possibly Pitt, wanted this task carried out without alerting either their political friends or their more vociferous enemies, many of whom were totally against the war with France. That provided the other reason for employing him; it was telling that even as powerful as he was, when it came to a task like the one outlined, Dundas had very few options, though Pearce was not so conceited as to think that, had there been an alternative, he would have been asked.

'I may need funds when I am ashore.'

That Dundas understood completely – he was a man who thought bribery an advantageous avenue to achieving his aims. 'I will draw upon the contingency fund to provide you with more than enough.'

'I am, as you know, at Nerot's Hotel. Please let me know when you have satisfied my other demands.'

'So you will do what I ask?'

'If everything is to my satisfaction, yes. Now I bid you good day, sir.'

It was a happy Pearce who exited the room, but he would have been less so if he had heard what Dundas said after the door was closed.

'One day, Master Pearce, you will pay for your arrogance, possibly just as your father did, with your damned head.'

'All the arrangements are in place, sir,' said Gherson. 'The men I have engaged will break into the offices of Mrs Barclay's attorney and clean out all his documents tonight. I will meet them at another location, where I can look for what we seek. Only when I have those court martial papers will I pay.'

Expecting hard bargaining with Codge, it had in the end been easier than anticipated and, happy with the conclusion, on the way back, Gherson had dropped into a Covent Garden brothel for a quick rut with a doxy, for in passing near the Carruthers house once more he had felt so primed by memory of the lady of the house that he required release.

'How much?'

'Thirty guineas is the price I agreed.'

Hovering around Ralph Barclay's mind was a pun about thirty pieces of silver, but he could not quite nail it. 'Anything else?'

'Yes, I want Devenow along.' That got Gherson a keen look. 'These are rough fellows and I may require protection.'

His employer was tempted to point out that would be because he would be carrying more gold than he would be paying out, but that was better left unsaid. It was also best left unmentioned, though it was worthy of a quiet smile, that if his rough fellows wanted to beat on him then Devenow would be more likely to join in than interfere.

That his two closest aides should despise each other suited Barclay well – there was no chance of them ever combining to dun him, albeit Gherson was about that now. Still, for what would be gained – the ability to put his wife firmly in her place – it was worth it.

That took the smile off his face; there would be a reckoning and a painful one for her. He had it in his mind to give her a severe whipping so she would never again doubt to whom she owed her loyalty. He would have her as well, as was his right as her husband, at his will and any time he so chose in future.

There would be no more gentility in his household, for it had proved with her to be a mistake. Her spirit had to be broken, just as sometimes at sea the same trait in a troublesome hand required to be crushed by a regular kiss of the grating.

'I am happy to see you, Michael,' said Emily, as she entered the parlour of the house owned by her landlady Mrs Fletcher. 'Would you care to sit?'

The Irishman shook his head, for he felt awkward, which for him was unusual. Really it was the parlour in which he stood, overfurnished and very feminine, with its cushions and comfortable settles. Besides, he did not know the lady well and could probably count on one hand the words they had exchanged, so different were their paths even on each crowded ship as they had shared.

Emily Barclay was likewise at a loss, for all she knew that this large man before her holding his hat in his ham-like fists was someone on whom John Pearce relied and a person he trusted absolutely. She wanted to ask about the letter she had received but somehow it felt wrong to do so, for he might know nothing about it.

'I just came to deliver a message, ma'am, from John-boy, to let you know he is back in London.' That got a raised eyebrow; the question as to why he had not come himself was immediate. 'He had a communication from Mr Pitt seeking his attendance at Downing Street and said to tell you he will come on here right after.'

'No!' The speed of her response shocked him. 'You must intercept him and tell him that is not wise.'

Emily spread her hands and silently rotated her head to indicate the house, which had Michael nodding in slow understanding – Mrs Fletcher, her landlady, was both curious and prudish – while Emily racked her brains. She did not want to go to Nerot's Hotel, that was too public a place and the notion of going to John's rooms even worse. Really there was only the house of Heinrich Lutyens where they could meet without risking comment.

It was only on exiting that Michael realised he would have to keep an eye on the door. Jockey's Fields was a narrow street, one carriage wide at best with houses to only one side, while the other consisted of a long unbroken brick wall too high to see over but with a tall building standing not far back from the far side.

Unable to stand outside the house – if it had not been stated, he knew that Mrs Barclay feared disgrace – he took up station some twenty yards up, leaning against the bricks with a view of the whole street, feeling very exposed.

'In the name of Christ, John-boy, don't you be too long.'

* * *

Much as he wanted to go to Emily Barclay, Pearce could not pass by the Liberties of the Savoy without he dropped into the Pelican Tavern to ask if anyone knew of a fellow who called himself Arthur Winston and where he could be found. Though he doubted it to be his true name, he was the man who had engaged him to go to Gravelines. It came as no surprise when the response was a flat no, leaving him wondering if he had been wise to buy so many pots of ale and porter to loosen tongues in the process.

He could hardly call into the Pelican without remembering that first visit, the foul night he had met the men who would become his friends, as well as the sods who had made up Barclay's press gang, or that he had been on the run himself from that very King's Bench warrant issued by the Government at the behest of the man he had just left, Henry Dundas.

Disappointed in his quest, not cheered by recollection, he left and made for the Strand, passing through the boundary of that part of London where there was no fear of arrest for debt or minor felonies, the confines of the old Savoy Palace. As usual there were men lounging round, with alert eyes and, no doubt, a good memory for a face, there to take up anyone foolish enough to set foot out of the sanctuary of the Liberties which kept them safe.

John Pearce had nothing to fear from these tipstaffs and his step became more jaunty as he thought of the destination to which he was now proceeding and who he was going to meet.

Michael was still standing with his back to the wall when the gang led by the Tolland brothers arrived. Full of ale and pie and with Franklin having asked discreet directions of the stable boys, they made their ways from the Cittie of Yorke to Jockey's Fields, which turned out to be no more than a short walk. Yet on viewing the street the same immediate problem surfaced for them as it had for Michael O'Hagan. Eight fellows could not just stand around without sticking out like a sore thumb, even if the light was going, for it was not a busy thoroughfare.

Jahleel left his lads at the base of the street – a mob of eight moving together was too obvious – and he and his brother walked up past number 18, narrow, three storeys high and brick built, but they did not linger and a little further on they passed a giant of a fellow, hat pulled low, who was doing just that and who did not react as he overheard one of them speaking in a gruff cracked voice.

'There's no way to watch the house close to, Franklin, so we must take station at both ends . . .'

The voice began to fade, which meant Michael missed what followed. '. . . though having marked it, we can keep a sharp eye out for the man so described to us by that gaoler, either in a naval uniform or not.'

'Four each end?' Franklin suggested.

'Aye, you go back and send three of the lads my way and keep the rest with you.'

In such a street, watching what happened, it was not hard to be suspicious – why was that fellow walking back so quickly? – and, after a very short time, there came three right hard-looking buggers who looked at him without a word as they passed. Apart from that, what rang the warning bell was that these looked to be the same fellows in dress and manner he had espied in Dover asking for a fellow with a bandaged foot.

Tempted to move, Michael was torn; the only point at which he was sure Pearce would appear was that doorway he was watching, but which way would he come? Having dug foundations in half the streets of London, which was in the middle of a house-building frenzy, Michael O'Hagan knew the place better than most and he reckoned Pearce had to come from the south end of Jockey's Fields.

Behind him, over the brick wall, the windows of the large building just behind it were beginning to be illuminated by lamps or candles, which somehow made the twilight in the narrow street seem darker. Above Michael's head the sky was still clear, which was more than could be said for the situation.

It did not take much thinking to work out why they were here; that Dover postmaster must have shown them the same letter he had let John Pearce write on, which meant that if he stopped his friend, Mrs Barclay would still be in the house, name known, and as a bargaining piece she would be peerless – he knew John-boy well enough to be certain he would not allow anything bad to befall an innocent woman, never mind this one.

Whatever he did involved risk, but doing nothing was scarce an option and he moved immediately to the door of number 18, which was opened once more by the lady of the house, who looked at him as she had done before, down her nose and reluctant to let such a fellow into her parlour; he was the kind who should come in by a back door and he would have been sent round to do so if she had possessed access to one.

'Could you call to Mrs Barclay, please, ma'am?'

'Again?' Mrs Fletcher replied.

'It is important.'

The face went through several expressions, none of them kindly, before she said, 'Very well.'

It was hard not to look up and down the street and just to stand there. Could those coves see which house he had called at, could they tell the number at such an angle? Did the lamplight from the hallway make him too visible? It was as if he could feel those eyes upon him and for all he was not a man given to dread it was with him now.

'Michael?'

She was dressed to go out and meet John Pearce and that was a blessing, and he spoke quickly and breathlessly. 'Mrs Barclay, sure you're going to have to trust me and I have no time to explain to you. Would you be after getting your bonnet and shawl and come with me?'

'Why?'

'Holy Mary you are in danger. Now, I admit to not knowing you as well as John-boy but he is that too. You just have to take my word and do as I ask.'

Jahleel Tolland, stood at the junction with the busy Theobald's Road and peering down Jockey's Fields, said to one of his men, 'Do you recall that Dover fellow said that Pearce was in the company of a big sod when he came for his letter?'

'No I do not, for I was not in the post house.'

126

The growl made the reply sound as if it was the fellow's fault. 'Well, if that ain't a big 'un we passes a'standing I don't know who is, and where he is now looks to me to be mighty close to the number of the house we're after. Best we have a gander.'

'Please, ma'am. I know you are good at a time of danger, for I have been told so, but this is worse than facing hell itself. You must come now!'

The street was in shadow now, dark enough for it to be hard to see one end from the other and still Emily hesitated, but there was light enough from Mrs Fletcher's lamp to see clearly Michael O'Hagan's face and that brooked no delay. She reached for her bonnet and shawl, both on hooks in the hallway, and stepped out, he holding out a hand to ease her down the two front steps, then without letting go, the hand moving to her elbow, setting the pace with a grip that was tight.

Jahleel Tolland was moving now, his men behind him, and as he saw the hurrying pair he yelled out, a noise that carried and echoed in the narrow confines of the street. Michael saw four men gather and move to look up to where the shout had come from.

'Are you able to run?' Michael asked.

'You must tell me what is going on,' she demanded breathlessly.

His voice carried the same quality, brought on by anxiety, not the pace they were walking. 'There are men at either end of this street who will kill John-boy if they get hold of him, and me too most like. Four of them up ahead – can you see them gathered?'

'Why?'

'There's no time, Mrs Barclay, for they will take you if they are given a chance. When I let go of your arm, run away as fast as you can and go to Mr Lutyens as you said you would.'

'What about you?'

Michael laughed, wondering if it sounded as false to her as it did in his head. 'Why, I am going to be right behind you.'

CHAPTER NINE

There was a sharp right turn at the bottom of Jockey's Fields, where the road dog-legged prior to taking another left turn that led to busy Holborn. Michael reckoned if she could make that crowded thoroughfare she would be safe – it was too busy a place for outright mischief against a well-bred woman, but getting to that would be hard. If the men before him had heard the shout so had he, which meant as well as those in front of him he had four more coming as fast as they could to join.

'Keep close to me, ma'am, very close.'

He said this as he let go of her elbow, necessary so he could put one hand on his hidden hanger. The odds were terrible, but he had his height as well as his strength to aid him and once he had got Mrs Barclay clear he would himself be looking for a chance to disengage and run.

'Would it help if I screamed?'

'Sure, it would do no harm.'

Enclosed as it was, the street echoed with that, a noise that was bound to bring folk to their windows; that it might bring aid was too much to expect, but unknown to both Emily and Michael the sound carried to John Pearce, who had left Holborn a minute before and was making his way through that first dog-leg. The sound made him stop dead so he could try to identify the source.

Having been walking with his head down, deep in thought, it also caused him to look straight ahead. The knot of four men in heavy coats and riding boots was very obvious as they blocked the southern exit of the street in which Emily lived. In his mind he was back at that inn in Lydden, reprising what he had overheard and cursing himself for not getting hold of the true import and meaning of the words that had been exchanged between those two fellows who did the talking; they too had been to the Dover post house and it was a fair bet they had either seen or been told of the address to which his letter was being sent. There was no pondering this; Pearce was already running, his fine long-bladed officer's sword swishing out of its scabbard, the sound of his shoes clattering on the cobbles.

Michael left the short hanger hidden inside his coat until the last moment, wondering as he began to pull it clear why those before him had suddenly diverted their attention. Whatever the cause, it was too good a chance to miss so he lunged forward, pulling out the blade and striking at the first man he came to, who, distracted, was too slow to draw his own weapon and found that before he got it clear the arm required was rendered useless by a deep cut. His scream was added to those of Emily Barclay as he fell back, mixing his yells of distress with expletives.

Another one had his sword out but was facing away, which left only two men with whom Michael had to deal, and the fist he pushed out, inside the metal guard of his weapon, caught another fellow on the side of the head and felled him. Emily, doing as she had been bid, ran straight into John Pearce, who pushed her to one side with no gentility and took guard, sword point level.

'Run, Emily,' he shouted, as the first of his opponents swiped at his blade, this while the last of the quartet was backing away from a furiously swinging Michael O'Hagan, who had stepped over another laying comatose. 'Get to Nerot's Hotel.'

Unaware if he had been obeyed – it was necessary to concentrate on what was before him – Pearce withdrew his sword from what was a much more substantial weapon, more like a cutlass, that might have broken through the thinner metal he was employing and severed it. But it did not go back far, only enough to let the other blade swish uselessly past, then in classic fashion he bent forward on his right knee, extended his back leg to the full and drove the blade into flesh, quick to twist it and withdraw.

'To me, Michael.'

That shout had to be heard over the crash of twin blades as they struck against each other, the next act of Pearce to slash at the face of the man now standing stock-still before him, eyes wide open, shocked by the fact that his body flesh had been penetrated.

'There's four more behind me, John-boy.'

Michael's warning came at the same moment as the

fine point of Pearce's blade, manufactory sharp, sliced down his opponent's cheek, drawing immediate blood. The huge Irishman was doing the right thing, using his strength rather than any clever swordsmanship to get to the right side of his opponent; by the time they were shoulder to shoulder the odds had gone to five against two, with the light fading rapidly.

'Franklin!'

The shout and the gruffness of the voice identified the fellow called Jahleel, and he bent over the man now on his knees holding his slashed cheek, blood oozing through his fingers, his groans likewise, this while the trio that had come running with Jahleel stood, swords out, not sure what to do. Pearce had no doubts.

'Run!'

No second bidding was required and both were off like hares – there was no time to worry about a damaged foot – the only sounds their boots and the keening of the man whose arm Michael had near chopped in half, but that did not last, for a great shout echoed in the confined space.

'You won't get clear of me, by thunder, Pearce. No one steals from Jahleel Tolland and lives to tell the tale.'

Aware that they were not being pursued, Pearce stopped at the corner of the street that led down to Holborn, there being just enough residual light from the windows behind the smuggling gang to show that the concern was more for those wounded than any chase. Chests heaving, both he and Michael watched as the man Pearce had skewered was helped to his feet, bent double over his first wound, while his brother pressed a handkerchief to his gashed face.

'How do I tell them we are not the guilty party?'

'John-boy,' Michael gasped, 'this is not the time, by Jesus.'

'There will have to be one, friend, for I cannot see them giving up. Twice we have had the luck to survive, it would be tempting providence to think there would be a third occasion.'

'Take the blessing the Good Lord has given us this night,' Michael replied, not forgetting to cross himself, 'for I tell you, John-boy, I did not expect to come out of this whole.'

Pearce felt his arm taken and Michael pulled him down the street, and immediately his thoughts turned to the whereabouts of Emily Barclay.

Not far from where they were and by the light of a candle, Isaac Lavery was reading the reply he had fetched earlier from Sir Richard Ford, the Bow Street magistrate and the man in charge of the now famous Runners. His alderman employer, having responded to it, was out at a Mansion House dinner, a male-only affair at the London Mayor's residence, which left his wife at home.

That the letter was in a locked part of his master's desk presented little difficulty, the key had been copied not long after he took up his position, it being axiomatic for the clerk that he should know as much as he could about the alderman's private affairs.

Not to do so was to preclude him being aware of any threat to his position, as well as denying him profit from knowing of certain speculations of a lucrative nature, which had to be kept secret, edging as they did on illegality – for Denby Carruthers, upright to those with whom he would now be dining, was not as pure as the driven snow; he was a man who used his wealth in many ways.

Having read it through twice, he decided not to take it to Mrs Carruthers and show her the contents, reasoning that that would not give him the leverage on her affections that he sought; it would also make her aware of his unauthorised access, which could be unwise. Instead he verbally related what he had gleaned, without saying how he had come about the information. Likewise he kept to himself that another low fellow had come to his master with an unknown message, though one he suspected was from Codge.

'The matter refers to the fellow who called yesterday, Codge is his name, and identifies him as a true villain whom the Runners and Sir Richard Ford would dearly love to lay by the heels.'

Catherine Carruthers had to hide her impatience; she was not in the least interested in the creature called Codge or the desires of Bow Street magistrates. But the whereabouts of the man she still loved, the man she had thought to be in cold ground, concerned her mightily.

'It seems,' Lavery continued, 'he is a criminal of some repute, but one who has never been caught in an illegal act himself. Sir Richard advises your husband to be careful in his dealing with the man.'

Patience ran out. 'Was Gherson mentioned?'

'Only in passing; it seems he has commissioned this Codge to commit some felony—'

'Felony?'

'. . . and your husband has suggested that once he has the details, which he will most assiduously seek, that the Runners can be alerted to catch them both in the execution.'

'Which means that Cornelius is alive.'

The enthusiasm with which that remark emerged, as well as her look, brought a frown to Lavery's unprepossessing face, but it also induced a degree of curiosity. 'You had reason to imagine him dead?'

'I fear you do not know my husband, Mr Lavery, he is a man of strong resentments.' She paused then, wringing her hands. 'You see, Cornelius and I were friends.' The next words, as Lavery tried to compose his features, were hurried and larded with excuse. 'No more than that, but my husband misunderstood.'

It was as well that Lavery was well practised in dissimulation, for if he had not been, he would have shown his reaction to this blatant untruth. Why was it that rich folk never understood that their servants knew everything, especially about matters untoward? It was they who washed the bed sheets, they who took care of the clothing and it was they who could not fail to see tender glances exchanged or hear a blazing shouted dispute in which every fact, most of which they were already aware, was loudly aired.

'I am told he was an engaging young man.'

'He was my soulmate, Mr Lavery, the person to whom I turned when I was in confusion.'

He could not resist it. 'Confusion, Mrs Carruthers?'

Her head was down and she was looking at her

wringing hands now. 'Little is done to prepare we young women for marriage, and my husband can be intemperate, as well as so jealous of my company that he allows me no friends.'

'Mrs Carruthers,' he said, his voice a touch hoarse, 'if you require someone to converse with, someone to share your burdens, a friend, then I would be only too happy to be that person.'

Blind and partially deaf, she could not have failed to pick up his meaning and Catherine Carruthers was neither. Isaac Lavery saw innocence, albeit corrupted; what he did not see, for she was not looking at him, was the expression of anger on her face, for if Catherine Carruthers had failed to understand the perils of marrying a much older man, and had found the conjugal part of her duties both painful and unpleasant, she had learnt some valuable lessons.

She wanted to spit in this old goat's eye, but that would not get her to where she wanted to be, so it was with both a simpering look and a crack in her voice that she responded.

'Mr Lavery, you have no notion of how such words comfort me.'

'I want for nothing more than to do so.'

'But,' she said, her voice firming, which stopped him coming closer. 'I cannot sit by and watch my husband cruelly take revenge on poor Cornelius for things that are part of his wild imaginings. Somehow, I must find him and warn him.'

There was a hint of an objection in Lavery's old face, until she added, 'So that he can get far away from such jeopardy, far away from this house and the unhappiness with which it is filled. For that, I require the aid of a dear friend.'

It was a long walk from Holborn to Nerot's Hotel, which lay in King Street, St James's, one in which the thoughts harboured by Emily Barclay were much troubled, for having left the house of Mrs Fletcher so suddenly she had not brought with her the means to pay for a hack. Several times, as she stopped at the roadside prior to crossing, so that a sweeper could remove the piles of horse dung and human muck, she considered turning back, but that atrophied on the thought of what she might be going back to.

Bodies perhaps, those of John Pearce and Michael O'Hagan lying on the cobbles, for she had seen the swords being drawn, had heard that scrape as they left their scabbards, knew the men they contested with to be more numerous, which made her feel like a coward for not stopping, even if she knew in her heart her presence would have hindered those seeking to save her rather than aiding them.

The other deliberations were just as confused: what had brought this on, who were those people from whom she had been required to flee, and what were John and Michael trying to save her from? Would she have been safer staying in her rooms? None of which had a conclusion, and on top of that it had begun to rain, so she was obliged to pull her shawl over her bonnet even if it did little to keep out the wet, as well as ignore the filthy sludge that stained her hem.

This meant when she finally arrived at Nerot's Hotel, the man on the door was halfway to refusing her entry, such was her state. John Pearce was pacing the lobby, frantic with concern as she was reluctantly allowed into the warm and dry interior. As soon as he spotted Emily shaking her soaking shawl he began to rush towards her, only to be stopped by the look of alarm in her eyes and a hand held out in protest; this was a public place and she was a married woman. That slowed his final approach and meant the words he used where uttered in a low voice.

'I wondered what had become of you?'

'And I wondered at the need to flee,' she snapped, made angry not by the thought alone, but by the fact that her state of distress had made her an object of curiosity to all the people in the lobby, staff and guests. 'And do not come too close.'

'Damn me, Emily,' he hissed, annoyed at her tone, 'Michael and I just saved your life.'

'A life, sir, I had no notion of needing to be saved.'

'Emily, we cannot talk here.'

'Will you address me as Mrs Barclay in public!'

'Your surname is not one that sits happily on my tongue.'

Her eyes were blazingly furious and she made to turn. 'I shall go back to Mrs Fletcher's this instant.'

He had to grab her arm regardless of what impression it created in those looking their way and trying not to be seen to do so. 'No. Take a room here.'

'Quite apart from the fact it would compromise me, I do not have the means to pay.'

'I do.'

'And how will that look?'

'It is not something that troubles me. Stay there.'

Pearce strode over to the desk, sorely tempted to slap the man who stood behind it, so supercilious was his raised eyebrow as he approached, as if to say 'Who is that foul creature with whom you have been conversing?'

'I have the wife of a naval officer acquaintance come to me in some distress, as you can no doubt observe. Please be good enough to find her a room and put her accommodation on my account.'

'Certainly, Lieutenant Pearce.'

The clerk signalled to a hotel servant, a crabbed fellow called Didcot, who was looking at the ceiling, not wishing to catch the eye of either party; he had served the lady when she came to see Pearce only a few weeks before, at a dinner taken by the pair in a private room, and he was thinking she looked a lot better then than she did now, with her bonnet off, soaked clothes and her auburn hair plastered to her head.

He was also speculating, as he responded to that hooked clerical finger, on the relationship, which had not ended that night as he expected, with a bout of rutting on the couch in the private room, a piece of furniture which had seen a great deal of that sort of thing in its time. No, the assignation had been cut short when she left early, clearly in a temper, which, looking at her now, seemed to be still her state.

'The lady's name, sir?' the clerk asked, as Didcot approached.

'Mrs Barclay.'

'Didcot,' he said, reaching for a key, 'there is a room

on your floor not far from that of Lieutenant Pearce. Show the lady up to number 17 and, I hazard, since she has been so buffeted by the elements, and is, as Mr Pearce says, in some distress, a maid should be sent up to see to her clothing and her toilet. Anything else, Lieutenant?'

'Yes,' Pearce snapped. 'Please prepare a room where she and I can take dinner alone.'

'No luggage, sir?' asked Didcot cheekily, before he got a look that would have felled an ox, which rendered him suitably obsequious. 'No, sir, quite, sir.'

Approaching Emily once more, still stood on what seemed to her like public display, he dropped his voice and told her what he had arranged, glancing at the clock.

'Will an hour be enough?'

'For what?'

'For you to get yourself fit to have explained to you why you have just suffered.'

'Those men, John, where are they now?'

'Seeking assistance at the nearest hospital, I shouldn't wonder. You have nothing to fear from them.'

'And you, do I have anything to fear there?'

'Only the depth of my affection,' he whispered. 'Now go with Didcot to your room, while I go down to where they accommodate the servants of the guests and tell Michael you are safe and well.'

The mention of the Irishman brought back some of her natural spirit; for all she was confused she knew that, had she truly been in danger, his actions had been designed to save her and he had been prepared to make a great sacrifice to achieve it, given the odds as they were

140

before John appeared – she was mortified that she had forgotten all about him.

'Please thank Michael for me.'

There was a silence then, as Pearce waited to be included; he waited in vain.

'In an hour, then,' he said finally.

The food he had arranged was simple, the explanation which went with it much more complex, but at least Emily was restored, her hair dressed, her garments dried, cleaned and pressed, her green eyes steady upon him and looking, as he had observed so many times, stunningly beautiful.

'I was at a low ebb, I suppose, not having as much money as I expected, my supposed prizes locked in dispute, a case I would struggle to bring and my need to care for you. This fellow I met was so plausible. The sum I was supposed to gain by helping him was fabulous, enough to—'

'I know, John, enough for you and I to live as man and wife, you said.'

'Not a prospect, judging by your expression, that fills you with joy.' Lacking an answer, he continued his tale. 'Anyway, the ship and cargo was not his but belonged to another, and those were the folk outside your house. I assume these Tolland people heard about my arraignment and came to Sandwich to try and get it back, for which you cannot blame them, given its value. It was only by luck they missed.'

'So you were a dupe?'

'Very much so, led by the nose like the ass I am.'

'And what am I to do now?'

'You have a room here.'

'Everything I possess is at Mrs Fletcher's house.'

'That we can send for.'

'I cannot help but feel that you and I are destined for nothing but unhappiness.'

'Because of my actions?'

'Not just that, there are my actions too.'

'Yours?'

'There is something I have to tell you, John, and when I do, I would not be surprised if it is you who wants our association to cease.'

'I would not choose to describe it as an "association", Emily.'

'Not yet, but let me speak without interruption and your mind may be set on a different course.' Which she did, to an amazed John Pearce, who had great trouble, as had Heinrich Lutyens, in matching her actions to the person he thought she was. 'I knew I was wrong to do what I did and I am sure God will punish me.'

'If there is a God and he inclined to punish anyone, then he will start with your husband.'

'Your papers are now lodged with Mr Davidson, to do with what you will and I, well, perhaps I should do as I said earlier and return to Jockey's Fields to live there like a widow.'

She was looking at the table and her empty plate when he started to laugh, a low chuckle, and that made her look up, her face showing perplexity as his laugh grew louder.

'My darling Emily, you are everything I thought you

to be, wonderful enough to be impulsive, honest enough to admit an error and make amends, and innocent enough to come to entirely the wrong conclusion.'

'Now you have the means to ruin my husband.'

'True, but do you not see, you and I also have the means to protect you against his wrath. There are many ways a husband who is cuckolded can take his revenge, a writ for criminal conversation, for instance.'

'There has been no such thing,' she protested.

'Not yet.' Seeing her shock he stood up and went to her, adding quickly, 'Should your husband even think of an objection, he has a choice. He can sacrifice his career or acquiesce in you and I being as one.'

'What about your case?'

'Damn my case, Emily.' He crouched down and looked up at her. 'You are worth so much more.'

Having said that, John Pearce was aware he may yet have damning evidence from the Mediterranean; that too could be used to keep Ralph Barclay at bay. He was also thinking how close her room was to his, but that would not serve; hotels were gossip mills, and besides, he did not want to shock or upset the woman he loved but to introduce her to the joys of having a proper and experienced lover in the right surroundings.

'You will sleep here tonight and tomorrow we will talk of our future.'

CHAPTER TEN

The first thing Horatio Nelson did, once all was ashore and set before Bastia, was to mount what he called a 'captain's piquet'. This he set up at the ancient tower taken on his previous landing, closer to the walls than his batteries, with sentries out front to ensure he was not surprised by a sudden sally by enemy infantry. The tent he put up to keep the Corsican sun off his head was within range of cannon fire from the nearest French bastion, so it was a damned uncomfortable place to be and one each midshipman was invited to partake of.

Toby Burns, when his turn came round, found himself sharing a less than comfortable dinner with the commodore, an hour past the normal naval time of three of the clock. Roasted goat and root vegetables were served to them by Frank Lepée, a man who, prone to grumble anyway, voiced the very thoughts the young man harboured.

'Madness and showing away,' he moaned, as he clattered a battered pewter plate in front of his master. 'Ship in the offing, a cabin sitting empty when we could be aboard and in comfort enjoying our vittles, instead of jumping every two bells to avoid a cannonball.'

'Do be quiet, Lepée,' Nelson replied softly, raising his eyes to Toby Burns, as if to say 'Hark at the fool!'

As yet Toby had not experienced any shot, but he was sure it was coming and the evidence of accuracy was easy to see, not only in the scarred ground but also in the repairs that had been made to Nelson's tent: square patches of canvas to cover the holes made by enemy fire.

He had been gifted a telescope by Captain Duncan, the artillery expert, and he could thus observe the activity around the closest gun position: stripped-to-the-waist artillerymen readying their weapon, taking their time, no doubt to get the charge right, choosing a ball that, chipped free of rust, would nestle neatly in the barrel.

'You can set your watch by them,' Nelson said, taking out a Hunter from his waistcoat and examining it. 'It's one salvo per watch. I fear we will have to shift from our chairs in a minute or two and take shelter behind the earthwork.'

The red-coloured mound referred to, behind the tent, did not, in Toby Burns' reckoning, amount to an earthwork, being so low that it was necessary to crouch behind it on all fours, which was silly given the amount of idle manpower around now that the battery positions were nearly finished. Behind that was where the food had been prepared – if Lepée was a sourpuss he knew how to cook over a charcoal pit, and the smell of the roasting meat had set the boy salivating.

Now that the food was in front of them, Nelson leant forward to confide in him. 'I swear Lepée has timed this so we will have to shift. He knows yonder gunners will certainly try to interrupt our dinner if they see us sat before it; they do it for the sport. They are loaded and ready to apply the flint, I shouldn't wonder.'

'Would it not be best to take your dinner further back, sir?'

'What, Mr Burns, and let them think us a'feart?'

'No, sir, of course not, sir.'

'Tuck in till we see the smoke. When that billows out we have just enough time to get clear before the ball lands.'

It was odd that Toby wanted to ask Nelson about fear; he hardly knew the commodore and he was sure he did not like him much, he being another one of those fools, and he had met too many, who sought out danger. Yet he had a feeling that if the question was posed he would get an honest answer, not some patriotic gibberish of the kind he had heard too often in the various berths in which he had laid his head.

He was just about to open his mouth, which was full of goat, which if it smelt wonderful on the spit was tough to chew, and ask the question, when the black smoke billowed out from the near white walls. Nelson moved quickly, his plate in his hand, to stand and look out for the approaching lump of black metal.

Toby had abandoned his grub and was scrabbling like an ungainly dog for cover, not caring one jot if he was seen to be shy. He just made it, roughly shoving Lepée further to safety in the process, when the damnable device landed, hitting the rocks to Nelson's left and sending shards of stone in all directions, up as well as out, before bouncing over the low earthwork to bound on until it came to rest in a bush, which immediately began to smoke from the heat. Slowly Toby rose again, to find the commodore once more sat at the table, carefully picking up and discarding bits of rubble.

'Stones in the food is bad enough, Mr Burns,' he said cheerily, 'but the dust in my small beer is the very devil for a parched throat.'

'You do not see, sir, that you take too many risks?'

'Why, Mr Burns, did you not know I have the Almighty to protect me! When I was not much more of an age than you I was vouchsafed a vision that I would one day achieve great things, that I would be the hero of the nation, and since that day has not yet come, I feel at liberty to tempt providence.'

'Foolishness,' groused a restored Lepée, hovering a few feet away.

'Recall the words of Shakespeare,' Nelson intoned, though to whom, Toby was unsure. 'Cowards die many times before their deaths, The valiant never taste of death but once.'

'A vision, sir?' Toby asked, trying not to sound too astounded, this while he felt tears of self-pity prick his eyes.

'A golden orb, young sir, which appeared before me when I was ill and abed while crossing the Indian Ocean, that and a voice which told me of my destiny. I will be entombed in Westminster Abbey, Mr Burns, or die in the attempt.'

It required a direct look from the youngster to ensure he was not being played upon, but Nelson's face was suffused with radiant certainty. This man, Toby thought, should be in Bedlam, not in the navy, and certainly not in command of an independent squadron of fighting ships.

The messenger came before they had chewed and swallowed the last of their goat; Hood's topsails had been sighted, which led Nelson to confide, rather boastfully, that he was sure the admiral would be pleased with his arrangements. An offer of terms was sent in from the C.-in-C., and that was rejected, so the next morning, as the sun rose, Toby Burns found himself lined up with every midshipman from the whole squadron, by the battery of twenty-four-pounders, waiting for the order to fire to be given, which would be a red signal flag at the main topgallant masthead of HMS *Victory*.

When it was sighted, fluttering in the breeze, Nelson had hoisted the Union Flag colours of his sovereign, King George, a sight which was met by the hurrahs from twelve hundred throats – the bullocks had been stood to for the occasion – soon to be followed by the boom of the cannon as they sought, by ricochet fire, to dislodge the weapons of their opponents.

With the wind in the north they were enveloped with acrid black smoke, and the odd burning thread of the expended wad might singe a coat or even skin. Each mid took it in turn, under supervision, to aim a cannon and give the order to fire, which was hazardous, given they were subject to the responses of the enemy.

Powder monkeys ran from the gunner's stores, set well out of range for safety, bringing up fresh charges, now of a regular weight – the range had been set – while a line of seamen kept the gun crews fed with the heavy iron balls, all chipped and painted black.

The fire went on all day and throughout the night, setting up a hellish glow of red from muzzle flashes as well as the fires that had long been started behind the walls, and there were captains and lieutenants on hand to explain to the youngsters what was being sought – something heartily encouraged by the commodore.

Ricochet fire was designed to skim over the parapet, either directly or off the glacis, to kill anyone foolish enough to show their head and take out the masonry as well. With luck they would breach an embrasure and destroy an artillery piece; if not, they would pass overhead to send crashing to the ground what walls or buildings were left standing, the debris of which went in all directions, forward and back, to fall upon the men working the guns, this while the high-firing mortars sent shells into the air to drop on the heads of the defenders.

That they were dismounting guns and killing the men manning them was not in doubt, but to totally destroy a cannon was rare. More often it was human flesh and the wood and ropes required to move and work it, and that could be repaired, while fresh blood was brought forward once it was remounted.

So it was not all one way – the French replied in kind and six of Nelson's gunners died from one well-placed ball. A Corsican guide and the brigade major of the 69th also died when the commodore led forward an observation party, foolishly getting to within a thousand yards of the walls, exposed to both grape and round shot, his aim to get a greater impression of how the bombardment was progressing.

Nelson did not escape himself, taking a sharp cut in his back from a rock splinter that sliced though his broadcloth coat and shirt. The wound bled copiously, though he was able to get back to a safer place without aid. It was while he was sitting, stripped to the waist, being bound up by Surgeon Roxburgh, that Toby found himself called forward.

'Mr Burns, this fellow I am about to introduce you to is Lieutenant George Andrews, who, apart from being a fine officer, has a very lovely sister, whom I am sure he will tell you all about. Mr Andrews is to construct a new battery much closer to the town and higher up the slope: a pair of nine-pounders, which can put shot right down the throats of the defenders. Since I promised Sir William that I would give you opportunity, I have selected you as one of the fellows to go with him, Mr Farmiloe being the other.'

'I fear my preparations will not go unnoticed, sir,' Andrews said, 'and at seven hundred yards distance I will need protection from a sally.'

'I shall ask General Paoli to launch a series of attacks to keep the enemy infantry honest. The guns, however, I cannot silence. That task falls to you and your men.'

It was only while on the way to that forward position that Toby found out what was afoot, this from Farmiloe, who he had been sent to fetch.

'We must press hard. The Foot Guards have arrived at

San Fiorenzo and once they have organised themselves they will come on to aid the siege. The commodore is anxious that Bastia should fall before they get here. It would be too maddening if they turn up just as the town is ready to seek terms when the navy had done all the toil.'

'Surely bullocks are better at such assaults than tars.'

'God Almighty, Toby,' Farmiloe responded, 'don't let Nelson hear you say that.'

The gun position being further up the slopes than the original batteries, they were too steep for the massive lower-deck cannon, but at a shorter range nine-pounders would be very effective and it was possible to manhandle them into position. Farmiloe and Burns arrived to find Lieutenant Andrews supervising the Corsican labourers working with shovels to flatten the ground so that the cannon could be properly worked.

Others, using the dislodged stones, were building a drystone parapet that would be backed by the dug-up earth, seemingly impervious to the musket balls seeking, albeit at extreme range and from careful skirmishers, to kill them. More worrying, from this elevation they could clearly see a pair of cannon being shifted to a position from which they could respond; they would be under a barrage before they even got their guns in position.

'Mr Burns, take a party of Corsicans and help clear the way for the men bringing up our cannon.'

As usual, when given an order, Toby Burns had to filter it through the many layers of his being, his first thought gratitude, for on that backward slope he was out of danger, which got a sharp response from a hitherto benign-seeming lieutenant. Andrews positively barked at him, and as he rushed to obey, with no idea of how he was supposed to achieve it with people who did not understand a word he said, he heard Dick Farmiloe excuse his behaviour.

'Cut him a bit of extra line, sir, he's always been a bit slow.'

The cry that followed had Toby turn back, just in time to see Andrews spin away, his hat flying off and one arm grasping across his body with Farmiloe rushing to stop him from collapsing. Clearly he was wounded, perhaps seriously so, for he had dropped to his knees. Toby Burns could not help but harbour the thought that it served the fellow right for shouting at him.

'In the name of God, Toby, attend!' Now it was Farmiloe shouting at him. 'Get a stretcher party up here and tell the commodore Andrews is wounded.'

For the same reasons of security, this time Toby was all speed, skipping down the slope with the loose screed flying from under his boots, dodging past the labouring and sweating sailors who were sledging the guns up the slope. He found Nelson where he always stood, right under the Union Flag, a sure target for the enemy, and passed on the information.

'Back at once, Mr Burns. Tell Mr Farmiloe the duty is now his and that you are to second him.'

'A stretcher, sir?'

'I will see to that and send Mr Roxburgh to attend to Lieutenant Andrews.' Then those bright-blue eyes took on an extra sparkle. 'You've got a double chance to find glory now, lad.'

Halfway back up the hill, Toby came across a party of seamen from *Agamemnon*, working under a very competent gunner's mate. Ahead of them some locals were already clearing the pathway and he suddenly had a notion to assert some authority in a place where musket balls could not reach him. Hands quickly thrust behind his back he assumed an air of command, careful, when he spoke, to merely support the man who had been in charge before he arrived. The stretcher-bearers and Surgeon Roxburgh passed him going up and, on their return, with a comatose and coatless Andrews as their load.

'Ball in the shoulder,' the surgeon called, almost gaily. 'Not too serious, so let's hope he had on a clean shirt.'

'Beggin' your pardon, young sir,' came a gruff voice, 'but would you shift, 'cause we can't move the gun, you bein' in the way like.'

Turning and looking into the fellow's eyes, Toby Burns could see no humour or understanding, while behind him the men on the ropes that led to their newly located pulleys were glaring at him; he was being told, even if the man could not say it, to sling his hook.

'Carry on,' he said, before making his way slowly up the hill, only breaking into a trot when he knew he would come in sight of Farmiloe, calling out with false breathlessness, 'You're to take command, Dick, orders from Captain Nelson.'

'The guns?'

'Not far off and I have given the men bringing them up a sharp order to shift.'

'Right, Toby,' Farmiloe replied, immediately removing

his coat. 'Let's show these locals we can shift too, the earth and rocks, as quick as they do.'

Toby Burns had no option but to do likewise; it was coat off and hard labour under a warm sun and no shade, though he found that the odd grimace got him sympathy for the arm that had taken a wound. Most of the time he made sure he was below that rising stone parapet, only occasionally allowing, and that was by accident, his head level to surmount it.

But that did not stop him shrinking into his neck every time a ball cracked overhead and he was far from grateful when Farmiloe called to say the first of the two nine-pounders was about to arrive. That meant putting on his blue coat again and standing up, making him a prime target for the French skirmishers hiding in the scrub between him and the town.

'Can we not get some of the 69th to see to those fellows?' he asked, as yet another ball cracked by his ear.

'It would be to endanger them for mere pinpricks, Toby.'

Which left the lad wondering how Farmiloe could say that when he had just seen Andrews near killed. Safety lay as far as possible from that drystone wall and fortunately it was the men who would work the guns, both of which had now arrived, who stood in most danger. They had to drive into the unforgiving ground steel stakes on which the restraining tackle could be rigged, this to stop the cannon recoil from taking the whole thing back down the slope behind.

A line of Corsican peasants were now bringing up balls and a barrel of powder, tars arrived with water butts slung on the swabbing and worming gear, this while men worked furiously to build around the cannon mouth a higher barrier which would form an embrasure. The notion seemed fine until the first French ball arrived and demolished one end of the parapet.

'In the name of the Lord,' Farmiloe yelled, 'get those flintlocks fitted and let us give the buggers some of their medicine back.'

The grins that accompanied the 'Aye, aye, sirs' told Toby what he already knew: Dick Farmiloe was a popular fellow and could josh the hands and they would smile; he could neither joke with them nor seem to get their respect, but he knew he must try.

'Aye, it's time to give them hell, boys,' he called, not really loud enough to be a shout.

Only Farmiloe responded, with a cheery agreement, leaving Toby to wonder how these men from HMS *Agamemnon*, whom he really did not know, were aware of the insincerity of his exhortation. Needing to show them he was as fearless as they, even if it was a lie and with his heart in his mouth, he stepped forward to stand by one of the cannon, as the gun captain fitted the flintlock, knowing in doing so he was exposing himself. All the saliva had disappeared from his tongue and throat. It took a great effort to speak, even more to smile.

'Come along, man, quick as you can.'

That got no more than a grunt; the lock was fitted, the long lanyard needed to fire it taken backwards and he watched as the gun was loaded, the charge, ball and wad rammed home, then the touch hole primed, until finally it was run forward, the muzzle peeking through the newly created embrasure. Speaking got no easier, especially when below him he could see the French gunners preparing to fire once more.

'Time to try the range,' Farmiloe called from his position beside the other cannon. 'Toby, as a guest aboard HMS *Agamemnon*, I give you the honour.'

The delay was like something in a staged drama – he could not speak, but someone else did: the gun captain, stood several feet away, line in hand. 'Might I suggest, young sir, that where you is standing, when I pull this here lanyard, my beauty here, on the recoil, is likely to take off your leg.'

Moving swiftly to one side, Toby croaked, 'Fire.'

CHAPTER ELEVEN

Emily Barclay, in her hotel room, was a victim of troubled dreams in which her husband had her in his power and in this it was Ralph Barclay as a slavering ravenous beast of a man, worse than the kind who had so cruelly taken what he considered to be his marital due in the cabin of HMS *Brilliant*, the final act in a long strand of his misbehaviour. The vision, which made her wake with a start, was of a grinning husband eating the papers she had given to Davidson, thoughts which melded into the faces of John Pearce, her hated husband and a mob of indistinct people in the hotel lobby pointing at her for her moral laxity.

Had she seen her spouse then she would have been more comforted, for Ralph Barclay did not sleep at all, pacing up and down his hotel room wondering if Gherson was about to succeed in the task he had been set, with the occasional discomfiting thought that the only thing saving him from blackmail was the complicity of the fellow, this mingled with forced asides as he tried to turn his mind to the needs of his forthcoming command, not least his shortage of hands.

If he was awake, so was Alderman Denby Carruthers, back from his public dinner, he having set in motion what he hoped would be an end to both Gherson and Codge; Carruthers might not know the latter well, but he sensed the evil in the man, so the Runners were out, keeping an eye on him, for he would lead them to Gherson and the evidence they needed, once they met, to lay the pair by the heels and see them out of his life for ever.

Sir Richard Ford had assured him as the sitting magistrate that they would come before him in the morning. His thanks for the information leading to their apprehension would see them both in a prison hulk waiting for the next transport ship to Botany Bay without a chance to speak to anyone.

Codge was relaxed, happy to sit alone and sip the last ale he would have that night, for a pair of those foolish enough to believe in him and do his bidding were out and busy. In his mind's eye he could see them digging with their jemmies at the mortar which held the bars on the attorney's rear window, before employing them on the sash itself and finally the lawyer's strongroom door, the contents of which they would sack up and take to the rendezvous.

That the thief-takers were out worried him not at all, for he had alerted them to the person of Gherson and his aims, who, just after matters were concluded, would be apprehended in possession of documents known to be stolen – any protest made would be ignored until Studdert, alerted to the theft if he did not already know of it, had attested they were his.

Codge would have the promise of the alderman's money and in his pocket the payment of twenty guineas; the rest, given there was bound to be more, would be purloined from Gherson's purse by the Bow Street Runners before they reached the basement cells, men who would deny such monies existed and claim it as a common lament of the collared villain to accuse of larceny those who had taken him up.

Codge might have a wealthy city alderman, maybe even a future Lord Mayor, at his beck and call, and in his criminal bank a slice of Bow Street's very valuable goodwill. Already his mind was turning to ways to profit from that, so all in all, it looked set to be a good night's work!

Cornelius Gherson was pacing too, nervously so, in an upstairs room before a fire he had not ordered in need of more coal – not that he intended to call for any, for he was not in the least cold; if anything he was too hot, his mood not aided by a bottle of foul-tasting wine. He had picked the place of rendezvous carefully in an area he knew well.

It was a tavern called the White Swan close to his father's place of business just to the south of the fashionable area of Clerkenwell, with its spas and theatres. That there were also prisons like the Bridewell and Coldbath Fields close by meant that it was also home to a less salubrious kind of folk and thus it was a place with which Codge was familiar.

These were streets he knew like the back of his hand, for it was here that he had grown up and played as a child; should trouble ensue, he was confident of being able to get away. Barclay's man, Devenow, who had done nothing but glower all the way from Brown's Hotel, was below in the busy taproom with an admonition to stay sober and another to keep out of sight the heavy cudgel he had brought along in case of violence.

The White Swan was surrounded by Bow Street Runners, hiding in doorways or set to watch the approaches, Sir Richard Ford having ensured that every one of his thief-takers was on hand for this major collar, their impatience, as well as their ache for a pipe to smoke, matching Gherson's.

Meanwhile the one in charge could not stop looking at his watch, even though the time was not right for Codge to arrive. That a felony, the break-in, was being executed not far away in Holborn just had to be let pass; the greater prize was here and after several cold hours news came that Codge was on his way, bringing with him two of his companions carrying large bulging sacks, which brought into the open a pair of the thief-takers to let Codge know they were, as arranged, in place.

The rest made sure they were out of sight as he passed under the flickering gaslight that illuminated the doorway of the White Swan, which, being close enough to Smithfield meat market, was open all hours for the porters and traders. They closed with the place once he was inside – not to enter, for that would be precipitate, but to wait for this Gherson fellow to exit. Once he was apprehended and the papers were found on his person, Codge, who would still be inside with the remainder, was doomed.

Men with bulky sacks in a tavern close to a meat market did not even merit a glance in the taproom, such a sight being a commonplace in an area where a shouldered side of beef was not unknown, meat purloined by the leather-hatted men who worked Smithfield – no one in London ate better than the family of a market porter – well paid, no more honest than any other fellows, given opportunity and doing jobs handed down from father to son in which the illicit take-home was considered a perquisite of the employment.

Codge was careful to keep his own hat pulled well down while Gherson was enquired for – not, of course, by name – and on the nod they made their way up the stairs to the private room above. As their legs disappeared, Devenow moved closer to the base of those stairs, easing the club under his cloak, thinking to himself that if anyone needed a belt with it, Gherson would get one too.

'Codge,' said Gherson, as they entered, which got him a scowl.

'Don't you know better than to name me?'

'There's no one in this room who does not know you.'

'Makes no odds,' he growled, before turning to his two companions and indicating they should close the door and empty their sacks. This they did, bundles of papers tied with red ribbons tumbling out onto the floor, that followed by an order to get back downstairs and wait, empty sacks included.

Gherson made to kneel down as the door closed behind them, but Codge's outstretched hand stopped him. 'I'll be seeing my payment afore you cast an eye.'

'And I will be seeing if you have what I came for.'

'No,' Codge insisted, head shaking as he pushed Gherson back slightly. 'Coin first, or you won't even get a look.'

Gherson considered refusal, but not for long. Codge's narrow blue eyes were hard and he was physically imposing, so a purse was produced, which was taken, weighed, then opened and the coins counted. Satisfied, Codge stepped back and indicated that Gherson should help himself, before moving to warm his hams by the dying fire.

'You're a right tight-arse with the coal, mate.' Rummaging through wills, property deeds and powers of attorney, Gherson replied that he was not cold, which got him a snorted response. 'Nothing beats a good warm fire, Codge always says, and Codge is never wrong.'

Giving no reply, merely carrying on with his task, the only sound to be heard was of rustling papers as bundles were torn apart and examined, those discarded now scattered all over the floor, until finally, after an age of rummaging, he threw a last bundle down in frustration.

'They're not here.'

'Since I ain't got a clue what it is you're looking for . . .'

Gherson nearly blurted out what it was, but stopped himself just in time, scrabbling through the scattered papers to no avail to make sure he had not missed the bundle. Had he been mistaken, had the papers never been in that attorney's office at all?

But that flew in the face of memory: the timing of Emily Barclay's first visit to her husband, she being followed by Devenow, and the subsequent delivery of those pages Barclay had demanded – on his instigation – the originals that identified Pearce as the writer. There was a terrible sinking feeling in Gherson's gut; what would Ralph Barclay say when he turned up empty-handed? There was only one thing that might mollify him.

'I need that money back.'

'You must be dreaming,' Codge replied.

'I must have it, Codge.'

That got no more than a hollow laugh, which told Gherson he was wasting his breath, but Devenow was downstairs and he had both the muscle and the means to force Codge to reimburse him. He stood to make for the door, surprised by the way a man bigger than him managed to move from the fireplace so swiftly to block his path.

'Now where would you be headed?'

'There's no point in staying here,' Gherson bleated.

'Wait awhile.'

'Why?'

The reply did not come at once, but the look in Codge's narrow blue eyes showed he was deep in contemplation. He was thinking, unbeknown to

Gherson, that this fellow walking out empty-handed would not suit and there was no way he could think of to persuade him to take something of those papers, anything, which would not arouse his suspicions. A wasted night out would not please the Runners, so he might find that instead of being owed a favour he was in danger of the opposite and that put him at risk. It would not serve if they came in here and saw this on the floor and they would be loath to go back to Bow Street empty-handed, so he might be had up instead.

'If you need an explanation,' he said finally, 'you ain't got a brain.'

Codge took Gherson's arm and led him to the far side of the fireplace, so he was between him and any hope of escape and there he had to stay while Codge gathered up the scattered mess and fed the fire for ten whole minutes until every last piece of paper was consumed.

What had been a dying blaze now flared as flames shot up the chimney, high enough to set the soot alight if it was in need of a sweep. Codge then took up a long heavy poker to break up any bits that were left, finally raking the mass of ashes so hard that tiny pieces of charred remnants were carried up the chimney and into the night sky, keeping at it till the fire died down through lack of material to burn.

'Right, friend,' he said, waving the poker under Gherson's nose, 'off you go.'

Gherson did not move – his mind had been racing and was still unsettled as he stared at the ash-filled fireplace. If he went downstairs and came back up again with Devenow, Codge's men were bound to follow, and besides, armed with that poker he might do for Barclay's bully before Devenow could do for him. That would leave him at the mercy of Codge and his men, yet he had nothing to show Ralph Barclay for his thirty guineas and it was only the direction of his stare that gave him a solution.

'Right,' he said. 'I shall.'

'And I shall rest here until you are well away.'

The two exchanged one last look, larded with mutual mistrust, before Gherson made for the door, in his eagerness to get clear taking the stairs two at a time. Devenow heard him coming and stood up so suddenly the club dropped out from under his cloak and clattered noisily on to the floor, turning every head in the place and stopping any conversation.

'Damn you, Devenow,' Gherson spat.

Half bent to pick up his club, Devenow straightened up quickly, his bully face furious, the cudgel held out as he towered over Gherson. 'Have a care who you damn, turd, or you'll feel this here club on your crown.'

'I'm sorry,' Gherson gasped, 'but we must get away from here.'

'Did matters go for the captain's wishes?'

'Yes,' Gherson blurted. 'Of course they did. Now let us get back and give him the news.'

He was heading for the main door before he finished speaking, leaving Devenow no choice but to follow, though he took the trouble to give the room a glare as he went. He being the size and build he was and an ugly bugger with it, few, even amongst these tough market porters, wanted to stare him down. Outside Gherson was breathing deeply, aware of the sweat cooling on his body. When Devenow exited he made to move.

'Hold there, friend, we want a word with you.'

Two men had stepped out of the shadows, burly fellows in heavy layered coats and big triangular hats.

'Who are you?'

'Bow Street Runners and we have a notion that you might have about you some stolen goods.'

Devenow's club came up, with Gherson protesting he should desist, not that it was needed, for one of the pair before them produced a pistol and aimed it at his chest. 'I should let that cudgel fall, fellow, for I have the right to put a ball in you if'n I am threatened.'

'Put it down, Devenow,' Gherson said, before addressing the pistol holder. 'You cannot mind a man seeking to protect his master.'

It was a testimony to Devenow's stupidity that he swore. 'You ain't my bloody master, Gherson.'

'Happen if you don't drop that club you'll be his cellmate.'

'Cellmate?' Devenow barked, but he did let the club drop to his side.

The pistol waved towards Gherson. 'You have about your person, friend, some papers which we have grounds to believe are not yours to own, valuable documents that were stolen this very night from the offices of a Holborn attorney.'

If Gherson's mind had been in turmoil before it was even more so now, yet it was not so disturbed that he could not guess what had happened. Fighting to control his breath, his ability to tell a barefaced lie with a straight face came to his aid, though not without a bit of a wheeze in his voice.

'There must be some mistake, I have nothing of the kind on my person.'

'Then you won't mind being searched, will you?'

'In the street?'

'As good a place as any, I say. Now if you will step back closer to this gaslight and this here window sill we will see what we will see. Empty your pockets.'

'I shall protest to the highest authority in the land,' Gherson cried as he began to take from his pockets everything he carried. 'This is an outrage.'

That got a gruff and humourless laugh. 'So it is, friend, but the only protesting you will be doing is to the magistrate in the morning, pleading for leniency.'

Amongst other things Gherson produced a small leather purse, which the second Bow Street Runner grabbed and pocketed. Tempted to protest, Gherson stayed silent until everything he had was exposed on the sloping stone of the tavern window sill.

'Now don't you go messing us about,' growled the pistol holder. 'For we can turn nasty if we so desire.'

'Shall I search him, Lemuel?'

'Search both of them, Mill.'

That took several minutes, for in not finding what they sought, they searched more than once. Cornelius Gherson had got his breathing under control and that was reflected in the mocking tone of his voice.

'I fear some fellow has led you astray.'

'What makes you say that?' demanded the one called Mill.

'Seems to me you would not be doing what you're about without some piece of deliberate malice set you to seek for what is clearly not there. You have been duped, I think.'

'What do you say, Lemuel?' asked Mill.

'He should say,' Gherson interjected, his voice now full of confidence, 'give him back his money.'

The response was weary. 'Do as he says, Mill.'

'You are Bow Street Runners, you say, and your names are Mill and Lemuel, which will do to identify you to authority. Do not be surprised to see in the first post of the morrow, then, in the hand of the magistrate, a written complaint bearing your names and the accusation that you were prepared not only to arrest an innocent man but steal my property, and I have my companion here as witness. Perhaps, gentlemen, it will be you who is seeking leniency. Devenow, pick up your cudgel and follow me.'

It was clear by the dropping shoulders there was no option but to let them depart and Gherson could almost feel the hatred in their eyes as they bored into his back.

'How the fuck did you pull that off?' Devenow whispered.

'Wait and see,' Gherson snapped, now so elated he felt he could be sharp even with the bully.

Behind them a whistle blew and heavy-coated men seemed to come from every doorway, making for the entrance to the White Swan, to join Lemuel and Mill, and gathered, they went in at a hustle. Gherson did not see, but he could imagine what came next, the rush up the stairs to confront the man who had sought to betray him. Whatever had happened – if he had been mistaken, or those court martial papers had been removed, and it made no odds how – he was safe, with only one more hurdle to overcome.

When the Bow Street Runners burst in on Codge, they found him with his back to the fire, drinking the remains of Gherson's wine, and were greeted with a wide grin.

'Welcome, friends.'

'Welcome, you snake,' Lemuel spat. 'You'll say welcome to a prison hulk when we is finished with you.'

Showing mock surprise, Codge raised his eyebrows. 'Whatever do you mean?'

'Lemuel,' Mill said softly, his eyes having surveyed the room, 'there ain't no papers here either.'

'Where are they, Codge, two whole sacks full?'

'Two whole sacks full of what?'

'You know of what I speak.'

'Step aside, Codge,' said Mill, sniffing the air, a command that was obeyed, though with no great haste. Mill looked into the fire, still full of blackened paper ash. 'Best cast an eye over this, Lemuel.'

That the other Runner did, standing over the near dead coals and broken ash, his head slowly shaking. Then he ordered everyone but Mill to leave the room and wait outside. Once they had gone he addressed Codge, his voice a hiss.

'I ain't standing for this.'

'For what?' Codge asked, his eyes twinkling.

'If you think I am going back to Sir Richard empty of

hand you have got another think coming. I will take you in anyway and think of something to lay against you that will satisfy our employer.'

'Take me in – so that was the plan?' Lemuel's face went blank; he had said too much, indeed he had virtually told Codge what the idea had been and who had set it in motion. 'Can't have you goin' in empty-handed, can we now?'

'No,' Lemuel spat.

'But you can't take me in, can you, for you have no evidence that I have done anything and I would walk out a free man of the morning. Seems to me, and not for the first time, that Old Codge has to come to your aid. There be a pair of lads down in the taproom with empty sacks by them. If you was to go through their pockets you might find that they had an item or two that was not their own, stuff that could be identified as being the property of a certain lawyer and taken from his premises illegal. If'n you don't mind, I'll stay in this here room and wait till you are done.'

'We have spent a night in the cold without so much as a farthing to show,' protested Mill.

Codge pulled out the purse given him by Gherson, now a quarter the weight it had been originally, for he had removed fifteen guineas, then held it out. 'That is a crying shame. Why not take this for your trouble?'

Codge was grinning now and not in the least worried about handing over the money; he had a very good idea where he would be able to not only replace it but acquire more, much more. After a decent interval he left the White Swan, having already composed in his head the note he

170

would send to Alderman Denby Carruthers, wondering, now that he had lost two of his drinking companions to the Runners, who to send with the message.

Not that it would be a problem; there was always some fellow who wanted to be his best friend.

CHAPTER TWELVE

'Burnt them? Ralph Barclay demanded. 'Why did you do that?'

Gherson had been rehearsing the words he needed to say all the way back to Brown's Hotel, which at night had meant skirting the closed city gates as well as thinking up the justification, so he replied with confidence. That it was a lie, that it might be exposed as such in the future, would have to be dealt with at the time, for right at this moment necessity was the mother of invention.

'You must understand, sir,' Gherson said, using the superior tone that mightily irritated the captain, 'that the people I deal with are not the type in which to repose any trust at all and Devenow will tell you how close we came to being apprehended.'

'Within a whisker, Your Honour,' the bully added, not fully in the picture of what had been intended or the errand on which they had been engaged.

'My concern was that there should be no evidence at all, sir, for that would serve your purpose and it was only the slimy nature of my felon that alerted me to what might happen. Imagine if I had not acted as I did, if the Bow Street Runners had found those papers upon my person.'

Slow realisation appeared on Devenow's face. 'So that's what we were about?'

'What the devil were thief-takers doing there, man?' Barclay snapped.

'My hired felon tipped them off, no doubt for a fee as a reward for my arrest. I would have been charged with stealing from Studdert, the court martial papers would have been in the hands of the Bow Street magistrate, which in turn, given the contents, would have implicated you and could have led to your arrest.'

'I am sure you would have kept me out of it, Gherson,' Barclay replied, not that he believed it; Gherson did not respond to correct that impression on the very good grounds that to save himself he would have dobbed in his own mother.

'As it is, sir, they are now black ash.'

Ralph Barclay nodded slowly and spoke with what he thought was sincerity. 'You have done well.'

'And your wife, sir, do you wish me to communicate with her the change in her circumstances?'

'No! I shall do that. Prepare to coach down to Chatham. *Semele* is near ready for sea as we speak. I will write to my wife this instant and tell her what she must do, on pain of destitution if she does not conform to my wishes.'

The decision to vacate Emily Barclay's room at the house of Mrs Fletcher was not a difficult one to make; with the Tolland gang knowing that address it could never be secure, and if they had backed away the previous night there was no knowing how long that would last. Michael was the one charged with the duty, a letter provided for the landlady plus an extra month's payment for rent, this while Emily began her search for new accommodation; she was unwilling to stay at Nerot's given it would be bound to cause gossip, she and Pearce being constantly in one another's company.

Michael asked, when hiring a conveyance to carry the fetched possessions, that the carter provide enough men to move the contents of a house, there being safety in numbers, and if they wondered at merely being asked to shift a pair of hastily packed trunks instead of sideboards and beds, the Irishman did not bother to enlighten them. Nor did he explain why he had in his waistband a pistol and the need to keep a sharp eye out for trouble.

While they were there a sealed letter arrived addressed to Mrs Barclay, not that Michael would have known had he not been told, he being unable to read, nor did he know that the wax seal was that of Brown's Hotel. He just stuck it in his pocket to be taken back to Nerot's with everything else, pleased to have seen no sign of the smuggling gang.

John Pearce had received a note from Henry Dundas with his breakfast to say that a ship had been found, a hired armed cutter called HMS *Larcher,* presently laying at Buckler's Hard in the Beaulieu River having a new mainmast fitted. He was required to call at the Admiralty where he would be given his commission to take temporary command of her, her present captain being sick and requiring to come ashore for treatment. As a fully manned vessel it had everything needed to engage of the suggested mission immediately he could get aboard.

A chest containing gold coins to the value of a thousand pounds would be sent down to Buckler's Hard under guard to await his arrival and he would be required to sign for the sum and account for its use on return, the balance to be paid back into the Government coffers.

He at once replied regarding Charlie and Rufus, asking that a demand be forwarded through the Admiralty to Ralph Barclay to release his 'servants' and despatch them to his new ship; the sods might refuse him, Barclay particularly, but they would not refuse the Secretary of State for the Home Department.

If, having been granted command of a vessel for the first time, he expected to be greeted by the Admiralty porters with respect, he was disappointed; ex-seamen of advanced years, secure in their positions, rudeness was their abiding quality, though Pearce was unaware, as he was subjected to the usual grudging welcome, that such treatment was meted to any officer on his way to receive a commission who did not see it as his bounden duty to slip them a *douceur* merely for the act of opening a gate and touching their hat.

What followed was the usual wait in the anteroom, full of officers who had only gained entry with a coin slipped to the doorman, lieutenants in the main in search of employment, though there were captains too, the condition of their uniforms attesting to time spent on half pay; as he had done on a previous visit, John

Pearce avoided any intimacy, not even introducing himself.

This he did for the very good reason that sailors gossiped like fishwives, thus his name was known throughout the service and it was not one held in high regard through a combination of anger at how he had been granted his rank and outright jealousy at what was seen as his run of good fortune, which they no doubt put down to some satanic influence. Whatever, he would not open himself up to their condescension.

Called eventually into the great room in which the Board of Admiralty met, he was greeted with little courtesy by a fellow he had first encountered only a few weeks previously – and that had been far from a pleasant experience. Phillip Stephens was the secretary to the Admiralty, a dry stick of a bureaucrat who seemed to be rendered more grey by the nature of his garments, they being of a not much deeper hue than his pallid skin, the only spark of brightness coming from a powdered wig. Certainly there was little life in the hooded eyes and his tone of voice seemed to reek of suppressed frustration.

'I will not ask how this sudden request from the First Lord came about, only observe that it is most unusual. How it would have been met had Rackham not fallen ill I do not know.'

'It will be a new experience for me,' Pearce responded with a cold glare, 'to depart this building having been given something for which I do not have to pay.'

Stephens responded in kind, the look implying that Pearce should never have been allowed to enter the Admiralty in the first place. On both his previous visits he had been obliged to pass over money, first to secure his lieutenant's commission and a few weeks previously the protections against impressment for his friends; those who wrote documents for the navy did not do so for free.

'Given your publicly expressed antipathy to the service, it is to be hoped this is only of a temporary nature.'

Delighted to be granted an opportunity to needle the man, Pearce grinned. 'Have you not heard, Mr Stephens? I have decided on a naval career after all, which is why you will find on your desk soon a request that my servants be allowed to join me.'

Stephens was not going to oblige him by saying 'damnation' in his presence, but on his exit Pearce was sure the invective would pass his lips, so baleful was his look.

Charlie Taverner and Rufus Dommet were working on the fore top rigging, finishing off the work there under the supervision of a second lieutenant and a bosun's mate who knew how to make sense of what, to a novice, would have been just a mess of hemp. Their hands were thankfully hardened enough not to become like those of the landsmen newly come aboard, whose palms were soon raw from the pulling they had to do on the ropes used to get aloft what the more experienced seamen required.

HMS *Semele* had needed miles of buntlines and leech lines for the shrouds, hawsers for the standing rigging that ran from the deck to the highest point on the ship. When it came to preventer stays to keep the masts from suffering too much strain, these were made of cables, three hawsers entwined. Everything ran through blocks – single-, double- and triple-sheaved, depending on the task each one had to perform.

Added to that were sister blocks and futtock plates, plus a myriad variety of knots, braces, rope pendants, parrals, working on the tensions created by one force and acting to control another, that applied once in place by a combination of human muscle and the windlass, the whole now near to being complete.

On the quarterdeck, speaking trumpet in hand and wearing an outfit that would scarce have differentiated him from a tramp, stood the premier, bellowing orders to the six naval and two marine lieutenants who had come aboard over the last week, while cursing roundly the numerous midshipmen scurrying to obey their instructions, many from the captain's home county of Somerset, others the offspring or distant relatives of fellow officers whose parents had managed to persuade the absent captain to take them under his wing.

The vessel smelt of tar, grease, linseed and human sweat, the first to protect the rigging against the elements that would insidiously wear away at it through weather and the inevitable motion, the grease easing the sheave pins, oil keeping the outer wood of the blocks from cracking through drying out, the perspiration coming from the fact that there was no machinery in the world that could carry out tasks only possible by the application of the muscles of sometimes as many as a hundred souls when it came to getting aloft the heaviest spars and canvas.

Beneath them there was a party on their knees caulking

the last of the deck seams, driving in oakum before sealing the join between planking with tar, while above them the most nimble men aboard, the topmen, were working to bend on the heavy canvas sails with the dexterity and defiance of death that was their trademark – sometimes they seemed to having nothing to attach them to the ship but a single finger or a couple of bare toes.

The carpenter and his party of mates were busy teaching men they considered dunderheads to put in place and remove the bulkhead panels. These shut off the open decks at the stern to provide both the great cabin and the wardroom, while inside those wooden walls more barriers were being erected to create the varied internal accommodation, the whole accompanied by a great deal of cursing as cack-handed novices struggled to understand the simple orders that required them to drive home or knock out a wedge.

The arrival of the captain saw the officers, mids and those marines working, ordinary lobsters included, rush to change into proper uniform and to clean themselves up enough to pass muster, with Ralph Barclay, who knew the drill, ordering his barge to row around the vessel, ostensibly to study her lines but really to give those men time to smarten themselves up. Once sufficient of that had passed he was piped aboard with all ceremony.

Then all hands were called aft to stand in temporary divisions so he could read out his commission. He stood on the poop, with the premier beside him, and in addition two faces that the pair of Pelicans had never hoped to see again. Ugly Devenow they had feared would arrive with Barclay, but much worse was the countenance of a fellow

179

who had been pressed with them, someone they had forgotten. The sight of the handsome-cum-corrupt face of Cornelius Gherson had them making doubly sure they were behind broad shoulders to keep them out of sight.

And there was Captain Ralph Barclay himself, with his glowering look and dark brow, with one pinned-up sleeve attached to the chest of his broadcloth blue coat, a man Rufus and Charlie knew only too well – and they had passed this onto their shipmates – to be a good seaman, if a miserable bastard, who was not averse to having his crew started regularly and flogged into what he considered good order.

He was looking over the complement of his new ship with that habitual glower on his dark-skinned face; this was intended to let them know that from now on he was God Almighty as far as they were concerned. Once this official act of taking over the vessel was complete, they would begin to hear about his list of instructions for the proper running of his command, his personal way of doing things, and that would tell them more than the Articles of War by which they were collectively bound.

Every captain had his ways and few of them were soft-hearted or indulgent, nor would those expected to abide by them want them to be too lax; a ship of war was not a republic. If they were to survive, let alone prosper, HMS *Semele* had to be properly run from kites to keel. Any other way would see them doomed before any of the cannon yet to come aboard were fired, for the sea was a dangerous element, unforgiving, and the enemy they would face as deadly as they intended they should themselves be.

Yet those captains' orders had to be fair also; men like Davy would not allow for tyranny and they had their way of letting those who led them know when they had overstepped the mark, and if it upset the buggers all the way up to their Lordships at the Admiralty, so be it. They would do as ordered, sail and fight the ship to the best of their ability, but they would not be treated as slaves.

'By the powers invested in me by the Lords Commissioners of the Admiralty . . .' On he droned, speaking words which some aboard had heard a dozen times in their lives, having been at sea since they were nippers.

Isaac Lavery had accepted the charge from Catherine Carruthers to find Cornelius Gherson the previous day, this imparted with the most simpering of pleas. In truth, he had a strong desire to see the fellow damned; if he could not penetrate into his employer's mind, he was as keen to see the back of him as the alderman.

The request had occasioned a night out ostensibly trying to locate and warn him; in reality he had sat the whole time out in a snug coffee house reading the latest journals, having no idea where the pair were who were due to be taken up, Sir Richard Ford's note not having said.

But the duty did allow him time with his employer's wife as he sadly reported his failure and was then granted an opportunity to show her some sympathy. Should she ask him to carry on, he would continue with the pretence as his other duties allowed, for each time he reported failure he would advance his suit a little. Seeing a naive creature, a near girl lost in confusion, he failed to realise what a scheming creature he was dealing with.

Catherine Carruthers might have lacked great knowledge of the world, but she did not lack acquaintance with attempts at seduction – moves which she had been subjected to since a tender age, when the pretty child had blossomed into the beginnings of womanhood. Having had the advantage of a rare physical precocity, looking and seeming older than her years, she knew what Lavery was about and could calculate just how much latitude to grant to the old goat so that he would do her bidding.

'Another low fellow called today, which you did not tell me.'

Aware of the sharp tone, Lavery was swift in his reply. 'There was nothing to tell. He came with a note for your husband.'

'Did he come from this fellow Codge?'

Lavery's hesitation nearly got him a blast of true temper; it was only by making a fist of her hand she stopped herself from actually issuing the kind of filthy curse which, even as a child, she had confined to times when she was alone in her bedroom.

'It seems to me, Lavery, that if we can find this fellow, he will lead us to Cornelius.'

She had not met Codge; he had, and he knew a bully boy when he saw one. His mistress was asking him to go to the kind of places a man of his type would frequent and that on its own was dangerous enough without he found Codge, who would not likely be happy about the unearthing. Thankfully he had an excuse ready to hand.

'It is difficult to contemplate such a course when my obligation to my master takes up so much time.'

'But you are so clever, Isaac,' she pleaded, before looking shocked, her hand to her mouth, her voice matching the look. 'Forgive me for using your given name.'

'You have no idea of how happy it makes me that you feel you can, madam.'

His hand inched out, but there was no way Catherine Carruthers was prepared to yet take it. Looking up at him, taking in his bulbous purple nose, the lined face enclosed by those big stuck-out ears and the age bags under his watery eyes, which were now full of pity, she wondered how far she could push; would he risk his position for an indication that his aim was progressing?

'You must find the time and I will help you do it, even if I risk the wrath of my husband.'

'No!' That response was emphatic, while the concerned expression changed to one of a near-fatherly look, which irritated her immensely. 'You must repose your trust in me and I will not disappoint you by any failure of effort.'

'How I hope you do not.'

'The fellow who called today may do so again. When he does and when he leaves, I will dog his heels until I discover from where the creature has emerged, which may well be the den of this fellow Codge.'

Her pale smooth hand finally came out to be wrapped in his, with its wrinkled skin and the large brown spots of age very obvious on the back. 'How I wish I was as brave as you.'

In a nearby room Alderman Denby Carruthers was

sitting staring at his bookshelves. He had received two missives this morning, one from Bow Street telling him of the failure to lay Gherson and Codge by the heels, as well as another less well composed from the latter, informing him that he would be calling in the near future for a little talk.

There was no doubting what that implied and the alderman wondered if Druce, his brother-in-law, having helped in the botched disposal of Gherson, was in a position to aid him once more. There was no doubt this Codge posed a serious danger; whatever it cost to get rid of him had to be less than he would extract for his silence.

About to ring for Lavery, who would take a letter to Druce's office in the Strand, he decided against using his clerk; this was a message best delivered personally.

Emily Barclay read her husband's letter for the tenth time, trying to make sense of it, while also trying to think how to respond.

> . . . *I decline to support you in any way and I hereby order you to return to Frome, where, upon your arrival you will find waiting for you a list of instructions regarding your future behaviour. Do not, under any circumstances, entertain an illusion that you can disobey me in this, for if you do I will denounce you as an adulteress and cast you from both my life and my responsibilities. Even should you end in the workhouse, I will not come to your aid. As for your family, they will suffer for your folly.*

Please address your agreement to me immediately, as I am preparing to weigh, care of HMS Semele, Chatham Naval Dockyard.

At a loss to know how to respond, her initial reaction, to reply damning his nerve, was held back by the changed circumstances of her life. She must await the return of John Pearce and seek from him the right way to react.

CHAPTER THIRTEEN

Emily got her answer quickly and that was a scoff at the mere notion that Ralph Barclay could do anything. He was, though he did not say it, tempted to respond with an outright threat but decided that such a thing, which he could hardly keep a secret, would only work on Emily's nerves and that was the last thing he wished to happen, for it would interfere with what he hoped to achieve. First he had to tell her what had happened with Dundas and the task he had been asked to perform.

'So I am off to a shipyard in the New Forest and I want you to accompany me – in fact, I insist.'

There was no need for him to add that, left behind, she might not be safe; the time had come for their future life to be decided and he suspected it would be he who would have to force the issue. This was not because of cowardice on Emily's part but the natural caution of one who had been raised in a society riddled with hypocrisy, one in which duty was counted as being above happiness in the human condition.

John Pearce had been raised in a different setting, as a young man taught to question every tenet and see them often for what they were: platitudes passed down from the powerful and wealthy who blithely ignored their constraints themselves, useful as long as they kept the lower orders in line.

How many landowners had he met in his father's company who went to church only to be seen and grovelled to by their tenants and socially lower neighbours, to exchange pious dialogues with the clerics whose appointment they controlled while privately happy to engage with the Edinburgh Ranter in philosophical discussions that questioned if there was a God in heaven at all?

'Insist?' Emily said, her brow furrowed with the beginnings of objection.

'For the sake of love,' he replied, smiling as she blushed, for they were again in the public lobby of Nerot's Hotel. 'And freedom.'

'John, I—'

He responded with a wicked smile. 'If you do not wish me to take you in arms this instant, you will cease to demur. I will bespeak a post-chaise to collect you from here and a separate one for Michael and I, both to go to Richmond Park, where we can combine in a single carriage to take us to a place where we are unknown and may seek accommodation as a couple without raising an eyebrow.'

'You seem to have planned everything.'

'Someone must,' Pearce insisted, 'for this limbo we are presently in does not satisfy you or I.'

'Do I not have a choice?'

'Yes, you can stay in London, take rooms as you did at Mrs Fletcher's house and await my return, for which I will ensure you are adequately provided. I cannot force you to join me and neither will I try, but I will say this, Emily, to say no to my project is only putting off an intimacy that must one day occur.'

That deepened the blush that had begun to suffuse her cheeks; well raised as she was and knowing to that which he was alluding it was impossible not to turn a high colour. What men and women did in the bedchamber was never mentioned in polite society; as far as she knew it was never even discussed between man and wife.

'Do you agree?' he asked.

The pause was long, with Emily examining her clasped hands as though, somehow, in them lay a clue as to the correct answer. Pearce was actually holding his breath, a fact he only realised when on her affirmative nod he was free to exhale.

'You will come to see this as one of the happiest decisions of your life.' A wan smile was all he could hope for to that assertion. 'I have things to attend to, the acquisition of charts and the like, as well as some seagoing clothing for Michael and I, for I have no notion of what is available at Buckler's Hard. Besides, I need to know that Dundas has done all he said he would before we depart and I must order the carriages.'

'So I have time?'

'You have, Emily, time to pack.'

'And you do not wish me to respond to my husband in any way?'

'No! Let him stew in his own juice.'

And what a juice that will be, he thought, *when I get my responses to those letters sent to the Mediterranean.* Once he had those he would know how to proceed and with luck they might well be available upon his return from the Vendée, a prospect that made him even more cheerful, especially if Emily's nephew saw his way to telling the truth for a change.

The collapse was inevitable – Toby Burns had struggled to sleep at night in his canvas tent, imagining what death or disfigurement he might suffer; if he did drop off, his dreams were even more terrifying. He had to face cannon fire all day every day under a blazing Corsican sun, which heated the land and made warm and suffocating every troubled night. He sweated in his cot and lived in terror in daylight, until finally he wilted under the sun's glare, passing out from sheer exhaustion.

When he came to, and he did that slowly, he was aboard HMS *Agamemnon* and there was a cool damp cloth bathing his face, the ship was rocking on a swell and the beams above his head, being painted bright white, made him wonder if he was in paradise.

'So you've come round at last.' The voice came from an indistinct face but it made him turn his head, slowly revealing the features of what must be one of the loblolly boys who aided the ship's surgeon. 'I shall call Mr Roxburgh presently to come and see you.'

'Where am I?' Toby croaked, not sure, when the reply came, if he was pleased or disappointed.

By the time Roxburgh attended upon him he knew only too well where he was, in a sickbay full of wounded men, some groaning in pain, others too badly hurt to make a sound and, despite the odour of vinegar, there was an underlying smell of corrupted flesh. His first non-medical visitor was Lieutenant George Andrews, his arm in a sling and with words of thanks to one of the midshipmen who had ensured he had been seen to so quickly.

'Did you have a clean shirt?' Toby asked, for the want of anything else to say.

'Oh yes, never go into a fight in dirty linen, Burns. Unclean clothes mean an unclean wound.'

'I shall not, sir.'

'Speaking of which, you have been in the same clothes for several days.'

'Days?'

'Oh yes, and not just manning the cannon, you have been comatose for a while, but I suggest we find you something clean before Captain Nelson's inspection. Do I have your permission to raid your sea chest?' That got a weak nod, given the last person Toby wanted to face was Nelson. 'Anyway, enjoy the breeze, which will at least keep you cool.'

They had rigged a scuttle sail to carry the sea breeze into the lower decks and he was grateful to feel it when there was a gust, not just for its cooling property but because it carried away with it the unpleasant odours. Roxburgh appeared for a second time and examined his tongue, before announcing he would need to see his stool.

'Take a pot to the heads, now that you can walk, and fetch it back, laddie, for there's more of a man's ailments shown in his excretions than will ever appear on his extremities. Two minutes with that and I will know if you are fit to return to duty.'

Those words struck Toby with his usual dread, until the surgeon added, 'Mind, I will insist on light duties for a while; can't have you pushing yourself too hard too soon.'

The light was going when Nelson did his rounds – he had eaten his dinner and written orders for the next day – something he apparently carried out regularly, leaving Toby to wonder at a fellow who landed himself with such a tedious chore as visiting the sick. He spoke with each man who could respond, stood silently and in prayer over those who could not and was animate with the ambulant, even sharing a joke with a leg amputee about his prospects for a post as a ship's cook.

'Well, Mr Burns, what a to-do. You fell to exhaustion from excessive effort, I am told. Young sir, we share some ailments, for Roxburgh will tell you there is not an affliction in creation that does not seek out as a victim one Horatio Nelson. Colds, recurring fevers that I have had since my time in the Caribbean jungles, disordered bowels on a regular basis, I am a martyr to them all, and what can a doctor do?' That got the surgeon a look. 'Nothing, sir, that is what. It is I who have the cure and in a month of Sundays you will never guess what it is.'

'No, sir,' Toby replied weakly, though having had his own dinner of portable soup and fresh bread he was feeling quite recovered.

'Action, Mr Burns, that is the cure. Battle, the mere smell of it restores me. Damn the quackery, I say.'

'Except when you are low,' Roxburgh growled. 'Then it is "doctor this" and "doctor that" and no end to complaint. You're worse than a woman!'

They all do it, Toby thought, *talk to him as if he was of no consequence. Even that amputee joked he might need a cook's post himself one day, the way he was forever putting himself in danger as if it was any of his business.*

Nelson just laughed, a response to amuse all present.

'Hard to know who is the enemy, Mr Burns, the doctors or the Jacobins, what?'

'How goes the siege, sir?'

'Be over in a day or two I shouldn't wonder. Lord Hood has received a request from the mayor to send in another white flag, which signals acceptance.' Nelson leant closer. 'The French fear to fall into the hands of our Corsican friends, for which one cannot blame them. But just as we have the prize who should appear but the transports full of damned Foot Guards. When the white flag goes up, it will be redcoats marching in to Bastia, not blue.'

'You do not seem angered by that, sir.'

'Peeved would describe it, but it's all one, boy, as long as we beat the devils, and we still have to take Calvi, which will be a much harder nut to crack. We will need you at your best for that, so get some rest.'

What Nelson foresaw came to pass: with a flute band playing the redcoats marched into the citadel and a revived Toby Burns was there to see the tricolour come down and the twin flags of Great Britain and Corsica rise above the battlements. He was also witness, as was most of the fleet, to Lord Hood in a towering rage as news came from Toulon that the French had slipped out of their home port and Vice Admiral William Hotham had failed to intercept them.

Slowly, as stores and equipment came aboard, HMS *Semele* had sunk lower in the water, her wide tumblehome disappearing strake by strake. This included the weight of her cannon, thirty-two-pounders on the gun deck, eighteens on the upper decks and nine-pounders on the quarterdeck and fo'c'sle including a quartet of carronades, turning her into what the navy required, a floating fortress with a massive weight of available shot.

Just getting those huge guns aboard – the thirty-twos weighed three tons – was an education in leverage and rope work, given they could only be shipped through the gun ports, to be set directly on their wheeled trunnions. Lashed at both muzzle and pommel end they were lowered from a crane then lashed to a set of lines and pulleys to ease them inboard, a manoeuvre carried out with no haste given they were more than enough in weight to crush a man, the operation overseen by an anxious gunner.

Once set, the cables needed to contain the massive recoil had to be fitted, and on all the decks what had been confusion was beginning to look like order as everything was stowed away as it should be. This made life a little harder for Charlie and Rufus, keen to stay out of sight, but fortunately for them the pair they feared most were not much given to parading around the decks; they were content to stay aft, while the captain himself was more concerned about getting his good furniture aboard unscratched, as well as his copious personal stores.

There was also the question of a cook and some proper servants, for Devenow would never be that, and it was with the wiles of years of service that he sought those types out, men who could actually reside in a naval port like Chatham and still avoid taking a ship that did not suit. They were not to be had up to haul on ropes or be messed about by petty officers.

These men had skills a good captain wanted if he had any desire to impress, and it also served to attach to a man who was prosperous; a rich man meant rich pickings. Word went out, and knowing to the near penny how much Ralph Barclay had coming in prize money, the men he needed made their presence known and were fetched aboard.

Now quite a wealthy man due to his prize-taking, Ralph Barclay could not but contrast this occasion with the commission he had received to command HMS *Brilliant*. After five years on half pay he had been hard-pressed to meet the needs of his cabin and that, compared to what he lived in now, had not been spacious.

Servants had come from what he had aboard, his furniture had been of the lowest quality, his stores meagre by the standards he felt necessary to entertain his fellow captains as well as his subordinates, albeit, encouraged by other, better-off naval wives, his inexperienced Emily had overstretched the budget and felt for the first time his wrath at her spending.

He had left behind in Frome a string of creditors – now all satisfied – many of whom had hammered at his door through the years on half pay. If he thought about that lack of a ship he would lay the blame squarely at the door of Sam Hood, who as the senior naval lord had controlled appointments. Barclay had been a client officer of Admiral Lord Rodney, a man Hood had seen as a rapacious opportunist. Rodney having expired and his influence lost, any officer attached to him would whistle for an appointment.

Now, thanks to Hotham and the patronage of the Duke of Portland, he had a command he thought matched his position on the captains' list. Pacing the carpet of his day cabin, now filled with highly polished furniture, set off by the light pouring through the casements, was a delight. He also had a dining cabin with a skylight, his own privy and sleeping cabin and, most pleasant of all, when it came to the masses of paperwork, which aboard the frigate he had been obliged to look after himself, he had Gherson.

Such a man was necessary; everything had to be accounted for down to the last nail, endless lists and reports sent to the Navy and Victualling Boards, where they were pored over by pasty-faced clerks looking for discrepancies, and dealing with them and their requirements was as close to a war as it could get. They demanded payment for any perceived losses while ships' officers insisted allowance be made for everything, from the depredations of rats to the need to condemn poor-quality beef and pork in an endless game of claim and counterclaim that never seemed to be settled.

In the favour of the men at sea, the Navy Board and Admiralty clerks did not work, as they did aboard ship, all of the day. Rarely at their desks before ten of the morning, lunch was no short affair and was taken with wine, so that the afternoons, never long in duration in the first place, tended towards somnolence rather than activity; their pay was not dependent on the discovery of peculation, and the amount of paperwork was excessive, so a clever man could bury his losses as well as other things in the mass of detail.

'I hope he has enough for Devenow's gullet,' Rufus said as pipes of wine were lifted on board from a whip at the yardarm, prior to being taken to the captain's personal storeroom. 'For he'll be tapping them as soon as they're laid down.'

'There ain't enough in creation for that throat,' Charlie replied.

The shout from the quarterdeck made them jump, which was wise given what the premier, Lieutenant Jackson, yelled. 'Bosun's mate, start those men, I will not have idle bodies on my deck.'

The captain's list of private orders, imparted to his lieutenants, had been passed down through petty officers and their mates, then on to leading hands and able seamen – instructions which had registered enough to make them cautious and evasive when it came to punishment. The poor sods that did not understand them, the pressed men and newly volunteered, suffered from an inability to see trouble coming or avoid it when it arose.

Lengthy, what it told those who knew was that Ralph Barclay was going to run a very tight ship and one in which the grating was inevitable given the number of offences that could be committed which brought on that penalty. No one groused; it was to be seen if he would meet the need to be fair, and if he came it too high, well there were ways of telling even a mighty naval captain that it would not be borne.

The pair had got their wish and they were part of Davy's eight-man mess, all of them proper seamen who would combine to work as a team on one of the great cannon by which they took their food. They worked the day, which was hard, and slept through the night, which was bliss, for all the crowding, farting, snoring and moans of those who could not settle or were troubled by screaming dreams.

All in all, it was as good as could be expected. They were in port so there were over a hundred women aboard, supposedly wives but in truth not, and the cost of their services was rarely coin: food, a bit of tobacco, a share of grog or some of their daily allowance of small beer. Illicit drink was fetched in from the Medway bumboats despite the efforts of the soldiers fetched ashore as marines to stop it, so there was much gaiety of an evening, with the fiddler never still. The food might have been monotonous, but it was regular and padded out by fresh greens.

It would not last so they made the best of it, for in the great cabin the watch lists were being prepared, which would divide the men and rob them of a complete night's rest, turning their slumbers to four on/four off, while in the Admiralty the question had already been posed to Ralph Barclay as to when HMS *Semele* would finally raise her anchor and comply with her orders to join the Channel Fleet of Admiral Lord Howe, which he would struggle to do before they weighed from Spithead.

When the day of departure came, it was time to shift many of the women ashore and to conclude the last trades with the local floating market, then man the boats and warp the ship downriver, out past Upnor Castle and the Nore anchorage for a temporary wait for the arrival of a Thames pilot with the ships of the North Sea Fleet. They were not there long and finally the order came to raise sail.

This sent the topmen aloft to let go of the topsails, which were sheeted home as men heaved the capstan round to haul the ship over the anchor and pluck it from the Thames mud. Surrounded by his officers, with the pilot conning the ship out into the main channel that would take them out to deep water, Ralph Barclay felt like a king.

He might have been short on his complement by a hundred and fifty souls, but that mattered not; every vessel in the fleet was short-handed. He had his ship and he would work up the crew until they knew their tasks, and punish into knowledge those who were slow to respond. Now all he needed was a successful fleet action to cement his joy and the good news was that his commander, Lord Howe, had already sailed from Portsmouth and was a-sea hunting for the enemy.

That was until he recalled he had received no reply from his wife and that brought on a black look that had everyone who caught sight of it wondering what they had done to displease the man who now ruled their lives.

Information on naval ship movements came in quickly to the prize agent partnership of Ommanney & Druce. When Edward Druce heard that HMS *Semele* had weighed and was on its way to join the Channel Fleet, he saw a partial solution to a troubling quandary, having felt pressured on the subject of Cornelius Gherson. He had declined to tell Denby Carruthers what he knew about the fellow and his whereabouts; Ralph Barclay had taken valuable prizes and was a cherished client who had turned scrutiny as to how his affairs were handled over to his clerk.

He had recognised the name the first time it was mentioned by Barclay; that was underscored when he had had the villain in his own office, for if this was a first meeting who could mistake the description, and as for the man's morality all doubt evaporated. Gherson had made it plain that he was not averse to accepting a bribe to persuade his master that whatever advice, sound or speculative, Ommanney & Druce proffered as to wise investments, it should be followed.

He was now paying the price for not telling his wife's brother right away that the swine had survived their plan to dispose of him in order to avoid a family scandal, yet only slowly had it occurred to him, after a visit from the troubled alderman, that he had become embroiled in a conspiracy the ramifications of which could lead anywhere. Thank the Lord the fellow was now out of reach.

It was all very well for his brother-in-law to say the man must be found and disposed of, and properly this time – he seemed to think that with his connections Druce had a ready fund of assassins on tap; and just who was this Codge fellow who had also fallen foul of Denby Carruthers, to the extent he needed to be permanently silenced as well?

* * *

Henry Dundas sat at a desk piled with papers: requests for preferment from any number of his fellow Scots, demands from political allies for their pet schemes to be brought forward or to fruition – all the business of parliamentary management which was his daily burden. He was not a man put off by the weight of such responsibilities, indeed he revelled in them, seeing himself as a large spider at the centre of a complex web, but in control of the whole.

Between them, by the exercise of a massive amount of patronage combined with threats and blandishments, he and the First Lord of the Treasury, William Pitt, commanded the votes they needed in the House to pursue their aims – the war with France, the raising of monies through customs dues and various taxes on goods sold or items traded. As well as that, they had to keep happy the faction of the Whigs who supported the Tory government and kept at bay the opposition.

Everything that happened or was proposed went through their hands: pressure that some relative be given a sinecure office with high pay and no actual work, that expeditions be despatched to this place and that, every demand sent in by some commercial interest seeking security for their trades, as if the nation had a bottomless pit of soldiers, sailors, ships and money, when in truth Britannia was stretched to the very limit in all regards.

As of now the greatest military problem was a vital French convoy coming from the United States, reputed to be of over one hundred cargo vessels, carrying food, mostly grain. The harvest had failed the previous autumn and intelligence reported Paris as being on the verge of starvation; at the very least bread was scarce and expensive, so the very factor that had helped to topple Louis XVI and the Bourbons was now bearing down on the regicides of the Committee of Public Safety.

There were reports to plough through from the West Indies, the Low Countries and the Mediterranean, matters relating to the East India Company and problems with neutrals such as the Dutch and the Scandinavians, all of them needing attention, as well as requests from French émigrés either resident in Britain or attached to the court of the Count of Artois in Koblenz.

Finally Dundas came to the letter he had from John Pearce, telling him he was on his way to Buckler's Hard. The funds he needed and had pointedly asked for had yet to be collected and despatched with a secure and well-escorted messenger, for specie was not easy to come by with so many outgoings to pay for, not least subsidies to allies, so he would have to wait a while for an answer to what was happening in the only part of France still rebellious. Still, the matter was in hand and that was to the good.

Such satisfaction did not last as he read on; it really was too much that the upstart sod was again asking him to concern himself with the fate of his two servants. Their names and the ship into which they had been sent Pearce had added in the margin as a reminder, which pricked Dundas somewhat since he had forgotten the initial request. The brief scribble he sent to Admiralty came back with a reply that made him sigh, though it was not anything to trouble him greatly. The ship on which the pair were serving had weighed from the Nore and was now at sea.

'To join the Channel Fleet,' the man he had sent to deliver his request informed him.

'Then send it on to Portsmouth, let Black Dick Howe deal with it, that is, should the old bugger ever be able to rouse himself from his septuagenarian slumbers.'

'Sir, Earl Howe's fleet weighed several days ago, if you recall, to seek to intercept the American grain convoy.'

God, Dundas thought, *I must be getting old*, for he had forgotten that.

CHAPTER FOURTEEN

Pearce was obliged to issue an apology as he watched the second of the four-horse carriages he had hired disappear down the forest track, and that was to his best friend.

'Michael, I have only just realised how cramped we will be in only one post-chaise with all of our trunks. I'll be damn near sitting on your knee.'

'John-boy, I have, thanks to you, a decent coat as well as a comforter and will do very well on the postillion's step, for it is not bitter. Besides, what would I be wanting sitting inside listening to you and Mrs Barclay billing and cooing and me obliged to keep looking skywards so you did not see me redden?'

The notion of any indulgence in such behaviour with Emily was not a thing John Pearce anticipated, but there was another concern and he hissed at his huge friend. 'We must stop calling her Mrs Barclay.'

He looked to see if the coachman had heard what had

been said, unsure given the man was looking straight ahead, only then realising that he had never bothered to ask Emily her maiden name. He would have to think of one to use, for there was no way of getting to Buckler's Hard in one fell swoop. They would have to stop frequently to change horses, for food as well as overnight and he was thankful he had the money from the sale of the Tolland mounts to pay for what was a rich man's mode of travel, albeit he was intent on reimbursing his expenses from the funds Dundas had promised to provide.

Entering the carriage, it was to join a companion who was still harbouring doubts, so it was not until they reached Hindhead – they had changed horses many times – where they would need to spend the night, that he was able to broach the subject.

'You are not suggesting, John, that we share a room in a travelling inn?'

The lie was swift and far from convincing. 'Never in life, Emily.'

'Then brother and sister will do very well to cover the journey.'

'And when we get to the New Forest?'

'I still have time to think on that.'

'Of course,' replied a frustrated John Pearce.

He was destined to remain frustrated even as they passed through the great hunting estate created by William the Conqueror not long after his elevation to the crown of England. Emily was more intent on soaking up the surroundings – pointing out the deer and ponies that abounded, as well as the specially planted oaks designed to grow wood for the navy – than responding to Pearce's diffident attempts to steer their stilted conversation towards how they would disport themselves in public.

At the last change of horses, in Lyndhurst, he learnt that the possibility of accommodation at Buckler's Hard was not good; it was a place wholly dedicated to ship construction and not the kind of riverside village to offer much in the way of quality lodgings. So they headed for Lymington, sat on the estuary created by the river of the same name, ending up outside an inn called the King's Head – there seemed to be one in every English town – which sat on a steep cobbled hill leading down the quayside and harbour.

'My maiden name is Raynesford.'

Emily imparted this as the coachman and Michael dismounted, preparatory to unloading their trunks. That required Pearce and Emily to alight and enter the inn, and not having time to think it through, that was the name in which he bespoke their best set of rooms, which included a tiny parlour, to which they were led by an innkeeper effusively happy to have such a fine naval officer and his lady wife staying at his 'umble establishment.

Instead of Emily feeling awkward it was John Pearce, and that was increased by the arrival of a man to light the fire, a serving girl with a bowl of fruit, followed by yet another with a vase of wild flowers, then a third more senior come to unpack their clothing and possessions, this while 'man and wife' stood awkwardly at either side of the parlour window.

'I shall pay off the coachman,' Pearce said finally, as the maid was bent over their open chests tutting in a censorial fashion at the way they had been packed, 'then go to Buckler's Hard and see about my ship.'

'Yes,' Emily responded, clearly relieved.

'Damn me, Michael,' Pearce protested once out in the street, a boy having been sent to secure them a hack. 'I thought I knew about women, but I find I am still a novice.'

Michael laughed. 'It's not just women, John-boy, you have a rate of things to learn in other places too.'

Buckler's Hard was an isolated place, and being at the very southern edge of the New Forest, the only way in and out was over a series of narrow bridges or a long trek through heath, bog and mainly open woodland, a landscape in which anyone deserting a naval vessel would mightily stick out, so there was little fear he would get to his destination and find a ship devoid of hands.

He had been told it was dedicated to shipbuilding and, even as widely travelled as he was, John Pearce had never seen a place so accurately described – it was literally two rows of workers' houses built either side of a sloping road leading to a pair of slipways. The unpainted hulls of a ship of the line and a frigate under construction dominated the skyline.

With the whole community employed in the task, the place smelt of the resin from freshly hewn wood, this carried on dust rising out of the deep saw pit in which one man stood in the ground with one end of the ten-foot-long blade while another, no doubt the senior of the two, laboured from above. There was a blacksmith forge, a rope-walk and a mast house as well, and in the process of being seasoned, the long fir trunks for the upper poles floating in the water beside it.

HMS *Larcher* lay out in the middle of the tidal river and Pearce knew enough not to just go aboard. He sent out a message to say he had arrived, this to allow those on the ship to prepare the required greeting for a new commander. It was the same whichever vessel was welcoming a new captain – the commission from the Admiralty as well as the Articles of War had to be read out to a crew assembled, and all would want to appear at their best; given the entire complement of *Larcher* consisted of forty-five souls, it seemed an absurdity.

Following that there were the warrants, to whom he was introduced by the master, in this case a fellow called Dorling. The gunner and carpenter went by the name of Kempshall, being twins, albeit one was fair with blue eyes, the other dark brown in both; the bosun was called Bird and the cook, oddly with two good legs instead of the more common one, answered to Bellam. The vessel did not run to a master-at-arms or a purser, the last being a task the sick Rackham had carried out himself; this now fell to Pearce.

Those offices accounted for a tenth of the crew but – and this was a good thing – the overall age was low, master included; the last thing he needed was some old wiseacre stirring up trouble or questioning his orders. On inspection she turned out to be a dry ship, ready for sea with her new mainmast fully rigged, cramped below decks but not damp.

She carried twelve three-pounder cannon on her single upper deck and for what was wanted, given she had a shallow draught good for inshore work, HMS *Larcher* seemed ideal, so, taking Dorling into his cabin, he advised him of the proposed destination with instructions to keep it to himself and together they pored over the charts he had brought of the Vendée coast.

'We shall weigh, I hope, within a day or two. Work out a course and I will consult with you when we have cleared the Needles.'

The 'tween decks being cramped, his accommodation did not run to anything approaching luxury. Michael would sling a hammock with the rest of the crew, taking a deck beam close to his tiny compartment to act as both servant and guard. The first task was to go over the various logs – muster books, lists of stores and the mass of paperwork that accompanied any ship of war – fed by cups of coffee fetched to him by his incongruous 'servant'.

'Do you think Charlie and Rufus will make it before we weigh?'

'Perhaps not, Michael, but if they miss us they can stay here and await our return. I will leave word and a sum of money to keep them accommodated. I dare not risk them going to Mrs Barclay at the King's Head.'

'An inn where you will be spending this night.'

'Yes,' Pearce replied, lips pursed, anticipating the salacious jest that he expected to follow.

'Sure, I can't wait to see your face of the morning or the skip in your step.'

'You have more certainty of either, brother, than I do.'

* * *

208

As soon as he saw her Pearce knew his pessimism to be misplaced; never having had to work hard to look radiant, Emily had taken the trouble to put in an extra effort. Her shiny auburn hair was high-dressed and plaited showing the elegance of her long slim neck; the green silk dress edged with lace was not indiscreet in any way but did not disguise that she possessed an alluring bosom and below that an hourglass waist, which it required no stays to exaggerate.

Without powder Pearce could see, as he bent to kiss her cheek, the fine, barely visible freckles that dotted them and it was hard to avoid looking at her lips without aching to meet them with his own. She had requested, while he was absent, a downstairs booth to eat in that cut them off from view, while the reserved attitude she had shown on the two-day journey to this place seemed to have evaporated to such an extent that no one could have mistaken them for anything other than man and wife, very comfortable in each other's presence.

They would have been utterly mistaken, for appearances were deceptive; there was still a reservation that John Pearce found impossible to break through, more in the nature of how they appeared to others, like the folk who served them, than in private conversation. Did those waiting on their booth notice how each exchange atrophied when they appeared, Emily being acutely conscious of their approach, as well as being rendered self-conscious by their knowing smiles, for, if they had not enquired, it was clear they saw the couple as either newly-weds or close to that estate.

'What passes for acceptable in Paris,' she hissed as the

soup tureen was removed, 'is not seen in the same light in England, John.'

Having only alluded to the way men and women consorted with each other in the French capital, flirting openly in front of those to whom they were married, Pearce had to stop himself from going into detail regarding how that flirting was carried to the bedchamber, indeed with the knowledge and indifference of marriage partners in most cases.

'I merely point out, Emily, that, as in this country, marriages are often entered into for reason of money, land or social position. Only very rarely does love trigger nuptials, more often in the novel than in real life. In certain circles, even in our country, people see no need to indulge in pretence.'

'Are you alluding to my circumstances?' she demanded, her lips pursed, an expression that quickly changed to a forced smile as a dish of dabs appeared in the hands of one of the serving girls.

'Would it apply?' Pearce asked, quietly, causing her to blush again; the presence of the girl did not bother him. She ignored him and concentrated on a too-fulsome thank you, which needled enough to have him go back to his previous point and expand upon it.

'And as for your allusion to England being different from France, I can tell you, for I have personal experience, that in the upper reaches of society there is no difference whatsoever.'

'Personal experience?'

'The ladies of the court act no differently to their counterparts in Paris.'

'No doubt, in time, you will relate to me this personal experience.'

'I will not, any more than had you had any I would enquire about your own, for it is none of my business.'

'You may satisfy yourself on that score,' she replied primly.

'Why are we arguing?' he sighed.

'We are not!'

'I'm damned if I can tell the difference.'

'I had many occasions, John, when I was required to remind my husband of his language, I did not think I would be obliged to do so with you.'

'Then don't.'

'Are you saying I should just accept a foul tongue?'

'May I take your plates, sir?' Emily's rather stern expression changed immediately and she nodded, as did Pearce, except he was not smiling, even when he was addressed. 'Meat course will be along presently, Your Honour.'

'Is it a fowl?' Pearce asked, grinning widely and suddenly at his pun.

'Why yes, sir, a chicken from our own yard.'

'Thank you,' he replied, allowing her to take their plates and depart, this while Emily tried but failed not to laugh, with Pearce reaching out to take her hand. 'That is more the lady I wish to see.'

'I deplore such language, John, as I was brought up to do.'

'Even after you have spent months on a variety of naval vessels?'

'What coarse expressions seamen use to each other

I dislike intensely, but I would not interfere with their discourse.'

'Then I ask to be treated as a common tar and be allowed to express myself as I see fit.'

'I do hope you do not run to the words they use, which are truly disgusting.'

'It has been known,' Pearce replied, yet adding quickly, 'but never in the presence of a lady. So let us eat our dinner and be friends, while talking of more pleasant topics.'

Which was tried, though there was no avoiding how the night was expected to end and that induced inevitable silences as Emily's mind wandered from whatever inconsequential subject John Pearce was dwelling on in a deliberate attempt to keep the mood afloat. That also induced the odd pained expression when some inadvertent word brought the issue back into focus, until the time came when the food was eaten, the plates cleared away and the owner of the King's Head, as a personal duty, was standing by with a candle to light them to their rooms.

Candles, too, illuminated those, while a copper warming pan had been placed in the great bed, the long handle visible though the open door. There was a fire in the grate to give heat and extra light to the cramped parlour, and on entering Pearce uttered the ritual good night to their host. The closing of the door and the falling of the latch seemed to be louder than required, while Emily's shoulders stiffened as she heard the key being turned in the big lock.

She did not move as she felt his hands on her shoulders, but she did react when his lips brushed the nape of her

212

neck, a shudder running through her frame. Did she know the rustling sound was of him removing his coat and his stock? If she did, she kept her eyes firmly on the flickering flames in the grate.

'Emily,' he whispered, as his hand encircled her waist and pulled her backwards, 'this will not be like anything that has gone before, I promise.'

Her voice was like that of a small girl. 'Should I not go and disrobe?'

'It would be my pleasure to do that for you, if you will allow me.'

Without waiting for a reply, Pearce's hands went to the hooks that held her green silk dress, starting at the neck and working his way down. He knew, without being told, that such an act was a wholly novel experience for her, just by the slight reaction to each disengagement of hook and eye, a greater one as his hands slipped under her shoulders to ease it forward and off, the dress dropping at her feet.

Underneath she wore only a cotton shift and, once he had eased the strap off her shoulder a hand came round, this time to cup one exposed breast, and that did induce a sharp intake of breath as his finger gently sought the hardened nipple, his other hand moving the second strap so that her shift joined her dress, leaving her, for the first time in her adult life, naked in front of a member of the opposite sex.

There was slight resistance brought on by shyness at that estate as he spun her round to face him, his lips coming down on to hers as he pulled her body close. He could smell her as much as she could smell him, and both

213

were conscious of the tremors brought on by desire and touch as John Pearce's lips moved down her neck to her breast, at which point he suddenly lifted her up in his arms.

'I believe it is customary to carry the bride across the threshold.'

Which he did, to gently deposit her on the top cover of the bed, where she lay, her hands hiding her nakedness as he removed his shirt. Then, seeing her embarrassment, he blew out the bedside candle, which left only the faint light from the parlour, not enough to show him entirely without clothing as, breeches removed, he lay down beside her.

Emily Barclay's only experience of sexual congress had been with her husband, a separate undressing and bashful entry into the bed followed by a swift grunting coupling, initially very painful, which conformed to the account from her mother of what she could expect. If the pain had not been repeated, every other facet had, more than once, and never could the act have been said to be pleasurable.

This was so different, not least in the time John Pearce took to arouse in her feelings she had heard and speculated with her friends about, but had never before allowed herself to experience. His hands had only soft fingers and like his lips sought out every sensitive part of her body. As his leg slipped between hers, to push them open, she was not in the least inclined to resist.

There was no weight in the body that then covered hers; nothing but a gentle nudge to ready her for contact, her gasp matching his as he entered her, and there was

214

too, even if she was not aware of it, anticipation; this lovemaking had been promised for so long, days and weeks, that when it came her every sense was already massively heightened.

Which was why, for the first time in her life, she knew what people meant when they whispered that there could be a pleasure so deep in the act that silence was impossible and screaming with delight not unknown.

Even in an old and solid-walled building, such sounds carried and those servants who heard it nodded knowingly. The owner of the King's Head was not one of them, for he was downstairs in his taproom sharing a drink with a regular customer, an old friend of a letter-writer who had another occupation part of his time, which was to report to the *Hampshire Chronicle* anything newsworthy that happened in isolated Lymington.

On the morrow he would inform the editor of the arrival in the town, to take up residence in the King's Head tavern, of Lieutenant RN and Mrs Raynesford, which would be reported in the social column. This would earn him a penny or two, as well as a free pot of ale for helping to tell the world outside the town that when folk came to stay in Lymington, this was the hostelry of choice.

The week that followed was one of near-unalloyed bliss: long walks, shared and secret jokes, and much lovemaking that was not always confined to the hours of darkness, in which John Pearce's still-shy bed partner was introduced to those variations which did not cause her to flinch. Her lover was in no hurry to cause such a reaction;

in time, and he now knew he had that, she would be brought to experience every form of the art in which he himself had been schooled by an older, beautiful and experienced woman.

Interruption did come from his visits to Buckler's Hard to see if there was any sign of the money he was expecting, but there was no frustration in the delay for someone normally troubled by impatience. Pearce was happy and that feeling was passed on to the men he now commanded by his endemic good cheer, as well as his allowance of shore leave in turns which were appreciated even in such a backwater, not in the least dented by the gentle ribbing of Michael O'Hagan.

Dundas's money man arrived eventually, a silent dark-looking cove, accompanied by a party of armed men who would not depart the shore until he was present, delivering a heavy chest that had to be fetched aboard, and with many a curious look at that, by a whip from the main yard. Michael carried it to his cabin, where it was secured to the deck by battens, Pearce preparing to add a chain and padlock.

The cabin was then cleared, the key was passed over, and the heavy bags of specie were extracted to be counted and signed for – Pearce did not trust Dundas one little bit when it came to coin and his fellow Scot did not trust him either, while it seemed the weather was part aware of the doubts in the transaction, for it was raining heavily and the wind was one to keep the cutter pinned in the Beaulieu River.

As well as the funds, there was a packet of papers – the latest intelligence from France on matters in the Vendée, which Pearce put aside for later reading. Michael was tasked, once the delivery was complete and the carriers sent on their way, to keep an eye on the cabin while Pearce went ashore and took the hack back to Lymington, he having extracted a sum to cover his expenses so far, money which, added to that he still possessed, would keep Emily during his absence.

CHAPTER FIFTEEN

It was with a less than light step that John Pearce had to leave his paramour and go about his business, for it was very obvious two days later in the morning light, the sky being clear and blue, that the wind, a steady north-easterly instead of the recent rain-bearing westerly, was favourable to his voyage. That they parted with regret was obvious, though he knew what he had set out to do, to show Emily Barclay that a part of marriage most women openly dreaded – thanks to old wives' tales and perceived wisdom – was the very opposite in reality.

He left her eating breakfast in their parlour, she wondering how to disport herself for the time John Pearce would be absent – as usual with any sea journey it would be a time of an unknown duration; money she had, he had left her well provided for, but she knew no one and was living under an assumed name, albeit her own given at birth.

This time the coming aboard HMS *Larcher* was not to be delayed and the sight of the master and commander of the ship on the hard, signalling for a boat, was enough to get those aboard preparing the vessel to weigh – they too could read a wind – it being the intention to impress him with their alacrity. The decks had been sanded, swabbed and flogged dry at first light, the hands had consumed their breakfast and the crew were ready.

'You may weigh as soon as you wish, Mr Dorling.'

John Pearce was impressed at the immediacy of what followed; the pawl poles were already in place on the windlass and if the men looked idle they were merely playing a role, as he found out later from Michael O'Hagan, for they moved with speed to their stations to haul the vessel over its anchor and pluck it out of the river mud. Within minutes those same hands had moved to the oars in the ship's two boats, taking up the strain on the cables already rigged to warp her downriver, aided by the falling tide.

'Impressive,' Pearce said quietly to Michael.

'Sure, it's only partly done of love for you, John-boy, more for loathing of the man you replaced.'

'Rackham?'

'Never, it is said, has a man so lived by his name. There are those here who are sure his maladies are their prayers answered or happen that he has gone to commune with Satan.'

'I had a look at his logs.'

'They won't have read pretty from what has been said.'

'If you were told about him, they must have asked about me?'

'They did, and I told them you are a fair man, if not always a wise one.'

There was a grin with that to take the sting out of the last opinion, not that Pearce would have disputed Michael's description; if he was pleased to be seen as fair, he knew himself to often act foolishly – impetuous perhaps rather than stupid – and what surfaced then, as his thoughts turned to that from which he had just parted, was a truth he had suppressed.

He would struggle to find the means to support Emily if his disputed prize cases were not settled. One was with a mother and widow in straightened circumstances whose husband had been his commander, suffering death immediately in the action in which the prize had been taken and, it had to be acknowledged, her claim had justification. The other dispute was very much less so: it lay with a clutch of French religious hypocrites, their lives saved by British tars, quite prepared to lie to achieve their ends, which was possession of a vessel not their own.

Such thoughts had to be put aside as the tow came round the last bend before the estuary opened out on to the wide Solent. Pearce gave the orders to bring in the boats, which had to be done given there was insufficient crew to both warp the ship and raise sail. Once back aboard, the boats secured, he was again encouraged by the way the hands raced eagerly to their duties. Canvas was quickly set and the falls sheeted home, and with the steady breeze on their larboard beam, HMS *Larcher* eased out through the deep water channel.

'Mr Dorling, a course to clear the Needles if you please?'

Once settled on that, John Pearce went below to reread the ship's log, and remind himself of what Lieutenant Rackham had been up to and what made him so unpopular.

HMS *Semele* had exited the Thames Estuary ten days earlier and turned south to weather the South Foreland in a cacophony of noise as those tasked to work the ship up to efficiency, leading hands, officers petty and commissioned, laid into the ineptitude of the majority of a crew who could barely be trusted to haul on a rope without it had to be explained to them the benefit of coordinated stop and go as the best way to apply their body weight.

For a fall to be laid tidy and coiled was achieved first by instruction, and when that failed, by the application of the starter. Then, once everyone thought a dolt was aware of the pain, the mere flicked threat of the knotted rope tended to be enough. Watching the way the poor souls were harried from pillar to post only reminded Charlie and Rufus of their own initiation into the ways of the navy, and while there was sympathy, there was also the knowledge of practical necessity.

The ship was out in the English Channel, which was a stretch of water as potentially dangerous as any in creation, with no way of knowing if their journey through the narrows would be one of calm or screaming tempest. The last thing anyone aboard could afford was to be soft, for if it was the latter and the men did not go about their duties with proper application, it was not unknown for vessels to founder even within sight of the home shore.

That men were sick was a given and it was not confined to landsmen; it affected every grade of those aboard, given the chops of the Channel, with short jabbing waves that created an uneven pitch and roll, were almost designed by the Creator to disturb a man's stomach. Ralph Barclay had to have a care and keep Devenow close at all times, for he was apt to forget his missing arm and reach out a non-existent hand for purchase.

The gun crews having been formed, it had been paramount to begin the act of teaching these folk to work the cannon, for battle was the primary task of the ship, sailing being simply to get her to where she could fight, and that extended to the nippers who carried the first cartridges from the master gunner's prepared stock. The whole thing was done in dumbshow and timed, the order to clear for action going out three times a day regardless of what else was being carried out on deck or below.

The great guns were freed from their lashings, hauled back for a pretence of loading, every act completed as much as possible as if for real, then hauled up through the opened ports for aiming, elevating and firing, by which time the gun captain, every one an experienced hand, was expected to have his flintlock attached and be standing with his lanyard extended awaiting the order to fire from his divisional officer.

It began as lumbering chaos but that was only to be expected, that it did not improve at anything like the rate required less so – even if the ratio of landsmen was greater than that which was considered ideal – which led to a spate of injuries to several feet and one badly broken leg. This led to silent reproach from the commanding officer, which did not lessen the impact; he would not be vocal except in private, it being a bad notion to openly undermine the authority of his officers.

As far as his premier was concerned, gunnery practice aside, Ralph Barclay spent an inordinate amount of time on deck; it was not pleasant to always be under the captain's basilisk eye and that, in turn, was passed on to those who worked the ship in both verbal and physical abuse. Men were sent aloft even if the prospect of heights terrified them, for there could be no allowing for fear and it was necessary to sort out those who could stand the duty and those who were either rendered useless by dread, or so cack-handed as to pose a danger by their mere presence on the yards.

Lieutenant Jackson was going hoarse from yelling and the ship's master was likewise suffering when it came to sail drill. The premier had met Ralph Barclay before when he was a senior midshipman, he and Jackson having served together under Captain – later Admiral – Rodney, but, even if they had corresponded, he had not shared a deck with him for over a dozen years, certainly not since he had been made post, and was not to know that his superior's presence was caused by anxiety; it looked to Jackson like a lack of confidence in his abilities.

This was doubly galling given Barclay had written to ask him to serve and Jackson had been deeply grateful for the offer, having spent many years without a ship, his every pleading letter to the Admiralty receiving what most such missives did, a stock reply that there were many officers seeking places and only so many available, so while they were sure he was a deserving case, the Board was sorry to disappoint etc., etc.

He should have recalled that his captain was a man sensitive to his pride and not much given to trusting his reputation to others till he was sure of them. The reason for his continual presence on the quarterdeck was the fear that something would go horribly wrong and he would not be there to correct it.

Having only one arm worried him, and not just on the grounds he may fall over; he saw it as a stick with which those who would like to diminish him would beat him and to Ralph Barclay's mind such people were numerous in the navy. The worst of his worries was that, with such a crew and short-handed with it, they would not be able to work up to any degree of efficiency and would appear like some lubberly dolt when he joined the fleet off Ushant.

His C.-in-C., Admiral Earl Howe, was a man with whom Ralph Barclay had barely exchanged ten words during the American War and thus an unknown quantity, not that Black Dick was a sparkling conversationalist with anyone. He was known to be taciturn by nature, a hard man to get to know and a very difficult one from whom to extract praise.

He would be surrounded by captains, most of whom owed their place to his influence, for he had been at one time both the political and naval First Lord, indeed he had held the office when Ralph Barclay was paid off from his pre-war commission due to cuts in the naval monies voted by Pitt's new government. Such memories and anxieties preyed on nerves already shredded by events in his private life.

His apprehensions were driven home by an early rigging of the grating, the man fetched up for the offence of abusing an officer in a bout of foul language, one not unknown with landsmen given to reactions which would not raise an eyebrow ashore. Later in the commission Ralph Barclay might have settled for a gagging, but an example had to be made, so it was a round dozen of a bare back turned to red mush; the crew now knew the rules and the consequences of transgression.

The day the two Pelicans were picked out was considered a bad one by both, even if they were out of the narrows and life was easier on the longer ocean swell. The bully Devenow stuck so close to the captain he was easy to avoid; Gherson was the culprit, for having got his paperwork up to date and identified a few opportunities for profit, he had enjoyed a full night's rest and was on the poop at first light when the deck was being cleaned.

His face was a picture of insensitive superiority as he watched the men below, working on their knees, pushing the sanding blocks to take out marks on the planking. It was a task he had once had to endure himself and, where the likes of Charlie and Rufus would have evinced sympathy for those still so occupied, he was wont to sneer at their inability to change their station in life.

They were members of the party flogging dry, moving aft for a second set of swings, the sweepers having cleared the fine sand, seeking to keep their faces hidden. They had seen him clear and were alarmed when a quick glance saw his eyes narrow, then a hand go to cut out the sun, that followed by a half-pointed finger, sharply withdrawn. Then he smiled and it was like that, as described later by Rufus, of a pageant snake he had once seen at the Lichfield Goose Fair, about to swallow a fair maiden whole to the roars of the crowd.

'He's got us, Charlie, I reckon.'

'Don't look up, don't give the sod the satisfaction of seeing concern.'

'What's the wager he'll be eyeing the watch lists afore long, and seeking us out at our mess table.'

'If he does there's nowt we can do, Rufus, and I, for one, will not seek to rile him.'

'Doubt you need to, Charlie, he's a man who hates long and easy.'

Gherson sauntered up to their table while they were taking breakfast, having, as Rufus had suspected, found their station in the lists kept in the great cabin. That he did so with a smirk came as no surprise.

'I thought I spied you two.'

'Bound to,' Charlie replied, flying right in the face of what he had said on deck. 'All you had to do was to raise your head out of the seat of the privy.'

'Still smells of shit, though,' Rufus added, grinning at Charlie with a look that showed he was glad to hear the insult.

'And who, for all love, would this fellow be?' asked Davy, eyeing Gherson up and down.

'An old acquaintance, mate, and one, for your own safety, I would scarce want to introduce you to.'

'A bad man then, boyo?'

'Few worse.'

'You do not see it, Taverner, as a mistake to insult me?'

'Gherson, I would not know how to address you polite.'

That did nothing to dent the man's superior smile. 'Perhaps I will send Devenow down to make reacquaintance, for I saw no O'Hagan on the watch lists.'

'You might find, Gherson,' Rufus spat, 'an' so might he, that we are not as green as we once was.'

'Next you'll be telling me you're not afraid of him.'

'I don't know who you are, mate,' Davy said, 'but I will be telling you that we are men who like to eat in peace, an' you are disturbing that.'

'So sling your hook,' said another of their mess.

'Perhaps I will tell the captain that John Pearce's arse-lickers are aboard and see how he likes it.'

'I got a piece of advice for you, Gherson,' Charlie growled. 'You'd best stay behind the great cabin bulkheads, and should we clear for action proper, do what you always do as the coward you are and hide somewhere, for if I find you alone and there is smoke to cover me, I will do for you.'

'Thank you for the warning,' Gherson replied, with a grin that appeared forced, 'it will render my making your life a misery so much more pleasant.'

'Happen you'd best tell your mates what all that was about?' Davy asked as Gherson walked away.

Which Rufus and Charlie did, relating how he had arrived aboard *Brilliant*, what they knew of the man's treacheries, which was only a fraction of the whole, a tale that did nothing to cheer anyone at their table, and they had not quite finished their damnation when the drumbeat to clear for action came before their allotted breakfast time was over, with Davy cursing.

'Look you, there it is again, the drum! Does this man Barclay never give up?'

'No, never,' the Pelicans said simultaneously.

Sitting in his cramped cabin and in need of a lantern to reread Lieutenant Rackham's logs, he saw once more what caused the crew to hate him – the man was a martinet. He flogged with little excuse and exceeded the allotted dozen of the cat with impunity, not that anyone was going to have him up for that, it being common for captains to go beyond the permitted punishment.

But Rackham liked stapling men to the deck as well, and for even a hint of vocal dissent he would happily shut them up with a clamp to the mouth and jaw. The stopping of grog was another of his punishments and that drove Pearce to the other ledgers, which listed the purser's stores for which, as the sole officer, his predecessor had been responsible. There he found that whatever was supposed to have been consumed had indeed been used up, either by Rackham or sold to line his pockets.

It took only a moment's consideration to realise that even if such peculations and punishments were sufficient cause for a complaint to a higher authority, with such a small crew in a tiny vessel to lay a grievance was hard. They would rarely see an officer senior to their commander and anything written would likely pass through his hands before being sent on.

John Pearce had strong opinions on the way to command men, by example and understanding rather than the use of the lash or arbitrary punishments, but he did have his own concerns of lack of experience, something an ill-disposed crew could exploit. Given what they had been through, he reckoned he could run them aground without a word of complaint.

'Mr Dorling's compliments, Your Honour, and there is a seventy-four in the offing bearing a commodore's blue pennant, escorting an outward-bound convoy by the look, an' he reckons a salute to acknowledge would be in order.'

Pearce looked at the youngster, a fresh-faced lad with an open freckled countenance under a tousle of ginger hair. 'A stupid and unnecessary waste of powder.' That got him a grin, which was pleasing, but still, a blue pennant meant a senior post captain in command and very likely a proud fellow to boot. 'Tell Mr Dorling to carry on.'

'Aye, aye, sir.'

Pearce went on deck, a journey of some ten paces, and lifted a glass from the rack by the wheel to espy the ship of the line, lifting it and focusing as the signal gun was loaded, that revealing distant faces on the deck, eyes fixed on him. The smell of slow match drifted back to him, the brass popgun had no flint, and as it spoke he had to acknowledge that it made for a fine sight, with its light-brown sails set against the blue of the sea and the sky, now filled with daubs of white powder smoke.

'Happen you might command one o' them one day,' said O'Hagan softly enough not to be overheard.

'God forbid, Michael, I am in danger of running this under the first big wave we meet.'

'Sure,' came the response, accompanied by a twinkle in the eye, 'I wish you had told me that afore I agreed to serve.'

CHAPTER SIXTEEN

Even with a very favourable wind it took John Pearce four days sailing to weather Ushant and get to a point south and west of the great naval port of Brest, safe enough in distance to change course and close with the shore. The last information he had, delivered with the chest of money, told him Earl Howe was at sea seeking battle, as were, very likely, major elements of the French navy.

This increased the risk to him, not necessarily from enemy ships of the line but the frigates they might have acting as a screen to warn them of danger, albeit their Royal Navy counterparts of the inshore squadron would shadow them if they were still active in these waters.

Nothing showed on the horizon, friend or foe – hardly surprising on such a vast area of an ocean that stretched west a distance of three thousand miles and many times more than that to the south – and it was only many weeks later that it was discovered that the enemy he feared to encounter was far to the west, out in the deep Atlantic, as was the Channel Fleet.

Dundas had also provided in his package of papers a list of names of those thought to be leading the revolt and, in addition, what constituted the latest information from the area to which he was heading, as well as what was known of the original uprising. Examining the list of names and the remarks appended to them, it was clear that the notion of who he might profitably contact was more than confused; it bordered on speculation.

Contact with the insurgent royalists was clearly patchy at best and quite possibly utterly misleading, and then there was the very nature of what they were trying to achieve – a return of the Bourbon monarchy, as well as the reconstitution of the venal church which had supported it.

John Pearce could imagine the look his father Adam would have produced to see his son engaged in such an enterprise, for if there were two things the Edinburgh Ranter hated, it was the overweening power of absolute monarchy and the greed of high-church prelates, be they Anglican or the agents of Rome. Yet he had come to hate equally the blood-soaked partisans of the Revolution for their hypocrisy, and it was they who had ended his life, so putting aside the thoughts of parental disapproval he turned to the latest intelligence.

First he had to seek to separate official revolutionary boasting in the pages of the *Moniteur* from that which came in from more reliable sources, often those same inshore frigates who now seemed so scarce. These ships regularly had contact with the local fishermen, a tribe whose loyalty tended towards foreign naval officers who paid well to take their fresh catch, always a higher price than it would fetch when landed to be picked and argued over by parsimonious housewives.

Much of what was in the documents Pearce did not need to read; he had been in the region the previous year when the war seemed to be going well for the insurgents and had kept his interest alive by reading what was reported in the British press. In the beginning they had either held off or defeated most of the forces sent against them, actually winning several important victories against more than one revolutionary rabble.

Yet to sustain such success against a more powerful and numerous foe over the long term had proved impossible, not aided by a lack of cohesion in their structure – those who wished to consolidate what they had against the more zealous who desired to bring down the tyrants of Paris, first of all by taking the major port of Nantes, which would thus exert a stranglehold on the interior.

Paris had responded by sending to Nantes not only strong forces, but also a General Jean-Baptiste Carrier. What that man had inflicted on the population he did not have to peruse at all, having heard the bloody stories from the lips of those who had been physical witnesses: the priests and nuns of a religious order he and men from HMS *Grampus* had helped to rescue in a ship they lacked the ability to sail.

Not that he thought of them with sympathy now, for they had sought to claim that same vessel as their property and were in dispute with his declaration that it should be awarded to him and the sailors he led as a prize. Yet what they had imparted, for sheer barbarity, had been hard to stomach; more importantly, as far as the Revolution was concerned, the siege had failed and Nantes had been secured.

In the new year the insurgents were defeated and their forces split; what followed led to the suspicion that they had either deluded themselves or been misled by their émigré friends who had previously fled abroad, or perhaps even by the British Government itself. One part of their army, as well as dependants, had headed for the north Brittany coast, expecting to be met by ships that would take them to safety in England.

None appeared and, lacking an alternative, they had been forced to retreat back south of the Loire in a forced march that took a heavy toll on women and children as well as the fighting men. Worse was to come; the Committee of Public Safety sent against them a much larger and better-equipped army and that part of the weakened Vendéeans were smashed as a fighting force.

His task was to seek to find what was left and how strong it could be in the face of relentless pressure from the Revolution. It was clear there was still fighting – no great battles, but endless skirmishing, which, by all accounts, was extremely bloody; it was a war of no quarter on either side.

'Mr Dorling's compliments, sir, he has raised the Noirmoutier.'

'Thank you, Jack,' Pearce replied, which got a smile, one that appeared every time this new captain used his given name. 'Tell him I will be on deck presently.'

Which he was, with a telescope to his eye seeking to read from what little he could see of the low shoreline if there was any need for caution. Conscious of his lack of nautical skills, Pearce had studied the charts for several hours on more than one day seeking to formulate a plan that would provide access to a safe landing with minimum risk at sea, in a place where HMS *Larcher* could anchor while he went ashore.

He had also wanted to approach the French coast along a simple line of latitude to avoid exhibiting a lack of confidence in his own abilities, aware that anything near Nantes and the mouth of the River Loire had to be avoided, that being the main route for French imports as well as slavers, and thus bound to be both busy and well patrolled.

Yet to the south of that lay an exposed shore consisting of long sandy beaches and little in the way of shelter, barring the odd saltwater inlet of questionable depth. Quite apart from the enemy he needed somewhere that would provide the ship with some protection against an Atlantic storm, which could whip up in no time and be deadly in the Bay of Biscay, a fact he knew from personal experience.

To seek a harbour was out of the question, given he had no idea of the state of affairs on land, so the long low peninsula of Noirmoutier, jutting out to the north-west, forming a deep bay that became a cut-off island at high tide, would allow him to anchor in some safety and also provide for the possibility, given the wind was not dead foul, of a wide escape route in case of trouble.

An added advantage lay in the shallows that lined the

inner shore: HMS *Larcher* drew little water under her keel and could steer close to the shoreline, so if anything in the nature of a frigate threatened danger, he could manoeuvre to avoid them in an area where they risked running aground. The tide was low at the moment, though making, which carried her in with little in the way of sail, which was just as well, for unusually in this part of the world, the wind was near to absent.

Requesting his master to tend north to clear the outer rocks and ordering *Larcher's* cannon to be loosed for action, John Pearce crawled deeper and deeper into the great bight on both the tide and those light westerly airs, sure he had thought of everything, his only concern, quickly set to rest, being that he might sight a sail or the poles of an equivalent or larger warship, a worry that proved unfounded, allowing him a degree of satisfaction that was soon turned to hubris.

'Gunboats.'

'Where away?' Pearce cried, looking aloft to where a lookout was pointing.

He had the sinking feeling of having misjudged the obvious in his mind as he followed the line of the lookout's outstretched hand and saw, setting out from the low inland shore of the Noirmoutier spur, four well-manned boats, low in the water but each with a set of four oars a side, as well as the black snout of a cannon in their bows. Added to that was a trail of smoke rising and drifting towards him that told him, as if his own slack canvas was not enough, that he was short of enough puff to easily avoid them.

Shallow water would not aid him now; if anything

they had the advantage, and on a near-windless day and unbroken water they could close with him and pick their spot from which to attack, which would be athwart the bows and dead astern, and with ample time to do so. To get up enough speed to get clear was made more of a problem by the fact that both the light breeze and the leeway were coming from the west, which would oblige him, if he wanted to get out to deep water, to slowly back and fill.

'Seems we are in a spot here, Capt'n.'

It took a second to realise it was Michael who had spoken, as ever careful of his rank on deck if others could hear and even, in so small a vessel, sometimes when they were alone in his cabin. Never had his Irish friend spoken a more obvious truth, for in thinking about the difficulties he might face between Noirmoutier and the mainland shore, Pearce had only calculated on a ship under canvas and one, thanks to its high masts, he would see well in time to avoid.

What he now faced made perfect sense for the forces seeking to contain people they saw as rebels, while at the same time securing the integrity of such a shoreline should any form of rescue be attempted. To acknowledge such a truth, however, did little to aid him in finding a way to counter it. Nor, because of the position he occupied, could he bring himself to seek an answer from all the eyes now upon him and waiting for instructions.

In the end, what came to his rescue was something he normally disdained, if in fact he did not go out of his way to avoid. He recalled a conversation he had shared with Lieutenant Henry Digby, one of the few naval officers whom he esteemed enough to afford a hearing when on the subject of ships and how to sail and fight them.

It had not been, as it so often was in a naval wardroom, an oft-repeated tale of some historical action – every battle was constantly relived by those presently serving, all the way back to antiquity. Digby proposed a proposition in anticipation of what they might encounter in the circumstances they were about to face in the delivery of some French revolutionary sailors.

These were men who had been taken out of Toulon, where they were a threat, and shifted to La Rochelle in warships stripped of cannon. It was an enterprise to which they had been assigned to get anyone honest who had served on HMS *Brilliant* out of the way of Barclay's farce of a court martial, and the possibility of gunboats coming out from La Rochelle had been discussed, as well as the means to counter them, which involved the ability to swing the ship.

'Drop anchor.'

Time was taken before anyone reacted and Pearce had to yell a repeat at what seemed like madness to even the most dim-witted brain on board and would probably look like that to his opponents.

'Mr Dorling, once the anchor is secure I want a spring on the cable from dead aft and enough hands on the windlass to move the ship on my command.'

'Aye, aye, sir,' Dorling replied, rushing to obey.

The youthful master had got it if others had not: for all his guns were mere three-pounders, they were numerous in comparison to a single weapon in the bow of a rowing boat, which could be not much greater in calibre given the size and the weight of the cannon. Also, he could reload his battery close to twice in a minute, while to do the same in what he faced had to be slow and very laborious, which gave him time to counter each threat individually.

'Mr Kempshall,' he called to the carpenter, whose given name was Sam. 'I will need you to have a party to hand with plugs and canvas for emergency repairs, for I cannot see us coming out of this without we are holed close to the waterline. And I need a message to your brother, Brad, to say I want strong cartridges in the coming action, for just wounding the enemy will not do, we need to blow these buggers out of the water.'

'Are we sound?' Michael whispered, as men ran to obey, leaving them enough room to converse in private.

'We are humbugged, but I doubt lacking a wind we can outrun these boats. Added to that, with the crew numbers we have there would be too few on the guns and too many aloft to fight properly. I am, I admit, doing what those sods least expect, which I hope will give them pause.'

'Sure, that is a long shot, is it not?'

Pearce grinned. 'When was our life ever different, Michael?'

'Where do you want me?'

'On a gun and aiming with care, for anchored we will be at the mercy of the swell, small as it is, which will make accuracy hard to achieve.' Reaching into his coat, he passed the Irishman a set of keys. 'But of this moment I would be obliged if you would open the rack of muskets and also the locker with powder and balls.'

The mere act of one of his enemies standing in his boat, obviously peering at what was happening on the deck of HMS *Larcher*, was, in itself, reassuring to a man who was thinking on the wing, for it hinted at confusion. Informed the anchor was ready, Pearce gave the order to proceed.

As this was carried out, the way came off the ship and he fixed the fellow standing in his telescope, which turned the distant figure into a close-up face and an outstretched arm, wearing a perplexed expression in his now stationary boat.

'Pick the bones out of that,' he said to himself as he heard the anchor splash into the water.

The cutter immediately swung on the tide, which was rising, stern to the shore, but the hands were not waiting for it to settle; the required cable, wrapped around the windlass, was being fed out of the stern hawse hole, to be run along the deck, and Dorling had put a party ready to bend it onto the anchor cable.

'Rackham did not know what he had, Michael.'

Pearce said this as the keys were returned and he watched those he now commanded working with a will, cooperating in a way that spoke of long sea-time, mutual trust, as well as faith in the man telling them what to do – a belief he was not sure he shared.

'He never stopped to find out, the heathen.'

Looking back to the enemy boats, he saw that their oars were working again and intensely, which led Pearce to suspect whoever was in command had worked out what he was up to. They had also split up, which he had anticipated, two heading inshore to come onto his stern, the others aiming for the prow. Right now he had to let them be, every man aboard was occupied, but having cleared for action prior to entering the bay, his guns were ready to be loaded and fired in half a minute, if that.

'Anyone able to fire a musket to me!' he shouted as soon as the work began to slack off. 'The rest on the capstan or man your guns as directed. I want them loaded and ready to fire on both sides.'

Two fellows came to him, knuckling their foreheads, an act he had to stop himself from barking at, for he was not one to revel in unnecessary courtesies. He led them into his cabin, where the musket rack was open, the chain that ran through the trigger guards hanging loose, half a dozen weapons with the short-sea-service barrels that rendered them near to useless at any range over fifty yards.

'Load and prime them all, take them out on deck and lay them where they will not kill or maim one of our own. Also, take the means to reload.'

Opening his desk, Pearce pulled out his own pistol, powder horn and cartouche of balls, while through the deck came the rumbling sound of guns being run in for loading, then run out for firing. Once the muskets were loaded, his pistol also, he led the musketeers back on deck, calling to the fellow who had been conning the ship to leave the wheel and make himself useful elsewhere.

Then, with a glance over the side that told him how little time he had, he looked along the deck to the men crouched beside their guns, with the captains peering through the ports at angles which indicated they would struggle to hit anything.

'Mr Dorling, stand over the hatch if you will and relay my commands. Jack, to me as a messenger.'

Pearce could feel the tension in the whole crew but it was not something to bring on concern, for it seemed caused more by eagerness than any hint of trepidation; these fellows were game for this and that in turn lifted his own spirits. He would not escape without damage, they might even see men dead and wounded, him included, from flying bits of wood or rigging as much as from a cannonball, but it was not going to be what those Frenchmen had anticipated: a one-way contest.

'Stern first, I reckon,' he said to Jack, before he called to his musketeers to head to that station. 'Heads below the bulwarks and do not open fire until the cannon in those boats have done their business, but once they have discharged their ball I want you to make it as hard as you can for them to reload, and don't worry too much about aim. A ball flying past an ear will do as much to disturb their efforts as an actual wound.'

The command went out and those on the windlass began to haul, bringing the stern of the ship round so that it lay square on to the making tide, this as the first of the armed boats fired. The thud as the ball rammed into the planking was replicated by a shudder that ran right through the ship, accompanied by the sound of smashing wood, but luckily, if there were splinters they stayed below the level of the bulwarks.

Slowly, as the stern came round, a second ball struck home, this aimed higher and taking out a great chunk of timber, most of which flew too high to do damage, but not all, and one sliver, shaped like a yard-long sword blade, shot across the deck slicing through ropes, but thankfully missing flesh.

'Muskets, now!'

The popping sound of them firing, half a dozen quick rounds, frustrated Pearce slightly; he would have preferred the shots to be more spaced, but there was nothing he could do but order a reload and a move to the bows, and that would take time. The bringing round of the stern was so slow as to feel dreamlike and it was taking place while the boats that had headed for his prow were free to inflict damage.

'Keep your heads down, lads,' he shouted, feeling very vulnerable, that being something his position obligated him not to do.

It was odd the way the two balls swished past in the air, low certainly but hitting neither side nor upper works. Then Pearce realised the sods were aiming to part his anchor cable or cut the spring and if that happened he would be in real trouble; clearly his opponent was no fool.

'Fire as soon as you bear,' he called, knowing there was no time for fancy gunnery, 'then man the guns to starboard at the double.'

Moving to look over the side, he watched as each cannon fired in turn, as interested in the effect on men struggling to load their own weapon as in the water that was churned up around them, turning from blue to spouts of white, at which point Pearce reckoned he had erred, given the range. Also the Frenchmen were rowing, not reloading, to get away from a broadside and back to attacking prow and stern.

'Jack, below to Mr Kempshall the gunner and say I want the cannon loaded with grape. And while you're below see if the second twin needs to report any damage to the hull.'

The starboard salvo, with more time to aim, was a deadlier effort by far, one of the boats, too slow despite its best efforts, disintegrating as a ball hit the side and split open the strakes like matchwood. With the weight of the gun, what remained went down like a stone, leaving flaying in the water men who could not swim by the look of their struggles and it was also the case that their comrades, busy reloading, were ignoring their cries for help.

The other boats had got out of his arc of fire and were safe to prepare a second salvo from their cannon, except for the odd musket ball. Pearce waited till his own cannon were reloaded, then called to his young master.

'Mr Dorling, first I want that cable to be let fly below, and secondly the cannon to fire on my command.'

They were not anticipating such a manoeuvre and were working their oars in those boats to hold their positions while getting the muzzles lined up to do real damage. Pearce could see them jacking up the weapons to fire low and knew the intent was to hull and seek to sink him, but they had failed to see that the tide, originally making slowly, had increased its rate of flow, perhaps something to do with the nature of the shallows, he did not know.

What he did was what decided the action; on his

command the cable was let fly, and with the spring suddenly released HMS *Larcher* spun much more quickly back to its original position with the prow facing out to sea. The men in the gunboats had too little time to avoid what was coming, even if the Frenchman in charge saw the danger and had his men hauling hard on their sticks.

'Fire!'

The two boats to starboard were swept with grapeshot in such quantity and at such a range that nothing could have survived it unscathed, and no one did. They got the third enemy with a rolling broadside as it was pulling furiously away, leaving three boats floating uselessly in the water, full of men who were either dead or dying, the oars as useless as they and their craft now drifting inshore.

'Man the boats. Let us see if any of those poor fellows have survived.'

CHAPTER SEVENTEEN

There had been no comfortable sojourn for Toby Burns in or laying off Bastia, no time to relax after the travails of investiture and capture; the news of the failure of Sir William Hotham to keep the French bottled up in Toulon had Lord Hood weighing immediately to join his second in command's squadron so they could face the enemy with enough force to crush them. Whoever commanded the French fleet was neither fool nor martyr – as soon as his screen of frigates alerted him to the presence of a superior foe, he retired to safety.

With Nelson gone off to Gibraltar to refit, Toby was thankfully back aboard HMS *Britannia*, even if it was a far from happy vessel, given the dressing-down its flag officer had received from the C.-in-C. and the way Hotham's mood seemed to permeate the ship to the point where even the planking groaned.

Hood had berated him in a voice so loud that his words

had been heard on the quarterdeck of HMS *Victory* and naturally the insults had been relayed with glee to the men in Hotham's barge, who in turn had passed them on to their shipmates.

Thus Sir William, who knew very well that what had happened in Hood's great cabin was no secret, had been taken back to his own ship by a crew of bargemen who made little effort to hide their knowing smirks, for he was not loved. From then on, for the next few days, every excursion he made on to the deck led to a change of attitude, a sudden silence so palpable it could only be occasioned by his presence.

The sight of a sloop, with a flag aloft telling the fleet it was carrying despatches, lifted the mood, for that meant letters from home as well as official correspondence. Even Hotham felt relieved by that; in amongst whatever mail there was would be the replies from his political supporters to his views of the way Hood was conducting operations.

There was even a faint hope in his breast that they had managed to contrive at the old sod's removal and his own elevation to command, so his barge was despatched to collect *Britannia*'s mail, rather than waiting for a boat from *Victory* to effect delivery.

Such a response did not go unremarked upon in Hood's own cabin; indeed, the air was blue with insults and not all of them directed at Hotham. The admiral was reading his own despatches from both the Admiralty and Downing Street without anything in the way of joy. It took care to discern praise between the lines of such official documents but it should be visible, and there was no evidence in them that his masters entirely approved of his actions.

Hotham was made much happier by his own private letters; matters were moving in his direction – Hood was not popular even amongst the ranks of his Tory confrères, for he had been intemperate in his demands and too brusque in his remarks to men like Dundas who found it easy to see an insult in any suggestion they were lax in the country's interests. While removal was, as yet, out of the question for Hood, the mood was encouraging.

The person least pleased with the contents of the mail sack was Toby Burns, though he was surprised to receive three packets. There was a letter from home which was the first to be opened, from his mother, wishing him well but wondering why he had not written to relate how he was faring to a family that worried for his well-being – obviously his own letter home had yet to arrive.

The next he opened with some trepidation, coming as it did from his Aunt Emily; he had some notion of what it might contain even before it was read, and in this he was not wrong. It was nothing less than a demand he tell the truth about both her husband and his own part in covering up his crimes. There was some guff about his eternal soul, as if God would care, a tone that grated so much he threw it unfinished to one side.

It was thus in a state of some annoyance that he opened the third letter from some legal fellow called Lucknor with a faint hope that it might contain news of a surprise bequest. When he read what it said it went near to stopping his heart, for, careful as it was in its legalese language, it was nothing less than a copy of that which he had just discarded, with one word striking home like that musket ball that had grazed his arm and that was 'perjury'.

He had to peruse it several times to make sense of the fact that this Lucknor fellow, a Grey's Inn lawyer, was not actually accusing anyone of that crime, he was only hinting that such an offence might well have been committed out of a misplaced sense of loyalty to a relative. This unfortunately did not militate against the transgression of the law, which came down severely on those who committed such an offence.

For a youngster lacking a quick brain, who had not shone at his school – his number work had been slow and his Latin and Greek close to dire – to extract a complete understanding of what was being said took time, and it was only much later, when he was on duty as midshipman of the watch, standing by the binnacle with only the light of that illuminating the quarterdeck and nothing happening but the odd toll of the ship's bell, that the full import of what Lucknor had alluded to struck home.

A court case was being prepared, but by whom? His Aunt Emily came first to mind, but that he dismissed after short consideration, which left only one person who might initiate such a charge: John Pearce. That was a name and a person Toby Burns had come to hate ever since he had first clapped eyes on the bugger. How pleasant it would have been to strike him that first day of sighting, as Ralph Barclay had done, and why, when they were both cast ashore in Brittany, had the sod not drowned, but survived to become his bane?

'Mr Burns,' growled the officer of the watch, 'I have

asked you twice to mark our change of course on the slate.'

God in heaven, the youngster thought, *I was so lost in fear I did not even register that we had worn ship*. Always quick to blame others for his failings, that was another mark and curse he put against the name of John Pearce, though thinking on that produced no notion of what to do about the lawyer's letter.

The man being cursed had just come back aboard a lantern-lit HMS *Larcher* with his party of armed seamen, having scoured Noirmoutier from the tip to the flooded causeway linking it to the mainland to ensure he could not be surprised again. Happily, the men who had manned those boats, only four of whom had any prospect of survival, constituted the sole evidence of French force on the island.

They were now being cared for aboard his ship, having been questioned, while his interrogation of the inhabitants, exclusively fisherfolk, had assured him that the chances of any warship coming by, outside of one seeking shelter from a storm, were remote. The island lay between the main French Atlantic ports and was pretty barren, barely anywhere significantly above sea level and continually swept by westerly gales.

They had come across a deserted chateau, a high, square and turreted building with an outward defensive wall. It had once housed a local aristocratic landowning family, but they had fled, as had the priest from the abandoned church nearby. There was also, on the northern shore, a redoubt with cannon to cover the approaches to the anchorage, although it contained neither men to man it nor powder and shot to work the cannon.

'You will have the ship as from first light, Mr Dorling, for I will be going ashore.'

They were, by the very nature of their location, dining on fish, which Michael, showing a skill Pearce had not known he possessed, had poached in an infusion of herbs he had picked while they traversed the island, the whole wrapped in seaweed to keep it moist. The wine which they drank with it was chilled from immersion in the sea, though even that did little to elevate it, Rackham, the purchaser, being no connoisseur in that department.

'It is as well you know the nature of my assignment, too, for you will be the sole judge of what to do should anything untoward occur.'

With a round kind of face not much given to being expressive, it was hard to tell if such a responsibility worried Dorling, but Pearce had to take into consideration that a man of his calling was not accustomed to dining with his commander and might thus be full of caution merely for his manners.

'You will need to keep a sharp eye out for any threat to seaward and have the anchor hove short at all times for a rapid exit.'

'It would be best, sir,' Dorling said, after a thoughtful pause and a mouthful of cod, 'to put a picket with a boat at that redoubt you mentioned to keep a lookout for ships in the offing.'

'A splendid notion,' Pearce replied, wondering why he had not thought of that, but he was quick to add his own idea. 'Get the gunner to make up a charge for one of

251

those cannon, with powder and slow match to set it off, to be used if the danger is pressing.'

'If the wind turns foul, Your Honour?' Dorling asked, his round face full of doubt.

'You have all the power which I am commissioned to exercise and that includes the authority to surrender the ship should there be no choice. Do not, for the sake of pride or my reputation, risk the welfare of the crew in an impossible fight.'

'I am not sure Captain Rackham would have said likewise, Your Honour.'

'He is not here, I am! Now I suggest I need a good night's sleep, so I will leave you to organise the watch.'

And sleep he did, not that Pearce had untroubled slumbers; it was unlikely to be the fish, maybe too much indifferent and sour wine, but he had frantic dreams in which he was being pursued through the streets of London by a gang of faceless men intent on doing him harm.

Codge had not rushed to put the screws on Denby Carruthers; why bother when he had his man dangling on the end of a rope? He had waited and let the alderman sweat for over near a fortnight, knowing that to do so would increase the price he intended to extract for his silence. There had been no more messengers, no contact at all, until the time had come to press and then he just called unannounced.

Expecting his man to dread his presence, Codge was surprised at the lack of apprehension – Carruthers was brisk to the point of being brusque, so all the words

Codge had replayed time over time in his mind were never given an airing, for he was unable to comprehend the way his mark perceived the problem he represented.

He was dealing with a man of business who faced investment choices every day and was accustomed to dealing with them swiftly, knowing that with trade there was always a gamble, as likely to lead to loss as profit, success coming from a higher incidence of the latter. He was also a man who had surmised this delaying game for what it was and he also suspected that Codge had never, in his life, possessed any great sum of money; for all his arrogance, he was no more than a petty thief.

'I suggest, Mr Codge, that we are required to come to some arrangement.'

'We are that.'

'You have a sum in mind, I take it?'

'A high one, yes, for it would not do to—'

'Please do not trouble me with facts of which I am already aware. I tried to have you taken up but failed, while you have discovered certain things that would cause me discomfort should they be investigated. That demands from me that I pay for your silence, yes?'

'Aye, and—'

He got no further. 'Now, I think for you to demand of me a large sum of money would not be wise. The possession of such, given your background, would raise suspicions and that might lead to a risk of official curiosity leading to disclosure, which would in turn affect me. In short, the Bow Street Runners know you too well.'

'I'm no blabberer.'

'No one is saying you are, but forgive me if I avoid the

risk, and what if your sudden prosperity creates jealousy amongst those with whom you associate?' Codge was not often confused, but he was thrown now; this was not going as he had expected. 'So I suggest instead a regular stipend, to be collected per calendar month, of say, forty guineas. That is a sum I can meet without damaging my business interests, which I would point out we are now both dependent on, and also one which, while keeping you in some comfort, could also come from your nefarious activities.'

'A hundred would be better.'

The lie was quick and delivered with speed, for such a sum would barely dent him.

'A hundred might lead to my bankruptcy and a complete cessation of payment. Forty is my price and any more means you must do your damnedest. Forty guineas to be collected by you personally, for I will not deal through intermediaries, on the first day of each month.'

The purse, produced from an open drawer at the alderman's right hand, landed on the desk with a thud. 'The first payment to be made this very night.'

There was a moment then when the alderman fixed his man, for to so produce that purse was like saying 'I have thought this through and made my decision'. Would it anger Codge? It did, but he was sure that getting his man to start payment was the key; the sum could rise later as he increased pressure, so he shrugged and nodded.

Denby Carruthers was thinking that making two or three payments was worth it to find out the habits of this swine, for once his movements were known, he would then become vulnerable, sure as he was that his brother-in-law could provide the means to terminate the problem.

'What about Gherson?' Codge asked. 'Happen I can find him for you.'

'Leave Gherson to me!'

Codge shrugged, for in truth he was indifferent; if this man did not want to pay for disposal, he had no interest. 'As you wish.'

'Then I suggest you take your money and go.'

When he left, neither Codge nor his employer had any idea that Lavery was following him, it being an act that did not last long enough to register. The clerk only made an appearance of doing so to please Catherine Carruthers; as soon as both were out of sight of the house, he abandoned his pursuit and went to drink coffee. It was his misfortune that his master wanted him about a half an hour later.

'Have you seen Lavery?' Denby Carruthers demanded of his wife. 'I have been ringing for an age.'

Knowing where he had gone she was hesitant, and in that state she could see suspicion grow in her husband's eyes, which led to a blustering confession. 'I hope you do not mind, I asked him to undertake an errand for me.'

'What kind of errand?'

'I need a repair made to a hat.'

'At this time of night?' She nodded fervently. 'Then why not send your maid?'

'It was she who damaged it and I was so cross I found I could not speak to her.'

'It did not occur to you to dismiss her?'

'It was a trifle, really, and she knows my ways.' She tried to sound confident as she added, 'Finding a maid you can trust is not easy.'

Nor is a wife, he thought, wondering what it was that made her words unreliable. The alderman stood for several seconds looking at her, she returning that with growing assurance, for he had not, as was too common, barked at her.

'Please do not use my clerk without my permission, Catherine. If you require his services, be good enough to ask.'

'I hope I have not got him into trouble.'

'No,' Denby Carruthers lied, for on his return Lavery would get a proper roasting.

Back in his own room, Denby Carruthers suspected there was something amiss but he had no idea what. After a while he went to a secret panel in the wall, which, once slid open, revealed his private strongbox, large and with a huge lock to which only he had the key. Opening it, he examined the leather bags of money, which represented only a small part of his wealth, most being lodged in various banks, given he did not trust any one not to fail. These were his ill-gotten gains, the money he made that he was disinclined to disclose even to his close associates.

It came from speculations that bordered on the edge of legality, the funding of dubious enterprises which sucked in dupes to part with their own gold and silver in the hope of massive profit – they always lost it all. It was a game he financed to take a share of the profits even if he did not need it. He could not help himself, a bag or two had to be lifted and weighed, for these were the riches he loved most, the profits no one knew about.

Access to muskets and the means to load them was essential, but the one key John Pearce did not leave with Dorling was that to the strongbox Dundas had sent to Lymington. Only Michael and he were in the cabin when it was opened before departure to reveal the pouches, each containing coins to approximately a hundred pounds value, some in the previous currency of France, gold louis d'or, others Austrian thalers and Dutch guilders.

The ties had been prepared in advance and these, knotted to two bags each, went over their shoulders, one pair for Pearce and a quartet of bags for the bigger stronger Irishman. Pearce had his pistol and sword, while Michael carried a musket and a powder-and-ball cartouche to go with his short hanger.

The naval coat and hat were necessary to John Pearce for the simple reason that, apart from the letters he carried identifying him as a British emissary, he needed to be seen at first glance to be whom he claimed, though it carried with it a risk: should they encounter anyone representing the Revolution, they might be shot at without even being challenged. Dundas's communication, the list of potential contacts, he kept up his sleeve, so they could be discarded quickly, for they could only lead to certain execution.

Added to that they had canvas sacks packed with clothing and food for a journey of unknown duration, for in amongst everything Pearce had read from Dundas's intelligence, the one thing missing amongst the many names of those to contact was any notion of where they might be. He did have a series of maps that ran from the Loire to La Rochelle, the notion being to head towards Challans, the nearest town of any size.

Rowed ashore, the ass he had bespoken the previous day was waiting for them, held by a man who would not let the lead rope out of his hand until it was required to accept payment, money which was examined by both eye and a hard bite of the teeth to ensure it was truly silver.

Trade completed, the canvas sacks were slung across the back of the beast, which required a solid belt on the rump to get it to move, and once in motion they made for the causeway, now visible and full of seawater puddles with the tide low, to farewells from the men who manned the boats.

'Not one of whom,' Michael opined, 'does not rate you mad, and myself alongside you.'

The mainland landscape was little different from that of the island: flat, featureless, with long chest-high seagrasses waving on a breeze from the north, stronger now than the west wind of the day before. But that meant if it was chilling there were clear skies, which in turn provided a good view of where they were headed: along a road that had never been in good repair in monarchical times and was now worse from the lack of any of the locals seeking to maintain it.

Michael was singing softly, in his own tongue, leaving Pearce to let his mind wander, and naturally part of his ruminations were on Emily Barclay and how they would fashion a future together. They had talked of how she would occupy herself in his absence, with mention of perhaps some sea-bathing, for there were machines available in Lymington. Then there was the whole New Forest to explore, either on foot or horseback and, as a woman who took pleasure in embroidery, should the weather prove inclement she had that, as well as several books to read.

Perusing the *Hampshire Chronicle* at his Winchester home, Admiral Sir Berkley Sumner was always alert to anything that referred to his profession. The depth of his interest was acute due to his being what was known as a 'yellow admiral', a man who held the rank and took the pay without the benefit of being asked to hoist a flag. Convinced of his own suitability for high command, it annoyed him that all his efforts to secure a fleet or a profitable station had come to nought.

To those who had known him throughout his years of service, and like many he had begun life at sea as a mere boy, it was a saving grace that he had not been entrusted with anything of importance, not even a shore command, for Sumner was held to be an absolute booby.

He had got his lieutenancy only because of the nature of the examining board. That body had been stuffed by his uncle, Captain – later Admiral – Sir George Rodney, with men who dare not refuse his nephew a pass mark, given they had relatives of their own needing a favour and he had likewise been made post under the same good fortune of family connection and client officers.

As time passed, he rose inexorably up the captains' list until at the top, in a round of promotions to fill the shoes of those who had expired, he was promoted to Rear Admiral of the Blue, a rise which had continued until he was now a Rear Admiral of the White Squadron, albeit he had not been at sea for twenty years.

His passion for the service manifested itself in a close attention to anything that even remotely related to the navy. Thus, when he read in his *Chronicle* that a Lieutenant and Mrs Raynesford had taken up residence in the King's Head inn in Lymington, he immediately reached for his copy of *Steel's Navy List* to pin the date of the aforesaid officer's appointment to the rank; that he did not find him drove him to his store of old papers to see when this fellow had been so recently gazetted, as he must have been if he was not on the list.

Not being able to find the name at all pricked him; he hated the notion of not knowing the minutiae of the service. Yet ignorance also presented opportunity and it was no trouble at all to dash off a note to Sir Phillip Stephens and ask for enlightenment, not forgetting to remind the secretary to the Admiralty that he was available, nay eager and skilled enough, to serve his King and country in any capacity commensurate with his rank and ability.

The two men who came to see Denby Carruthers at his favourite coffee house were brothers and strangers, but very different fellows indeed, the older one gruff and coarse both in countenance and manner, the younger-looking not only more refined but pale of face as if recovering from an illness; he also had a scar on his cheek so fresh the stitch marks were visible, an angry and straight red weal that had been made with something very sharp indeed.

Franklin Tolland would have left such an appointment longer if his brother had let him, for he did not feel fully recovered, having not long been treated for a sword wound at St Bart's hospital by an odd-looking cove of a less than gentle surgeon called Lutyens, who had, thankfully, left the stitching of his face to a more tender colleague.

Forced to stay in London till Franklin recovered enough to move, Jahleel had been busy and was, as ever, impatient – they needed investment if they were to return to making a living for themselves and those who depended on them. The connection to this city worthy was through a mutual acquaintance, a fellow who knew that Denby Carruthers was not averse to wayward investments, and, to avoid anyone knowing about their presence, had arranged that the meeting be held away from his house.

Not that the associate ever knew the details of any transactions, but in the world of discreet ventures that was as it should be; the alderman had a sound grip on inside information of certain stocks on which he could make a profit for both without anyone ever knowing who had supplied the privileged information or the money to buy.

'You will be aware, sir, that the price of certain goods has rocketed of late as supplies from France run out.'

'I have a wife, Mr Tolland, who is very fond of Calais lace.'

'We are in need of a ship,' Jahleel growled, getting a

frown from his more diplomatic brother. 'And investment to fund our trade, which is beyond our own means.'

'So I gather.'

Carruthers picked up the note he had received about this enterprise, hand-delivered and discreetly, as well as the information that these two brothers were very experienced in the smuggling trade, which begged the question, given it was massively profitable, as to why they needed him, a question he posed.

'We had our cargo and our ship stolen from under our nose,' Franklin wheezed.

'Why tell him that?' Jahleel barked, which had him get a sibling sign to keep his voice down.

'Because I would have found out,' Denby Carruthers said to Jahleel, before turning to his brother. 'And what good enterprise begins with lies?'

'Well?' Jahleel demanded.

The alderman actually laughed, rocking back to do so which made an already flushed and heavily poxed face go very red. 'Forgive me, but your directness I find amusing.'

'It is,' Franklin frowned, 'a habit of my brother to speak as he finds, and it is not always the best course.'

'Facts and figures are more important than manners, so let us turn to those.'

Here both brothers were on safe ground; they could price contraband to the farthing in both purchase and sale, quantity depending on the size of vessel that carried the cargo, albeit that had a round per-ton figure. Denby Carruthers listened with the attention of the man of business he was, able to make silent calculations of profit on investment without speaking or writing anything down.

This was a proper use for those secret bags of specie, risky certainly, but the profits were likely to be enormous. The Tollands would take no monies from the first cargo, only paying the men they led, and from then on it would be payment on a sliding scale until Denby Carruthers became a long-term partner on ten per cent of any smuggled cargo at no cost to him, by which time he would have at least doubled his investment.

Against that, these two were not honest men, but then neither in truth was he; his contact said the proposition was sound, with the caveat of interception by the excise. A risk, but a worthwhile one, and to protect himself he would keep ownership of the vessel provided, which would be claimed as stolen should these two be detained.

'Please be sure,' Carruthers said, 'that I have the means to deal with those who seek to . . .' he paused, that face had gone deep red again and the eyes were fierce '. . . shall we say "fail to meet their obligations". I am adept at finding people if I am required to.'

'Would those means extend to finding that sod that stole our ship?' Franklin asked.

'They might.'

'Name's Pearce,' Jahleel barked, 'and he wears a lieutenant's coat of the King's Navy.'

That surprised Denby Carruthers; he never thought naval officers as necessarily honest, but smuggling or the theft of contraband seemed extreme.

Franklin, for the first time of speaking, was as animated as his brother. 'Find him, and you can have our second cargo on the same terms as the first.'

'You want him that badly?'

The way Franklin Tolland gently fingered the scar on his face told the alderman why, and a look at Jahleel got a firm nod.

'My brother-in-law has good contacts at the Admiralty, so I will ask. Pearce, you say?'

'Given name John,' Franklin hissed. 'And a right bastard he is.'

CHAPTER EIGHTEEN

The route Pearce and Michael followed was dictated by water, for what they were traversing was sea marsh, with channels regularly inundated, which meant reed beds, salt pans, bird life, especially gulls to begin with, cackling ducks with that squawk which sounded so like a derisive laugh, but no sign of humans.

The road, if it could be called that, was a raised causeway that was never more than half a dozen feet above ground level; where disrepair was acute it disappeared entirely, obliging them to cross areas of grassland between the numerous rivulets and then look for a footbridge to get over.

These narrow wooden planks at least were numerous and looked to be well maintained, evidence of human activity – harvesting the salt, cutting reeds for roofing, no doubt grazing sheep with a high incidence of fishing too – so there was the feeling, impossible to avoid, that out there somewhere were a pair of eyes, maybe more than one, wondering about these two strangers, a possibility that had to be voiced.

'From what I recall, John-boy, do the French not wear blue coats as well as the navy?'

'Infantry and the National Guard, yes.'

'Then from a distance you might be taken for one of them, which, if you're telling me right about how bloody this fight is, would be likely to lead to you being shot at if those who have risen up have a gun.'

'I am hoping that no one will just shoot me without asking questions first.'

'Then, not being much for hope, you will not object if we halt for a moment while I load this musket. And I would suggest that pistol of yours might be better in your hand than a holster.'

'That would be asking for a misfire, Michael.' Pearce looked around the barren landscape, as much at the open sky, as O'Hagan acknowledged there was truth in that; powder got damp easily and there were all sorts of additional problems to bearing a loaded weapon for any length of time. 'Besides, this is not a place for the military – anyone armed out here will be loaded with birdshot, which might sting you but it will not kill or maim.'

It was as if he had sent out a message; his words were followed by a sudden flurry of wings as a flock of birds, disturbed by their approach, rose out of the long grass and fluttered noisily into the clear blue sky. As soon as they reached a decent height, the blast of a gun rent the still air, which had the ass Michael was leading jerk to a halt, feet splayed, while both men reacted by immediately dropping down to a crouch.

'Where away?' Pearce shouted, his eyes searching the horizon to left and right from a crouched position.

Michael pointed ahead of them to a rising puff of smoke, where the residue of black from the discharged powder showed just above the tips of the swaying grass. Tellingly, the shot had been successful, as one bird folded its wings and dropped to the ground halfway between where the shot had come from and where the pair stood, that followed by the sight of a dog leaping through the fronds to collect the carcass.

Michael was on one knee loading his musket and Pearce was doing likewise with his pistol; fowling piece or no, they had little desire to be shot at. That completed and both weapons at the ready they began to move forward slowly. They had not gone far when another group of disturbed birds rose up, bringing forth another blast of gunfire that seemed to connect right over their heads, for this time the prey dropped a few feet in front of where they stood.

The dog was not long in arriving, large, brown and white with drooping ears and a long tongue in what had to be a soft mouth, nosing around looking for what its master had just downed. Spotting them, it stopped, lifted one paw and eyed them for several seconds, but since they did not move it carried on with its task, located the shot bird and picked it up so gently it hardly disturbed the feathers, before running back into the long grass.

'A hat, John-boy,' Michael called. 'I swear I saw a hat.'

He was pointing right ahead with the muzzle of his musket and aiming along the barrel with Pearce following the line. It was just visible, the crown and wide brim of a dark-brown headpiece that stood out from the straw colour of its wind-blown surroundings. Then came the sharp whistle of the hunter calling his dog, which had taken too long about its task. Reasoning the first thing this fellow would do was reload, Pearce lifted his pistol in the air and fired; he had no notion to be peppered, for close to it could take out an eye.

That brought the head up higher, to reveal a face that promptly disappeared again. Pearce ran forward following the dog, Michael dropping the lead rope of the ass to do likewise. Bursting through the high grass Pearce nearly went headlong into a watercourse, stopping himself just in time, and he saw a few yards distant a flat-bottomed boat being rowed hurriedly if unevenly away, with the dog, still with the bird in its mouth, swimming to catch up.

'Stop!' he yelled.

Pearce signalled to Michael to chase up the bank and threaten the rower, at the same time holding out his discharged pistol on the grounds that the person at whom it was aimed could not know it was lacking a ball, just as, whatever language they spoke, they could not mistake the command. It was the musket that stilled the oars, which were dropped and the hands that had held them raised, one taking off the hat to reveal a very young face. It also released a cascade of long fair hair.

'Mademoiselle?'

Pearce asked that in a way that underlined how thrown he was, because the clothing was entirely male and of good

268

quality, while the person wearing it was quite obviously a young girl who could not be more, he reckoned, than twelve years of age – pretty, with pale clear skin and bright eyes to go with her golden hair.

The question was met by a look of confusion, his own clothing being examined up and down, with Pearce indicating the boat should return to the bank, which got a glance at the still-levelled muzzle. Michael dropped it when requested to do so, which produced even more visible confusion in this young Amazon. The oars were picked up to sweep the boat into the bank, the dog dragging itself on dry land to shake its fur dry, still holding the bird in its gentle jaw.

'Michael, the beast.'

'Sure, John-boy, it is not inclined to move when it should, so I do not think it will run off when it has grass under its hooves.'

Eyes swivelling from one to the other at this exchange, it was clear the girl's bewilderment had increased. Hard by the shore now, Pearce could see the fowling piece in the bottom of the boat along with the other bird carcass already fetched in by her dog. He addressed her in French, asking her name, aware that in this part of the world she might only know some local dialect.

'*Marie-Louise de Chalus, monsieur*,' she replied, not only in the right language but also with an accent of some refinement; this child was educated, which brought from him a slight bow as he responded with an introduction that had her eyes opening wide.

'John Pearce, *Lieutenant de vaisseau dans le service du roi d'Angleterre*.'

Mention of the King of England had her putting her hands to her mouth. Continuing, for he knew he was taking a chance by being open, Pearce informed her that he had arrived by sea and was looking for the forces fighting the Revolution.

'Sure it would be a kindness, John-boy, to let me know what you are on about.'

The reply to that gave the girl time to think and she quickly crossed herself and began to respond with a stream of words that left Michael O'Hagan high and dry once more. Pearce stopped the flow with an upraised hand, accompanied, to soften his interruption, with an understanding smile.

'We have struck gold, brother; it seems we are in country controlled by the very people we seek. There is a village not far off called Beauvoir and there, in an old priory, resides a priest who can lead us to those we need to find.'

At the mention of the word priest it was the Irishman's turn to cross himself, which attracted a look from the girl, who once more launched into an explanation with the rapidity that went with her years, the upshot of which was that she would row down to the nearest wooden crossing, then tie up her boat and lead them by foot to the village.

A sharp command had the dog leap into the boat, where it finally dropped the second dead bird.

The curé brought out to meet them was young, ascetic-looking, poorly clad in a severely worn cassock and he reassured them they were in territory safe from the forces of the Revolution, protected by a deep belt of marshland held by the insurgents, into which the army sent to subdue them feared to enter.

Beauvoir was not much better found than the priest, a tiny hamlet in a featureless landscape set around the Romanesque priory and the remains of a fortress that, though it might have once been substantial, was a ruin and one that seemed to have provided most of the stones for whatever non-clerical buildings the place possessed.

The arrival of a British naval officer in full uniform did not go without comment – the girl let everyone they met on entry know how and where they had met. In time, as word spread, a small crowd gathered setting up a babble of chatter, which had the curé suggesting it would be best to talk inside the church.

On entering through the low arched doorway, Pearce, who was not religious, felt awkward where Michael did not, the Irishman rapidly genuflecting, dipping his fingertips into a font and crossing himself again, which received a nod from the appreciative priest, who no doubt thought anyone not French was a heathen. The interior was cold, the walls of long-hewn stone whitewashed to maximise the shortage of natural light from slit windows, the statuary and carvings of a design that spoke of its ancient provenance and centuries of peaceful contemplation.

Gentle questioning followed as the Frenchman sought to nail their exact purpose, his disappointment that the two men were not the precursors of a substantial force of redcoats or fellow Frenchmen very obvious. Pearce was interrogating him too, to find out where the rebels could be found, which was frustrating because the fellow would not oblige.

Eventually he agreed to lead them to the leaders of the revolt personally, without admitting where that might be, apart from telling Pearce it was in the wet marsh – it seemed where they were was considered dry – and also that they would have to leave the ass, as part of the journey would be by boat.

Eager to be off, Pearce was frustrated when Michael asked if he could have his sins heard, which he had not done since Toulon, and given the curé spoke no English or Erse Gaelic it was necessary for him to translate the request, though not the actual confession, which left him wondering at the sense of it; it did, however, seem they managed to communicate both the transgressions and requisite penalties.

'Sure, I feel a better man for that,' Michael declared, as he emerged from the curtained confessional booth. 'Though it would have been grand to take communion as well.'

'Just as long as you're ready to kill if need be,' Pearce replied, in a jaundiced tone.

'You don't understand, John-boy, it's about being ready to die.'

By the time they emerged from the priory church, the curé was outside and waiting, now wearing a wide-brimmed hat and thick, brown woollen cloak. The whole of the village had gathered to stare, and before they got clear young Marie-Louise tugged at Pearce's arm and whispered something in his ear. They were on their way east when he told Michael what it was.

'Seems her father is one of the leaders. She wants me to give him a message of love.'

'Careful how you word that, John-boy,' Michael joked, being shriven having left him in high spirits. 'You being in naval garb an' all.'

After an hour of trudging the two sailors found out exactly what the priest meant about wet and dry, for they were no longer crossing a salt grass landscape similar to that which had brought them to Beauvoir; it changed completely to dense and forested wetlands in which what light penetrated the canopy shone on dappled patches of water and undergrowth which smelt of rotting corruption.

Trees filled the higher ground, but each wooded rise led to another still and silent watercourse or deep pool that had to be crossed by logs or stones, given any bridges had been destroyed, their gaunt remains a stark reminder that such demolition had been deliberately engineered to close off the region to straightforward access.

That was easy compared to the lower-lying ground, which was mud at best and ooze at worst; there was no way of keeping their feet dry. Sometimes that included their knees and thighs as they traversed the sodden landscape, their guide weaving through these areas with an admonishment to stay close and keep right behind him, indicating there were bogs into which they might be sucked whole.

It was a place that those who lived within its confines would know, which made it a deadly area for an army of strangers to fight in. Leeches soon found bare flesh and sucked their blood, swelling until replete then dropping off back into the water or mud. If this was a bad place now, it would be tolerable in high summer, but Pearce wondered how anyone could exist here in winter, when perhaps all this wet turned to ice and snow.

Thankfully the last part of the journey was, as promised, made by boat, which the priest located from an inlet where it had been carefully hidden – the same broad flat-bottomed sort in which they had found the girl. Pearce was doubly thankful; the bags of coin around his neck had seemed to grow heavier with each step and he had looked at Michael many times half hoping he was suffering likewise. If he was it did not show.

Even sat in the boat there was little respite; the damp made the line around his shoulders chafe and before long they were walking again until, finally, the curé indicated they should halt, putting his hands up to cup his mouth and calling out like an owl. There was a half a minute of wait before the hooting was returned and only then did Pearce sense by the pauses that it was some kind of coded message. When silence fell, their guide turned and spoke softly to Pearce.

'We wait here, Michael, until we are fetched.'

With darkness approaching, the wetlands had taken on a diabolical aura, which had Michael crossing himself repeatedly, his head jerking to each sound: a fish flapping its tail in a nearby pool, the splash of a wild duck entering the water, the cry of what might be a bittern, which was the kind of bird that relished these surroundings and, it seemed, a great number of owls – or were they humans?

'Holy Mary Mother of God,' Michael hissed when the lights first appeared, playing around in the dense foliage, appearing and disappearing like some ethereal presence, making strange shapes that seemed to assume human form and playing havoc with the Irishman's superstitious nature. 'The devil is in this place, John-boy.'

With sore shoulders and tired from the long march in his heavy broadcloth coat, John Pearce was in no mood for what he thought was Michael's credulous nonsense. Normally tight-lipped about any other man's religious beliefs – it was their concern what they believed and not his, unless they tried to persuade him to their way of thinking – he could not keep quiet now, even with a man he highly esteemed.

'Michael,' he growled. 'There are no devils here and no God either. What you can see are torches.'

There was enough natural light left to observe the doubt in his friend's face and to see him cross himself again, as another owl hoot filled the air, to which their guide replied. Within seconds the small clearing was full of light and humanity, men clad in dark clothing and low flat hats who seemed to emerge like chimeras from the surrounding undergrowth, every one of them armed. That was when the curé raised his hat to show his face, Pearce doing likewise, even if he would not be recognised.

There was no response to him, but one of the new arrivals did approach the young priest, and head bent, listened to what he had to say, a whispered exchange Pearce could not hear. Then he took a torch from one of the bearers and approached the pair, shining it in their faces but saying not one word. It was the curé who spoke once the examination was complete and the fellow had stepped back to talk to him. That was to tell Pearce that these men would take him on from here.

About to open his mouth as a torch changed hands, Pearce stopped himself; it was near to dark and there was no way this young man could find his way back to Beauvoir by torchlight through the kind of terrain they had traversed, regardless of how well he knew it. The reason for not speaking was simple; they had been led a merry dance on a circuitous route to ensure they could not recall how they came to be where they were. Beauvoir was a lot closer to this spot than they wanted them to know.

'Michael,' he said, 'would it surprise you to know they do not trust us?'

'Sure, John-boy, they would have to mine deep to find mine own.'

'*Au revoir, monsieur.*'

Pearce just nodded at the priest, whose face, in the light of the torch he held, looked other-worldly now, but there was no lingering. The men who had come to find them were already moving out in file – not all, for half of them were waiting for him and Michael to do so; they would bring up the rear.

Now they were on well-worn forest tracks, dry, with evidence of much use; the undergrowth had either been cut back or worn away by passage. No one spoke but it was certain that if they made an untoward move there would be a reaction, which left Pearce wondering if this was a trick they had experienced before. Perhaps it had not been a British naval officer and his seaman companion who had come with offers of help, but some emissary claiming to be on their side, while seeking to find them only for the purpose of betrayal.

Now they were on land carpeted with pine needles, the trees higher, straighter and the undergrowth sparse, finally entering a large clearing lit by several bonfires and surrounded by wooden huts and a large cabin, well constructed. It was a fair guess they were near the middle of the wetlands on some kind of elevation, given the air was drier than hitherto.

A mass of torches, fuelled by pine resin judging by the smell, illuminated the surroundings, and it seemed there were lanterns in the cabins. The clearing ground was worn flat by much use and all around them people emerged from doorways, not only men but women too, visible in the flickering flames.

Their escorts had fanned out to form a torchlit circle and to reveal a fellow standing in military garb, tricorn hat edged with feathers, a dark-green coat with brocade edges, white breeches and long waistcoat. He wore a sword at his side, while behind him stood several others who also looked to be soldiers, as well as a fellow in high-value canonical garments, obviously a bishop by his decorated crook, whose fingers flashed with his jewellery as his hand moved a fraction.

It was almost comical, the way the leader, a man Pearce took to be in his forties, swept off his hat and gave a deep bow, with a courtesy that would not have shamed the manners of a Bourbon courtier. His speech was as cultured as the bow was elegant, the introduction naming him as 'Joseph-Geneviève, *le Comte de Puisaye.*'

Tired, dirty, with his breeches black to the knees and

his coat streaked with mud, John Pearce could not but respond in kind. He too swept off his naval scraper and executed a bow, naming himself, as he had to young Marie-Louise de Chalus, as Lieutenant John Pearce.

The female cry that rent the air made him stand upright abruptly.

'Jean, c'est pas possible – c'est toi?'

It took a while for the lady who had cried out to emerge from the crowd and he did not recognise her till she threw back the cowl of her cloak to reveal her features, but once she did there was no mistaking a woman he had last seen in Paris over a year before.

'Amélie?' he responded weakly.

'Chéri!' she cried, rushing forward to embrace him.

CHAPTER NINETEEN

It was not necessary for Cornelius Gherson to do anything to wear down the nerves of Charlie Taverner and Rufus Dommet; he just had to appear at odd times on or below decks, stare at them, then disappear, which they put down to devilish malice, unaware that their man was pondering how to make use of them, not being one to waste what he saw as a very good opportunity, or that they barely registered to him as any kind of pest.

The person he most wanted to be shot of was Devenow, a nuisance he saw as inimical to his relationship with Ralph Barclay. His captain having rated the bully as a servant, Devenow was a constant if useless presence in the area of the ship they both occupied, hard by Barclay's own cabin, where he saw it as a duty to make sure his man was safe, regardless of the marine sentry.

If Barclay found Devenow's presence a trial – except on deck where he was on hand to prevent a fall – and

Gherson suspected he did, the others who had been employed by the captain as servants were in no doubt. They saw him as an interfering menace, useless in the pantry but forever looking over the shoulder of those who were competent at serving dinner or preparing light late-evening meals, as though they were trying to poison the captain.

When it came to cleaning the place Devenow was as likely to drop anything his master had paid highly for as keep it safe, and when he was not doing that his sprinkling of vinegar was carried out with abandon and took no cognisance of what it might land on to mark the French polish on a table, the gleaming wine cooler, an inlaid chest, or stain the very valuable Persian carpet that was laid to soften the sound of feet on planking.

The first time he had served at table during a formal dinner for the ship's officers brought those who knew the duty to the blush, and that included the men drafted in from the wardroom, though it was to be lauded that the captain had quietly called him aside and insisted he find other more suitable work to occupy him.

Worst of all, he was dead against the little privileges being exercised that cabin servants usually enjoyed: good food, for it was a custom to have the cook prepare more than was necessary, while to be seen to take a sip of wine before it was served to ensure the quality was a duty Devenow forbade, just as he would not allow for any unfinished bottle to be consumed when the meal was over. When it came to what a sharp-eyed man could whip away half full, these he confiscated for his own consumption.

So dark murmurings were to be overheard about the need to see Devenow's back; let him pull on a rope to haul on an oar, for that he was suited to, but God forbid he should enter the great cabin when Ralph Barclay entertained, as he must at some time do, the flag officers and his fellow captains of the Channel Fleet.

Finding the fleet at sea was not expected to be easy and Barclay relied on running across a string of Howe's frigates and sloops – the first he encountered had told him that the Channel Fleet was no longer in the Bay of Biscay looking for a grain convoy, but had headed out into the Atlantic in pursuit of the French main fleet, now at sea.

Such news lifted the spirits of everyone aboard who knew what it portended, and eventually of those who were in ignorance when they were told. If *Semele* could join in time they might be part of a fleet action, which if it brought high risk of death or a wound also presented the prospect of a great victory and prize money.

From then on it was a case of following the smoke on the horizon, the truth emerging when they encountered another friendly frigate: that what they were seeing – usually something which had sunk by the time they closed – were Dutch merchant vessels from a convoy that had been taken by the French fleet.

Retaken, they were burnt; Howe was short-handed – there were no men spare for crews to man ships that, being neutrals, would have to be handed back to their owners without profit.

When they finally did join, HMS *Semele*, as the newest

addition to the fleet, was ordered to take station astern of Lord Howe's flagship, HMS *Queen Charlotte,* and not long after Ralph Barclay found himself hanging on with his one good hand to the mizzenmast shrouds as he sought to hear what was being shouted to him, through a speaking trumpet, from the frigate which had come alongside in a sea that was running high as the result of a spent storm to the west.

He was, it seemed, required to read and absorb the orders about how the admiral wanted to fight a battle, should they be able to make contact with the enemy – instructions every other captain had been exposed to as they lay at anchor off Spithead, apparently too complicated to be conveyed to him by signal flags, while the flag captain was averse to launching a boat in mid-Atlantic or allowing a somewhat lubberly ship of the line close enough to his taffrail for a shouted exchange.

This left Ralph Barclay wondering at the necessity; the Admiralty Fighting Instructions were quite clear and everyone knew what was required of them in a fleet action, so what was Black Dick Howe on about? He was about to find out; with no more than twenty feet between ships the throw was easily accomplished, the bag and papers, weighted with lead and with a safety rope attached in case of failure, landing on the higher quarterdeck with a thud to be picked up by one of the midshipmen.

Taken to his cabin and opened for him by Gherson – Barclay could not manage the clasp or ties – he was left wondering, as he read, if the old admiral had lost his wits; Howe was proposing a very strange set of manoeuvres indeed, nothing less than the complete opposite of the regulations which had, for decades, ruled the conduct of warfare for British sea officers.

Being an island and without a standing army, it was axiomatic that Britannia required the protection of her wooden walls to be secure. The Lords Commissioners were as keen on naval victories as the rest of the nation, less so on the possibility of some flag officer whom they could not directly control losing a fleet through imprudence or some mad impulse, which could leave the country exposed to invasion.

Hence the promulgation of the Fighting Instructions, which enjoined admirals to assiduously seek out and do battle with the nation's enemies, but at the same time to avoid any exploit which would risk a serious loss of ships. Possession of the area of battle was to be considered a victory; as long as the enemy retired and the Royal Navy did not, that was a win.

'They seem to be of some interest, sir,' Gherson said, having stood silently, to his mind, for too long, yet aware that to seek to sit without permission was forbidden.

'They are very much that,' Barclay replied, not happy to have his thoughts disturbed.

'Might I ask, sir, what the orders contain?'

The reply was utterly lacking in grace. 'To what point, Gherson? You would struggle to understand them, for they are concerned with fighting at sea, a subject you know nothing about.'

It had been like that almost since the moment they had left Brown's Hotel, another shift in the terms of their relationship, indeed a reversal; gone was the man so recently dependent upon his particular knowledge and contacts, back was the irascible Ralph Barclay he had previously served.

'I am sure you have other duties to attend to,' Barclay added, once more looking at Howe's written orders, which included a reminder that they would be operating under a set of signal flags designed specifically by him to cope with the way they were to be executed, these included in the supplement to the signal book. That was handed over. 'You may take these to the wardroom, Gherson, for the signal lieutenant.'

Dismissed like some low skivvy, Gherson thought bitterly as he exited the day cabin, passing the pantry on the way to his own hutch opposite that of the master, running straight into Devenow, as usual hulking around uselessly. The supplement was immediately thrust out.

'Captain wants these delivered to the wardroom.'

'I ain't your post boy,' Devenow growled. 'Do your own runnin' about.'

Needled, partly with the captain, more with this lout, Gherson reacted, unusually for him, without giving his words much thought; it was enough to put this bully boy down.

'It's a good job I do some running about, Devenow, unlike you, and because of that I see threats to the captain that you do not, for all your damned attention to his well-being.'

'What you on about?'

'You don't know, do you?'

'Know what?'

'Who is aboard the ship?'

284

The look of confusion on Devenow's face only confirmed to Gherson how dense the man was, a level of stupidity so irritating he could not help but continue.

'A pair of Pearce's men, that's who.' Still that did not produce an enlightened response. 'You do remember who John Pearce is, don't you?'

'Course I bloody does!'

'Then ask yourself what would a couple of his Pelican friends be doing aboard, and volunteers at that?' God it was hard; if Devenow had a process of thinking there was scant evidence of it. 'If there's one person John Pearce hates it is Captain Barclay, a man he would dearly like to ruin. What better way to do that than to put a couple of moles aboard his ship.'

'For the love of Christ, to what end?'

It was only then that Gherson realised he had gone too far, had been more forthcoming than intended, which required him to come up quickly with something this oaf would easily comprehend, words he later considered to be quite inspired.

'What would happen if they were to cause a mutiny?' The lips moved to silently repeat the word, like a child. 'Taverner and Dommet are aboard and right now they are at their mess on the gun deck, no doubt planning an uprising.'

'You know that fer certain?'

'Of course not; they are not foolish enough to let their intentions be known.'

Gherson pushed past the bigger man and went on his way, leaving Devenow standing still, trying to make sense of what had been imparted.

In the cabin behind them, Ralph Barclay was feeling lonely, for what he had just read from the admiral was a document it would have been prudent to discuss with another, which was not an option open to him as the kind of captain he was. Really there was only Jackson, but the impulse of confiding his reservations about Howe's orders to his premier went right against the grain.

Yet what the doddery old sod was asking him to do carried with it great risk. *It is my intention to seek out the enemy and bring them to battle*, he read for the tenth time. *In order to inflict as much damage as possible, it will be necessary to close with them and engage . . .*

There was much about getting the weather gage, which was standard, and forming a line to comply with that of the enemy, but that was the point – and it worried Ralph Barclay – where the earl deviated from the compulsory course of action.

Once achieved, it will then be the responsibility of each captain, responding to my signals as listed in the supplement, to close with the nearest ENEMY SHIP *. . .* The capitals were revealing; there was to be no dithering about looking for a target *. . . and seek to either capture, destroy or sink that ship by an exchange of close-quarter gunnery.*

'With no indication of what happens if it all goes wrong?'

Barclay dropped the instructions on his table and posed the question to the deck beams above his head, for the history of the service was rife with examples of junior captains taking the blame for a superior's folly. He had only participated in one fleet action, the Battle of the Saintes off Guadeloupe, and that had been on the fringes

286

as a signal-repeating frigate. Yet he knew well that even an astounding victory, which it had been, was not free of dispute in hindsight.

Hailed as a great success for his patron Lord Rodney and, it had to be admitted, for Sam Hood as his second in command, it had become the subject of heated debate and much controversy, because Rodney had not abided by the Fighting Instructions. He had used a sudden change in the wind to do what Howe was proposing and closed with the fleet of the Comte de Grasse, humbugging the Frenchman completely, taking a number of ships as prizes.

Had he not succeeded in doing that, George Rodney could have found himself in the same steep tub as had faced Admiral Byng, shot by firing squad for his perceived failure to bring the enemy to battle off Minorca. Yet there was no mention of flukes of wind in Howe's instructions; these were to be employed regardless of conditions.

Ralph Barclay thought – and he was sure he was not alone in this opinion – that if it did not succeed, the repercussions might swallow more than the reputation of the man who issued them. Not that he would openly air his doubts, even if the opportunity for a personal meeting presented itself, unlikely in mid-Atlantic and an enemy somewhere about.

But he resolved then and there to be exceedingly careful about implementation should the aforementioned signals be displayed. Richard Howe was already famous for the relief of Gibraltar and an inconclusive battle at Cape Spartel, said to be much cosseted by King George.

Yet even that association would not save him from disgrace if he lost his fleet or rendered it incapable of defending the home shore. Ralph Barclay was damned if he was going to allow himself and his career to be put at risk for a man near retirement and already wealthy and titled; he had his own future to consider.

The sharp rap on the door broke the train of thought, that followed by a head popping round his door. 'Signal from a sloop to windward, sir, enemy in sight.'

The enemy in question proved to be a French frigate, which immediately sought safety in flight, its British counterparts in pursuit, signalling to the lumbering line-of-battle ships following in their wake. Whoever the Frenchman was, he seemed to be no genius; instead of leading Howe away from his main body, he led the Channel Fleet straight to them.

'Signal from flag, sir, clear for action.'

The next two days were frustrating in many more ways than one, HMS *Semele* being only an observer to what took place, this while she struggled to look anything like the fighting vessel she should be, showing itself most obviously in the rate of sailing she could achieve with a crew not fully worked up and in variable weather conditions and a changeable set of winds.

This was not aided by a lack of sleep, given that was reduced to catnaps in a chair in a ship in which all his creature comforts, including the bulkheads that provided his cherished privacy, had been struck below.

Several times signals with *Semele*'s number had been

hoisted aboard *Queen Charlotte* demanding that she keep proper station, as the flagship cracked on, hoisting everything she could carry aloft to close with the ships doing the fighting, exclusively on the first day of contact the six fastest 74s, the workhorses of the battle fleet, detached by Howe and led by Rear Admiral Pasley.

Even with two good arms Ralph Barclay would have been obliged to rely on what was reported to him of the distant fighting by a sixth lieutenant sent aloft with a long glass; he had never been one of those agile captains – to his mind nothing but show-away fellows who went aloft as if they were still skylarking midshipmen instead of responsible commanders.

Added to what could be distantly observed, there were also flags to read, those sent by Howe as well as the replies coming in from the repeating frigates and sloops to windward with news of what was happening. Palsey had caught up and engaged the rearmost French 110-gunner, which in royal times had been the *Bretagne* – like every vessel in the enemy fleet, having been renamed, she was now the *Révolutionnaire*.

The air reverberated with the thud of distant explosions, moving slightly as the repercussions swept across a deck full of its own sound and fury, this of shouted orders, lost tempers and pained shoulders as Barclay sought an extra knot of speed. A great cloud of smoke rose miles away where the fighting was taking place, hiding to the naked eye, even from the very top of the masts, what was actually taking place inside.

As darkness began to fall the same just-visible cloud was pierced by endless, more obvious flashes of red and orange from which emerged, one by one, the ghostly shapes of various ships of Pasley's squadron as they disengaged, evidence of damage to rigging and masts reported. Yet not all had broken off battle, someone was still engaged and the booms of cannon fire were still audible, until eventually, in moonlight, even that fell silent.

It was dawn, after an uncomfortable night for the whole crew, that brought the news that *Révolutionnaire* had been forced to strike her colours and surrender, yet it was a measure of the nature of the ignorant majority of Barclay's landsmen crew that they had to be encouraged to cheer.

Increasing daylight and a telescope aloft once more produced a less uplifting sight. *Révolutionnaire*, tricolour re-hoisted on the stump that remained of her mizzen, was limping away to the east with an undamaged 74 in company – not the prize all expected, but a crippled vessel heading for home that it would have been folly to pursue.

Full dawn also showed the state of the British ships, most notably HMS *Audacious*, which had suffered equally badly. More worryingly, there was no sight of the main enemy fleet. Thankfully the frigates had kept contact and soon flags were again peppering *Queen Charlotte*'s masts, the news passed to Barclay by the signal lieutenant.

'The French have set a course due west, sir.'

'West!'

Barclay responded with such surprise it produced what was, for him, a public and uncharacteristic outburst; he had expected, as had Howe judging by their course, that the enemy would run for Brest and safety. Whatever the reason that had not occurred, there was no time for speculation; the flags were shooting up the flagship halyards to indicate a change of course to pursue.

Later, after much hullabaloo to get on the new course, Ralph Barclay had time to ponder the tactics of the enemy admiral and the first thing that came to mind was the behaviour of that original frigate which had led them towards the French fleet; had that been, as he had thought, foolish, or was it really calculation? And why retire to the west, a manoeuvre that was unlikely to go undetected, if it was not to draw the opposition either towards or away from something?

'Are we being humbugged?'

'Sir?' enquired Lieutenant Jackson, on deck when he wanted not to be. In much need of a snatched slumber, he was there because of Barclay.

His captain nearly opened up and aired his thinking, but he stopped himself just in time, not least because he might be wrong and it would never do to be seen as that. The final despatches he had received before he weighed from the Nore had emphasised the need to look out for a huge food convoy coming from the Americas.

If that was truly as important as had been implied, then the best way to protect it was to draw off the risk of contact with the British warships who would wreak havoc upon defenceless merchantmen. Deducing that might be the case changed nothing; he was a subordinate captain and it was not his task to do anything other than obey.

However, a note in his log mentioning the possibility was paramount; never a direct question as to the nature of the orders he received, but a carefully worded hint that they might be misplaced, such allusions could be the difference between being perceived as wise, instead of being tarred by the same brush as a fool coming up seventy and long past his prime.

CHAPTER TWENTY

If Pearce was shocked to discover his one-time Parisian mistress hiding out in a Vendéean marsh, it at least had the effect of establishing his bona fides: there was now no one questioning that he was who he claimed to be, while beyond the fond remembrance of someone he thought might be dead he was here on a mission.

So after a brief exchange of affectionate remarks, which included the information that Amélie Labordière was now a widow, and an unkind thought that a year of age and deprivation had not done anything for her beauty, he was obliged by the people assembled to greet him to turn to matters more important. That he might be tired from a long day, which started at first light, of crossing marshland and bog, did not seem to occur to his hosts.

He was led to a large if roughly constructed cabin, which, given the abundance of coarse-hewn seating, seemed to act as some kind of meeting place. Hot because of the fire, as well as the numbers who crowded within to hear what he had to say, smoky through the lack of a proper chimney, Pearce was made doubly ill at ease by the proximity of many of those assembled, as well as still having about his neck the heavy bags of money – something he was determined to keep concealed until he knew they would be of use.

'Stay right beside me, Michael,' he said as he prepared to sit.

'Sure, John-boy, I have no notion of where I might be going if I do not.'

'I will be talking in French.'

'And I will be watching the eyes of these folk while you do.'

That made Pearce smile and wonder what these Frenchmen would make of being carefully examined, for he had no doubt that Michael's scrutiny, even if he could not understand a word of what was being said, would be acute. The amused look was still there when he turned to address the Comte de Puisaye and outline his reasons for being here; he was not given a chance.

'I hope, monsieur, that you are here as the precursor of a much more numerous force of men and material?'

'No, monsieur, I come as an emissary only.'

That produced an immediate reaction from the assembly and it was not a heartening one; they were looking at each other with dismay, some of it rather theatrical in its intensity. What had been benign looks changed when the hubbub diminished and were now quite hostile, though the count made an effort to be diplomatic both in his countenance and his words.

'We have sent messages to England over many months requesting aid.'

'And, monsieur, they have been heard,' Pearce responded, without being exactly sure that he was speaking the unvarnished truth, the sudden feeling he had been despatched by Dundas as some kind of sop impossible to suppress. 'Which is why I am here.'

'Surely more than just two men and one musket?'

'There is a ship off the coast,' Pearce lied, not prepared to say that he hoped it was still at anchor in the Bay of Noirmoutier.

'A large ship?'

'No, it is an armed cutter.'

That description required further explanation, which in turn set off more loud murmurs around the hut, more looks, none of them pleasant, a few downright hostile, the most telling coming from the high-ranking prelate, which brought a whisper in his ear from Michael.

'Are we in a tub of trouble here, John-boy?'

Pearce could do no more than gesture his uncertainty with a shrug, given he was unsure if there was anyone present who spoke English. He was given time to do so by the heated whispered conference being entered into by those who led the assembly.

'This,' the count said finally, when he turned once more to Pearce, his face no longer that of the bland mediator, but now with pursed lips and a stare of deep displeasure, 'does not make us content.'

Pearce replied with a query, to which he was sure he already knew the answer. 'I am here to find out: what would?'

He was not disappointed, even if the number who tried with loud voices and many gestures to give him an answer overwhelmed any clarity. They wanted an army of redcoats sufficient to overcome their enemies, cavalry, artillery, muskets, food and transport – not enough to just secure the Vendée but to reverse the gains of the Revolution, nothing less than to take the whole west as a prelude to reinstating the monarchy.

'Messieurs,' he cried, holding up his hands, about to explain that the British did not have the resources for what was being demanded, given their other commitments, before engaging in a rapid rethink, brought on partly by a reluctance to explain the position of Pitt's government.

That was not his position either by inclination or design, but the other feeling was the greater; he had been tasked to find out the situation here and what were the chances of success for some kind of military intervention. Such an investigation would not be aided by a purely negative response, and to that was added his impression of his audience.

John Pearce liked the French; he knew they had as many good qualities as other nations, but an excess of rationality was not one of them, and that did not just apply to the mobs of Paris or the other cities where the Revolution had produced riots and endless beheadings.

Before him, and the Count of Puisaye was one of the number – the overdressed and bejewelled prelate even more so – were the representatives of a body of people who had brought the mayhem of the last few years on their own heads and all they seemed to want was that which they had once had restored.

It was interesting but not helpful to recall that these were the opinions of his late father: that if the privileged did not see a way to gently surrender what they possessed, then those with nothing would take it by force. That Adam Pearce had been wrong about the ability of the lower strata of society to rise up on their own did not obviate the fact that there were people fired by good intentions as well as opportunist rabble-rousers willing to provide the required spark.

Probably few, if any, present had been to the Versailles of Louis XVI and Marie Antoinette – neither had he, but like them he knew of it by import, just as he knew what it represented: a monarchy and its supporters utterly out of touch with the citizenry, an institution bankrupt not only financially but politically, a polity who could not see that their protection of their advantaged existence stank in the nostrils of their fellow countrymen.

The French Church, no doubt the bishop now glaring at him too, sat like a great octopus on the nation, deluding the pious, sucking out money which it lent to the King and his ministers – not for good purpose, but so they could maintain their hold on their rich and corrupt benefices: their gold, their bejewelled chalices and their garments stitched with precious thread, as well as their perfumed mistresses.

'Sure, I don't know who is looking more grim,' Michael said, 'you, John-boy, or they.'

Pearce relaxed his jaw, aware that he had let his thinking run riot and that must be obvious by his countenance. 'If their thoughts are anything like mine it will be moot, brother.' His eyes ranging round the room, he saw the sad eyes of Amélie through a gap between two men engaged in voluble complaint, and he knew he must, for her sake if no other, produce some encouragement.

'But,' he said in a voice loud enough to overcome the hubbub, added to a confidence wholly manufactured, 'if I can take back to England a positive report of the prospects for my nation's arms in assisting your revolt, I am assured that aid will be forthcoming.'

'A mere naval lieutenant?' demanded the bishop. 'And such a decision?'

'A very well-connected one, Your Grace.'

The pause was long, the nod slow, but the prelate understood more than most how good connections made men of seemingly low rank important; if any institution favoured such arrangements, it was the Catholic Church – what else could they do with their bastard offspring?

'I must be made aware of your strengths,' Pearce added loudly, 'and, sad to say, where you are weak. I must also be able to assess what it is you face and, should an army land here, how you are going to both aid and sustain them, and I would humbly suggest that cannot be done sitting in this hut.'

If Pearce was glad to get out of that stifling cabin and be shown to a smaller less stuffy one of his own, the arrival, after only a few moments, of Amélie Labordière was not so cheering. Indeed he was grateful – and not only to protect his funds – that no one had suggested that Michael O'Hagan rest his head anywhere else but in the same place.

She entered through the wicker door with purpose, but that was immediately put in abeyance by the presence of the huge Irishman. She looked from one to the other and in that moment, because she was close to a lantern, Pearce could see just how unkind what she had lived through had been since he last saw her; there were lines where previously none had existed and an air about her that smacked of desperation.

'You'll be wanting a bit of peace, John-boy,' Michael said, looking from one to the other.

Pearce just shook his head; she did not speak English, but there were words and the way of delivering them that required no knowledge of language. Sadly there were gestures too, and it was clear by the look on her face that she had picked up the gist of the exchange. Pearce covered his embarrassment by indicating she should sit on the cot provided for him to sleep on.

'Does your fellow speak French, Jean?' she asked, receiving another shake of the head in reply. 'Then perhaps you will tell me why I am not welcome?'

'How can you think you are not that?'

'Do you intend that he should leave us alone?'

The reply was as feeble as the expression that accompanied it. 'I would not want to inconvenience him.'

'It is less trouble to inconvenience me, then?'

It was time to be a little more forthright, even if he kept his tone muted. 'How am I doing that?'

She laughed then and time fell away for Pearce, for if there had been one thing apart from her evident loveliness that had made her an attractive companion, it had been that: the ability to be amused where other women would have been irate. He was back in those gilded salons where wit, beauty and the high intelligence of both sexes combined to produce sparkling conversation. Michael's voice swept that away.

'I have no notion to stop your pleasures, John-boy, nor am I one to spill what you have been about when we get home.'

'Did you have to mention that?'

'I sense, Jean, I am no longer the object of your interest I once was.' He made to protest but Amélie kept talking. 'When I met you first you were an engaging young man, but lacking in experience, yes?'

Pearce nodded. 'And the fact that I was not made me a desirable companion, as well as a bed partner to cherish.'

'It was more than that, Amélie,' he replied, his voice slightly hoarse.

'One of my experiences, Jean, was to know and recognise what it is like when a passion cools and one is no longer the centre of a lover's affections. Who is she?'

The thought of saying 'no one' did not seem wise. 'Does it matter?'

'No, but it is a pity, nevertheless.' She laughed again.

'Or is it that I am free of constraints now that those swine have killed my Armand?'

'How did he die?'

'Fighting, which was odd, for he had never used a weapon other than a pen or an abacus in his life. What, you might ask, was a tax gatherer doing with a sword in his hand? Was it that he had a cause?'

'I'm sorry.'

'So, Jean, am I,' she replied, before turning and leaving.

'Was that you being noble?' Michael enquired.

'Stupid more like,' Pearce snapped, which only made his friend laugh. 'Now let's get some sleep, we will have a busy day on the morrow.'

'Just as well, then, John-boy, you turned down a busy night.'

If it was dark outside the windows of the Admiralty it was not quiet, for London was still busy at night, not only because of those about their revels, but with the noise of endless carts, all the produce being brought in to feed the world's greatest metropolis. Sir Phillip Stephens was going through the last of his mail, the letters that came in daily from supplicant officers, those who pleaded their case in search of employment, most of which would be passed to a clerk for a polite refusal, to be signed by whichever naval lord was available to do so on the morrow.

The handwriting of Sir Berkley Sumner he recognised immediately from the frequency of the missives the dolt sent in, but these too had to be given a response. As he opened it, Sir Phillip let his mind drift once more to the prospect of his upcoming retirement; if he took pleasure in affairs of moment he would not be sorry to see the back of this task, one he dare not delegate, given that to ignore some well-connected fellow or his powerful patron would only rebound on his head.

Sumner's letter was, as usual, larded with compliments to the Admiralty secretary's sagacity and unquestionable ability, while politely enquiring as to his health, which the old admiral hoped was sound given his burdens and long service. Then there came the list of Sumner's achievements, acts seen in the light of his undiminished vanity as worthy; others who had witnessed them saw them as black marks against any notion of granting him future provision. Then it came to the nub.

'Raynesford?'

Sir Phillip mouthed the name with an air of uncertainty. He was a man who prided himself on his memory, and he could recall no lieutenant of that identity being granted a commission at any time in the past, never mind recently. But he was, he knew, past his prime, so he rang a bell and, when that was responded to, asked one of his clerks to enquire.

The information that came back made him wonder if old Sumner had finally lost what few marbles he retained, but it drove him back to the letter again and the fact that the information from the senile ditherer had come to him from the local county newspaper, not in itself a source of utter reliability, but one nevertheless he should take cognisance of.

302

Was it an error, a person wrongly named, or in fact an impostor? If it was not unknown for dubious types to pretend to be naval officers, so Sir Phillip reasoned that such a possibility was best acted on. A polite reply was sent to Admiral Sir Berkley Sumner, thanking him for the information, with the added point that no such person existed and, as a precaution, in case of chicanery or an attempt at fraud, word would be sent to the local justices to investigate the matter.

Sir Phillip was, however, sorry that there were no suitable places available, even for a man of such high rank and exceptional talent.

In Lymington, Emily Barclay, if she was alone was not lonely, occupying herself during the day with long walks and in the evenings with reading and embroidery, taking her meals in the small parlour and generally being extremely discreet in any exchanges she had with the locals, who were naturally keen to make the acquaintance of the wife of a naval officer from without the boundaries of the town, who rumour insisted had come directly from London.

Given that connection, her clothing was examined closely to discern what must be the latest fashion, which led to much stitching and altering in many another parlour, to copy the style of what Emily wore, both in her dresses and her bonnets, those who did so unaware of their provenance, which was actually her hometown in Somerset.

The only other thing she had undertaken, and this went with her daily walks, was to engage a local artist to teach her to draw and perhaps in the future paint with watercolours or even oils. He, an elderly fellow, would accompany her in her hack with his boards and an easel to oversee and comment upon her efforts.

Each evening, of course, she would take another stroll, to look out from the harbour to the estuary, wondering about John Pearce, not only where he was and what he was doing, but whether her actions in agreeing to come here to Lymington had truly been wise. Then she would feel a sensation in her lower belly, and that would produce a private smile.

Determined to impress him, the servants who attended to the leaders of the revolt had been required to take away and clean their visitors' clothing, as well as to replace what they could not launder. They also provided the pair with more appropriate hunting clothes, Michael's rough cloth, Pearce given garments of high quality, so it was with smart leathers and well-brushed thigh-high boots he appeared before them.

There was to be no more walking either; they were each allotted a sturdy pony and provisions, the saddlebags of which were perfect for Pearce to keep out of sight Dundas's specie. Once mounted they were led away into the wetlands, this time on well-used tracks that kept them out of the bogs and ponds, their route due east into the still rising sun.

That the marshland was extensive he did not doubt, but Pearce reasoned it was easy to skulk within the confines of such an area and occasionally exit to prod an unprepared enemy, much more difficult to mount a full-blown campaign of the kind being proposed; this was no landscape with which to progress through a fully equipped army.

These were, however, notions he kept to himself, instead content to praise the precautions they took against being surprised themselves. He was shown cunningly concealed mantraps, covered deep ditches as well with tops strong enough to support an individual, but into which half a dozen enemy soldiers would fall through their combined weight.

One of their number had fought with the American Indians against the British, he being unmistakable by both his loose buckskin garb and the extremely long-barrelled musket he carried, which meant cunningly laid ropes that would see the victim hauled up to hang from a tree. There were whips of wood with sharp stakes attached both in the forest floor and tied to trees, coops in which geese were kept and fed so that, alarmed and noisy, they would alert the defenders long before anyone could harm them.

There were hides where a body of fighters could lay invisible, waiting for the enemy, forced to come along the narrow paths in single file, unaware of the oil-soaked straw and leaf bundles that, ignited, would trap them and channel them in an area in which they could be mown down to a man, for it was made plain to Pearce that the taking of prisoners by either side was rare and only done to extract information by the most barbaric methods.

Eventually the swamps ended and they proceeded through dry forest, where the tracks were wider and, judging by the slow progress, the possibility of an enemy presence needed to be guarded against. Then at last they were traversing more open country, a mixture of open heath dotted with woodland.

Finally they came to a string of hamlets. The mounted bishop, if he had discarded his gilded garments for an outfit of hunting corduroy, still carried with him his gilded crook – as well as his glittering rings – which told everyone in each village they entered that their prelate had come amongst them and the effect was profound on the priests that served them and their parishioners.

Like the first habitation to which he and Michael had been taken, it seemed the clerics were the leaders, obvious that the dominating lever to keep the local support firm was their adherence to their faith. If these people had risen up against Paris, and would continue to struggle, it was as much to uphold their church as any other motive. That none of them seemed to mind, as they kissed the bishop's ring, that there was wealth enough meeting their lips to keep them for life, they did not react, which disgusted John Pearce.

'Michael,' Pearce said, in a slightly querulous tone, as the bishop performed yet another short open-air mass – he had to, as every church was a burnt ruin – 'it is not required for you to kneel and pray every time the local peasants do.'

'Said like a non-believer,' Michael shot back, in no way abashed. 'For you cannot feel the power of the man as I can.'

'His power is in the imagination of the deluded.'

'Sure, I doubt, should we die, John-boy, we will be meeting in heaven.'

'Now there, Michael, I can agree with you.'

Progress was slowed by all this clerical flummery, as well as the desire of the peasantry to feed and care for those they saw as saviours of both their bodies and souls. It was also noticeable that the party, at each halt, was in receipt of recent information regarding the forces of the Revolution, equally apparent that such intelligence became less reliable the further they went from the swampy base.

They took to moving with increasing caution, only entering any clutch of huddled dwellings after a proper reconnaissance, until finally they came to a more sizeable community of some thirty dwellings by a bridged river, close to a destroyed and, in the gathering gloom, eerie-looking manor house, where he was informed they would spend the night.

'Tomorrow, Lieutenant,' said the Count de Puisaye, when Pearce enquired as to the risk, 'we will be coming very close to the ungodly. You will see their main encampments, the ones that ensure we are confined to the swamps.'

'I need to know their numbers, monsieur, and the state of their defences.'

'We will tell you the former and show you the latter,' Puisaye said, his eyes flashing. 'And we will show you their quality, which is low, then you will see how easy they will be to defeat if we are given the means to do so. Now join me in prayer, so that our cause will prosper.'

'Forgive me if I decline.'

'You do not believe in God?'

'Let me quote you Lucretius, when he says that religion is sublime to the ignorant, helpful to the ruler and profitable to the man of business. Since I am none of those things . . .'

'As you wish, but I will say a prayer for you nevertheless.'

'There are others who need your prayers more than I.'

CHAPTER TWENTY-ONE

If the first day of battle had been exasperating aboard HMS *Semele*, the second was even more so; with what looked like a superior rate of sailing and Ralph Barclay still harbouring thoughts of Howe being humbugged, the Channel Fleet had closed enough with the enemy for the entire van and the forward section of the centre squadron to engage. That left HMS *Semele* once more as an observer, not a participant, yet so close to the action she was enveloped in drifting smoke from the guns of *Queen Charlotte*, which served to cut off from view much of what was happening ahead.

They were witness, though few aboard knew it, to the frantic signals from the flagship to the lead vessel in the van, to obey what orders had already been sent out to close with the enemy. Ralph Barclay, informed of their meaning, was thinking that in Captain Molloy of HMS *Caesar* he had a man who shared his caution, a sea officer who doubted the wisdom of Howe's instructions in the first place and was not willing to put them to the test and risk destruction when unsupported by the whole weight of the fleet.

This was underlined by what information was being relayed to him from aloft about the positions of the opposing forces; Barclay could reckon that imposing a decisive conclusion seemed unlikely given the wind, the sea state and the positions of the opposing fleets. It was, in the main, long-range gunnery, the return fire doing some damage to the rigging of the flagship but little or none to the hull.

Such was being suffered by another flagship, that of Rear Admiral Gardner in HMS *Queen*, one of only two 100-gun first rates engaged, but despite the best efforts of Gardner and Lord Hood's brother and fellow admiral, Alexander, in HMS *Royal George*, the enemy was in no way threatened with the kind of battle that would either pin or destroy them.

When battle was finally broken off, Black Dick Howe issued orders that presaged a wager on the fact that the prevailing wind from the south-west might hold and possibly increase. If his gamble paid off and the French held their course, he would get to windward of them and be able to choose whether to attack or not; if the wind changed, he would look like a dunce – such were the vagaries of sea command, so slight the margin between success and failure, knowledge that filtered down from the quarterdeck to those below.

'Word is we will get a proper fight on the morrow,' said Davy.

'How can you be certain?' asked Charlie Taverner.

The question had the men crowded round the table leaning forward, for this was a popular mess and Davy seen as something of a sage, so many left their own tables to gather round his. The gun deck was cleared from prow to stern, lit by lanterns, the bulkheads that cut off the wardroom struck below, so the accommodation of the lieutenants, as well as the master and the purser, was visible to all, the deadlights rigged on the casements cutting out even the light of the moon and the stars.

'I heard the words of a man who stood close to the premier while he was talking with Barclay. Capt'n says if Old Howe has it right and the Frogs have not seen what he might do, he will be able to force 'em to fight, like it or no.'

There was no questioning of the source, for there were few secrets on any ship, size being of no consequence. Men-o'-war were crowded spaces, and when it came to the spreading of rumour or fact it was as if the scantlings had ears, or to some officers' way of thinking that there was a spirit presence on board – a superstition most of the hands rated as a certainty – an entity easy to cross and one that had to be assuaged with proper behaviour.

'Your young mate has been gone a while, Charlie, happen he is a touch gravid.'

'Bit soon for that, Davy,' Charlie responded, though it was common enough, given the diet, to be tight-bound when it came to evacuation. For all his seeming unconcern, the Welshman had touched on a truth; Rufus

311

had been gone longer to heads than was normal. 'Happen I will go and see what he's about.'

'Bein' his age,' an Irishman called Byrne opined, 'I reckon we know what that is.'

'A trip round the bay by way of a ready hand,' joked another of Rufus's messmates.

'Don't you go getting all righteous,' Charlie responded, rising to go, but grinning. 'There's not a man here who ain't seen your hammock rocking of a night.'

No seaman could just leave the gun deck to go to the forepeak without a marine gave permission, and with their redcoats being bullocks not lobsters there were occasions when the soldier on duty took delight in refusal as revenge for the endless ribbing they got from the sailors aboard, mostly for the fact that, even being at sea for a while, many were still green around the gills.

Tars were not too fond of marines in any case, but when they were saddled with army men for the shortage of true lobsters, that was a cause for more friction, given they, like the landsmen on board, were clueless about the duties they shared with the seamen. Yet in that area, as in relation with those pressed, matters were settling down with familiarity.

Most men had found their level, or more importantly those who ordered them about had sorted out the ones who would learn their tasks from those who never would. So it took a mere indication and a nod for Charlie Taverner to pass through to the heads, his shoulders hunched as he reached out to the door to the windswept forepeak, pitching and rolling in the long swell.

It opened before he got to the latch and the man who exited rushed past swearing loudly and clutching his ducks, while on his face was a look of alarm close to fright. In the light of the moon and stars Charlie saw the three-quarters outline of Devenow, which gave him pause, until he realised that gripped in one of his hands – the other was slapping to and fro – was a limp Rufus Dommet.

The door, under pressure of wind, slammed shut, cutting off the scene. There was no time to look for support and Charlie spun round to seek a weapon, his eye going to the nearest of the great guns bowsed up against the closed gun port. With the ship cleared for action, all the implements needed to work it were ready for use, not stowed away; the only one he thought of use was the handspike, which would be employed in shifting the weapon from side to side.

A solid block of wood, square at one end so it could grip on the deck planking for heaving, it was just the right size for what was needed. Holding it in one hand, Charlie reopened the door and went through swinging. Devenow saw him coming and dropped Rufus, who fell in a heap, but the bully was too slow.

The first blow took him at the back of his knees, with Charlie ducking under the haymaker fist aimed at his head. The handspike was a weight and it was that rather than the effort behind it that caused Devenow, with a screaming curse, to drop to one knee. The temptation then was to crown the bastard, but even with a red mist Charlie had no notion to hang for the swine.

So it was a vicious jab to the side of his head with

the square end instead of a full-armed swing that was delivered, yet that, given the force with which it was driven, was enough to fell Devenow completely, he emitting nothing but a low groan as he crumpled and passed out. Dropping the handspike, Charlie knelt beside Rufus, noting the blood on his face, black in the available light.

Devenow groaned again within seconds; the bugger was coming round, so Charlie pulled Rufus up on to his backside, pleading with him to respond and get to his feet. That took some doing, for the youngster was not much help, but eventually he was upright, groggy for certain but able to move with aid, enough to get him to the other side of the forepeak door.

Charlie sat him on the cannon and went back for the handspike, picking it up and looking down at Devenow, who was whimpering, then grunting. There was no time to muck about – he had to get Rufus to safety and himself too, for he had no notion that, even with his weapon, he would be able to take on this sod fully ready. Back through the door he went, where he dropped the handspike, picked up a slightly recovered Rufus and harried him back to the mess table past a soldier-marine who showed no interest at all in the fact that the youngster was hurt.

'How much did you take for that duty, you bugger?' Charlie demanded over his shoulder, suddenly sure that Devenow would have cleared his way for an assault too dangerous to carry out without a bribe.

The sentry just grinned at Charlie's retreating back, his voice loud enough to carry. 'Happen you lot won't be quite so sharp with your needlin' now and will show us some respect.'

By the time Charlie had got back to the table it was clear; the watch was changing and all his messmates were going to their stations, but Davy, last to depart, saw the state Rufus was in and rushed to help.

'Best get him on deck and out of sight.'

'Weren't his fault, mate.'

'Makes no odds, Charlie, boyo, he has the marks of a fight on him an' that is enough to earn him the cat if he is seen to have been bruising.'

The sight of Devenow, with blood streaming from a split ear, staggering with a discernible limp into the corridor that led to the great cabin, brought joy to Gherson, whom he woke up with his noise, that compounded by the yelling which came from his still-awake master when he caught sight of his man; the captain naturally assumed he was drunk.

Despite the loud dressing-down, the surgeon was roused out from his slumbers to attend, so that when Ralph Barclay appeared on deck before first light he was attended by a very groggy Devenow, his head wrapped in a bandage. Gherson, having no duties to do with fighting battles, had gone back to sleep, only occasionally roused to curse the bells that ruled the naval day.

It was not long after five of the clock, when a man could see a grey goose at a quarter mile, that the rigging of the enemy began to show to leeward, proof that Howe's manoeuvre had paid off handsomely; he had the weather gage and could enforce the battle he so desired unless the French fleet ran away. Feet planted wide apart, knees giving to take the movement of the deck beneath them, Ralph Barclay had to his eye a telescope that had been opened for him with which to examine the opposition.

In numbers of ships the French were near equal, but it was in weight of metal that they had the edge, their first rates carrying a superior number of guns to their counterparts in Howe's fleet. Added to that, their vessels had been in port for some time and were in better condition than many of their opponents, which had been at sea on and off for a year, their bottom fouling up in the process.

To counter that superiority in weapons, the Wooden Walls of England had better worked-up crews, so it was in the article of rapid gunnery and slick seamanship that the difference should show, the odds would be evened up and the success or failure of the battle be decided.

'Signal for flag, sir, all hands to breakfast.'

'Mr Jackson, make it so.'

'Now that, boyos,' cried Davy, 'is an admiral who knows how to treat his men, who would struggle to fight on a rumblin' gut.'

'Either that,' Charlie responded, 'or we's in for a very long day.'

By the time the first guns from the upper deck opened fire at maximum range, eight bells had been rung and the two opposing fleets were strung out in line ahead. Down below, the gun ports were closed to keep out the water from the strong Atlantic swell in which the ships were straining for every ounce of speed and would remain so until the enemy was yardarm to yardarm, so that the crews were crouched around them in near darkness, relying on whispers from the running powder monkeys carrying cartridges and quills to tell them what was happening.

HMS *Semele* was exchanging fire with several French vessels as the Channel Fleet inched forward to overhaul an enemy that had only two options: to hold line and accept battle, or run north to avoid it. Again Ralph Barclay was wondering at the French tactics, for it seemed that the enemy admiral had no intention of avoiding a contest, even if his position was the inferior one in which he could not have been blamed for avoidance.

Howe was favoured by the wind should he decide to bring his line closer, the second advantage being that the smoke from his broadsides would obscure his ships, which was not a favour the French would enjoy; quite the reverse: the southerly wind would leave him fully exposed throughout the coming exchange and at some point it was to be expected, under the normal rules of engagement, he would choose to acknowledge his difficulties and grant Howe a victory by declining to continue.

With such an obvious advantage Black Dick had seemingly forgotten about his questionable manoeuvres and was holding his line as dictated by the Admiralty Fighting Instructions; Barclay expected he would be required to close the range to distance fire, which could be achieved with what canvas was set and sheeted home, topsails and topgallants, by the use of the rudder.

It therefore came as a shock to see the flags go aloft to tell every ship in the line to immediately change course and do as had been outlined in those orders thrown over from that frigate. *Queen Charlotte* began to turn into her own gun smoke, her yards braced round to take more of the wind, bringing an instant increase in her rate of sailing, prow aimed directly at the French flagship, the 110-gun *Montagne* – an act which rendered useless her own broadside cannon, which fell silent.

'Madness,' Barclay swore, for it was obvious that Howe would take a real battering as the range closed without being able to reply with anything other than his lightweight bow chasers; his main armament would remain useless unless he bore up on his original course, which a watching *Semele* captain was sure he would be obliged to do.

The rate of sailing was no more than four knots, so it was with increasing foreboding that Ralph Barclay watched as the wood began to fly from his flagship's forward bulwarks, that seconded by the amount of gunfire that was shredding Howe's rigging, and yet the old sod held his course, aiming for the gap that separated *Montagne* from the nearest ship astern, the 74-gun *Jacobin*.

With the aid of that wind, the reaction of the other British ships was easy to see, and as usual Barclay had better eyes than his own aloft to report. What he was told induced caution, for not everyone was blindly obeying Howe's order, either as they had been previously outlined or as were now flying from the *Queen Charlotte*'s halyards. *Bellerophon* and *Defence* had responded as required from the van squadron, but HMS *Royal Sovereign* was labouring due to the damage she had previously received.

Astern, *Royal George* and *Glory* had likewise reacted but it was plain to Ralph Barclay that the majority of his fellow captains were either avoiding compliance, or were perhaps not in a state to do so due to damage sustained in encounters over the last two days. He was also aware that his officers, not least his premier Jackson, were looking at him waiting for the required instructions.

All right for them, he thought as he watched, aghast, at the punishment being inflicted on *Queen Charlotte, they do not carry the burden I do; never mind what Black Dick Howe orders, he might well never get near his chosen target. If he does not, he will have thrown away a certain victory and there will be only one consequence for that, opprobrium for those who complied and praise for those who showed more sense.*

'Flag making out number, sir,' called the signal midshipman. 'Signal reads: Engage the enemy more closely.'

In raising his head to look at the fluttering line of flags and pennants, his thinking troubled, Ralph Barclay slightly lost his balance, his mind telling an arm he no longer possessed to steady him. Thankfully for his dignity, Devenow was there to save him from an ignominious fall, but not from the feeling of dread that filled his breast.

He was not afraid of death or a wound and never had been; that had to be accepted if a man was to enter into his profession. The only thing Ralph Barclay feared was disgrace, the notion that he might be hauled before a court to account for his actions in battle, and not of the benign kind he had faced in Toulon. Yet to disobey a direct order from the flagship was to bring on that very thing, so it was with a hoarse voice that he responded.

'Quartermaster, put up our helm to close with the enemy; Mr Jackson, we will need the sails trimmed to give us as much speed as possible.' It was under his breath that he added, 'And may God have mercy on our souls.'

'Aye, aye, sir,' cried Jackson, full of the enthusiasm of a man who saw the possibility of elevation in the coming fight, as did all of Barclay's lieutenants; nothing brought on mass promotion for lieutenants quicker than participation in a successful fleet action.

The orders went out that sent men running to the falls, abandoning the upper deck cannons to loosen the ropes and swing round the yards, men called up from below to assist, for, short-handed, HMS *Semele* did not have the luxury of sailing and fighting without hands being required to perform double duty.

The prow came round slowly, for it was not a neat manoeuvre; in fact it was, Barclay thought, shoddy and would be observed as such from every other deck in the fleet. Out of the men who had come up from below, two were Charlie Taverner and Rufus Dommet, his face black and blue; never having seen an enemy fleet in the offing, it was hardly surprising that they were given to staring at such a wonderful if fearsome sight.

'Bosun mate, start those buggers,' Jackson called, which drew Barclay's attention to where he was pointing; that they were not alone in their reaction made no odds.

'Do you see who those two are, Your Honour?' growled Devenow in his ear.

With so much on his mind, not least that half a dozen

ships in the French fleet had seen him turn and were concentrating their fire on his ship, their sides suddenly billowing with smoke as they discharged their cannon, Barclay nearly shouted at his man to stay quiet; the next words from Devenow killed that.

'Two of John Pearce's Pelican sods, come aboard to do you mischief.'

The response to that was muted by the black cannonballs ripping into his hull, while above his head chain shot shredded the rigging; in the midst of a battle he could not concern himself with John Pearce or anything to do with him, yet it did delay his response to Jackson's request, made as the two identified were ordered below and back to their cannon.

'Permission to open the lower gun ports, sir.'

'No, Mr Jackson, every ounce of speed is vital and the guns cannot bear. Keep them closed until they can.'

CHAPTER TWENTY-TWO

HMS *Semele* shuddered from the long-range shot that hit her bow and ricocheted off her scantlings, yet everyone on the quarterdeck knew there was worse to come: case-shot, close-quarter cannon fire and musketry, though given the number of vessels seeking to halt her progress – in essence half the rear squadron of the enemy fleet – the fire was less than had been anticipated, certainly insufficient to impede her progress or deter the approach, and much of it was missing its target.

'Ragged gunnery, would you not say, Mr Jackson?' Barclay said with manufactured cheer. 'I fear our enemies have not worked up their gun crews enough in the time they have been at sea.'

The nod of agreement was quick enough, though it did leave unanswered the unspoken question in the mind of both men: HMS *Semele*'s gun crews were not much better trained and would show that as a fact when the time came to open fire. But Ralph Barclay was determined to adopt an air of insouciance he did not feel, to show a confidence in the outcome that went with his rank and the traditions of the service.

He put his mind to checking on all the other factors like ensuring the soldier-marines in his tops knew what to do, his hope that they would at least be better shots than most true lobsters, aided by the fact that their Brown Bess muskets were of the standard forty-two-inch barrel, more accurate than the shortened sea service pattern, albeit loading and aiming was difficult when surrounded by rigging.

'Captain Percival,' he called to their commanding officer, a pompous oaf to his mind who had bought his rank, not earned it as would a naval officer. 'Ensure your men play on the enemy gunners and the men who command their batteries, as well as the sharpshooters. The quarterdeck matters little and I do not want them seeking a braided trophy just so they can boast of the feat.'

'My men will do their duty, sir,' Percival responded, his tone arch if not actually insubordinate, 'as I order them.'

Barclay was happy to release some of his pent-up frustrations on a man for whom he had little regard, so he yelled back with no politesse at all. 'I want them, sir, to abide by my needs and those of my hands, as will you if you do not wish to face a court.'

'Well said, Your Honour,' Devenow murmured.

'What! Hold your tongue, man.'

'Aye, aye, Capt'n,' came the unabashed reply.

'Where is Gherson?' Barclay spat, looking around the quarterdeck.

'Cowering amongst the bilge, I shouldn't wonder, the lily-livered bugger.'

'He should be here, with me, on deck.'

That was not true. The quarterdeck of a ship engaged in battle was no place for a clerk, who would at best aid the surgeon, though even that was doubtful, but to Ralph Barclay it was only fitting that the supercilious swine should face the same risks as he. Gherson was, he knew, shy when it came to danger. He had lorded it over him in the business of getting those papers; now he could exact some revenge.

'Mr Jackson, send a mid to find Mr Gherson. I want him on deck with quill and paper. And we need to fetch a chair and board on which he can rest.'

'As you wish, sir,' the premier replied, surprised.

'If he shows reluctance, he is to be fetched up by force.'

'Well done, Your Honour.'

'Devenow, if you open your mouth again I will have you gagged.'

The mid, with two mates to the master-at-arms in tow, found Gherson in the sail locker, lying on the rolled-up canvas and looking pallid even though the battle was hardly joined. His response to Barclay's orders was a furious headshake that got him nowhere; clerks were not loved by the likes of midshipmen and warrants – too often they were denied things by such people and dismissed out of hand with it – so the mid, not yet fourteen years of age, had great pleasure in seeing him hauled out bodily and near carried up the companionway.

'Would you look at that, Charlie,' cried Rufus, who even in the dim lantern light could see the struggling Gherson by his fine blond hair; he could also hear him whimpering as he went by. 'They've collared Corny.'

'Happen they're going to chuck him in the briny,' Charlie yelled, pleased to see Gherson's head jerk in reaction.

'Belay that,' his divisional lieutenant, Mr Beresford, shouted. 'Attend to your duties.'

'Ain't got none, Your Honour,' Charlie replied softly, for Beresford was a good soul and tolerant. 'Not till them gun ports open up.'

Carried right up into the fresh air, Gherson was set down beside Ralph Barclay, who fixed him with a cold stare just as the ship was once more struck by half a dozen round shot.

'I may be in bad odour with the admiral, so I want this action clearly recalled and the best way to achieve that is to have you write down what you observe, when and as it happens.'

'Not much with 'is eyes shut,' Devenow jeered, which got him a hard look requiring a response. 'Beggin' your pardon, Your Honour.'

'My duty does not extend to that.'

Barclay's grin was like that of a wolf. 'Your duty, fellow, is what I say it is and, never fear, Gherson, I have already sent someone to fetch for you the means to pen your account. For your own sake make it both accurate and interesting.'

'We are gaining on *Queen Charlotte*, sir.'

That concentrated Ralph Barclay's mind, taking it away from spiteful revenge to the pressing needs of what was happening ahead. Newly refitted, with her clean copper bottom and being smaller than the massive three-decker, *Semele* was indeed overhauling the flagship at a fair rate, which tempted him to shorten sail – that was until he considered the quality, as well as the numbers, of his crew; it would not serve.

Howe's flag captain was obviously aiming to get across the stern of *Montagne* and really he knew he should be doing likewise with the *Jacobin*, the ship astern, but his head was falling off too much, besides which to be too close to the 100-gun flagship was to risk taking some of her fire when she opened up on both sides, as she would surely do; best leave a gap and another vessel between them to absorb any stray fire.

'I believe the enemy we should engage is *Achille*, sir,' Jackson said, when his opinion was canvassed, merely a courtesy of which both men were aware.

'Make it so, Mr Jackson. Put me across her stern.'

Time lost meaning and what noise had existed fell away as there came a pause in the level of the enemy gunnery; all that could be heard was the groaning of the working timbers, the wind whistling through the rigging and finally, when firing was resumed, the occasional thud as a ball struck the hull. That was until something aloft, a heavy block as well as half a spar, sliced from their lines by chain shot, fell to the deck and hit someone below, which produced cries of pain.

'Make sure the deck stays clear of men spilling blood, Mr Jackson.'

'Parties are already organised, sir, your own servants plus those from the wardroom.'

'Do 'em good,' Devenow spat, congenitally unable to stay silent.

'Why I do not send you to join them, I do not know,' Barclay sighed; but he did know.

The man in command of *Achille* soon sensed what was coming and set more sail, achieving a slightly increased speed, but attention was distracted by a cry from the masthead which focused attention on HMS *Defence*, the first British warship to breach the French line. Well ahead and beyond Howe's flagship, she was immediately engaged by at least two enemy vessels in a cascade of both gunfire and smoke.

'Sir, *Vengeur du Peuple* has increased speed as well,' the premier called.

Barclay replied, fixing his gaze on what was obviously the truth. 'God in heaven, the ridiculous names these Frenchmen give their vessels. She was originally the *Marseillois*, you know, which would have been fitting enough given their damned martial chant.'

Really that was said to give him time to think, for again he had a dilemma: if he could not, short-handed and with an inefficient crew, cut his speed to let *Queen Charlotte* lead the way through the enemy line, neither could he increase it to close more speedily.

What he was facing now was a set of very fine calculations; could he make the gap between the two Frenchmen and rake them head and stern? That would be deadly, certainly to *Achille*, with the flimsy deadlights covering her aft cabins offering scant protection to the open gun deck full of hundreds of men, along which any fired balls would travel and cause havoc.

'Hold our course, Mr Jackson, and let us see how it plays out.'

The closer HMS *Semele* got, the greater was the punishment to which she could not really reply, the same applying to *Queen Charlotte*. True, both were firing their bow chasers but these were mere pinpricks against the returned broadsides, even if they were badly aimed and coordinated. The topmast sails on both ships were full of holes, ropes hung loose that Barclay lacked the hands to send aloft to repair, and it was a miracle that nothing vital like a mast was carried away.

'Flag is through!'

The cry from the masthead took every eye on deck; *Queen Charlotte* split the enemy line and was immediately enveloped in the smoke of its own rolling broadside, which pounded to flinders both the deadlights of the *Montagne* to one side and the figurehead of *Jacobin* to the other, but the huge French three-decker, which had swung away to protect its vulnerable stern, took the most telling punishment.

She seemed to stagger as her hull was hit by some fifty cannonballs, including Howe's sixty-four-pounder carronades. Two more broadsides followed in the space of less than two minutes, with *Queen Charlotte* seeking to get to leeward, and immediately the French flagship began to fall away, obviously badly damaged, but no more attention could be gifted to that; Barclay had his own problems.

His attempt to head-reach the *Vengeur* was not going to work and again he was in trouble from an inability to quickly react by changing his sail plan, the trouble being *Semele* was committed, unless he wanted to range alongside with water in between and engage in a duel of equal versus equal.

This was not to him a promising prospect, with the chance that the French ships to the rear of *Vengeur* might manoeuvre to get onto his open side and trap him between twin broadsides. Suddenly he wanted all his hesitant confrères to do their duty to Howe's orders and damned quick.

It was like riding an unwilling horse, the way he sought, by bodily knee-jerks, to get that extra tenth of a knot that would put him in front of her bowsprit – that was until he realised it was not to be and gave an order to the helmsman to alter course slightly so they would meet bow on bow, calling to everyone to take a firm hold in the face of a coming collision.

This would not matter as long as he stayed clear of getting tangled and could manoeuvre by shaving her off her bowsprit. Once to leeward and having given her a dose of gunnery, he could take men off the cannons to increase sail if the rearmost Frenchman, the *Patriot*, showed signs of seeking to trap him. In the end he failed on both counts, neither getting to leeward of his enemy nor staying clear of him.

HMS *Semele* fouled the French 74's fished and catted anchor with her own foremast shrouds. This had the unfortunate effect of fixing his bow to that of *Vengeur*, which in turn swung his stern so that *Semele* crunched into her side, he standing no more than fifty feet from his opposite number on the enemy quarterdeck.

'Mr Jackson, get our gun ports open on the lower deck and fire as soon as they are.'

The shouts that followed sped down the companionway as the order to fire the upper deck cannon was obeyed; loaded with case they swept the enemy deck, killing and maiming dozens until the smoke obscured any more immediate observation. HMS *Semele*'s deck was likewise swept by enemy shot, two of the men on the wheel spinning away as it splintered in their hands, while Captain Percival was cut in half by a cannonball.

Ralph Barclay felt his own coat tugged and looked to see that the end of his empty sleeve was ragged where a case-shot ball had pierced it, and since his blood was up and he was now zealous for battle, that brought forth a huge cry meant to encourage his men.

'My God, a lost arm can be a gift, for it cannot be lost twice.'

That was followed by a more fractious request to enquire as to why the thirty-two-pounders beneath his feet were not firing, that answered above the din of gunfire by a stripling of a midshipman who popped is head up above deck level.

'We are too close to the enemy, sir, and cannot get the ports open.'

'Damn it, boy, tell the gunners to fire anyway, for if we do not the enemy surely will.'

Jackson, standing close to him, dropped like a stone as Barclay shouted that, a hole appearing in the very centre of his forehead, his hat flying off as he jerked backwards to splay on the deck, arms and legs outstretched. There was no doubting his condition.

'A message to the second lieutenant too, boy: he is to take over from the premier who is killed.'

There were bodies all over the quarterdeck and foredeck, but if *Semele* was being pounded the enemy was suffering more, for the main deck carronades had already removed the bulkheads opposite and were now firing huge balls across the open deck, seeking to blast the mainmast at its base.

The mid had disappeared with his message, running down to the dim red-painted main deck to deliver. The guns were already loaded and run right up to the ports, which only had to be hauled up, the problem being that they would not move more than six inches before they struck on the side of the enemy tumblehome, and heave as they might the gun crews could do no more.

The order to belay and fire regardless took a moment to sink in, but the crew on Davy's cannon, of which he was the captain, Charlie and Rufus included, leapt to the restraining tackles as he yelled they should do. Once they were set, feet splayed to restrain the recoil, he pulled the lanyard and set off the flint.

All along the deck the same thing was being acted out and the ports before them splintered and disintegrated as they were smashed by the great, solid, 32-pound rounds of iron. More gratifying was that those same balls, at such close range, demolished the scantlings on the *Vengeur du Peuple*, reducing the outer layer to matchwood and in a couple of cases exposing the carpenter's walk.

Even better, where they met an opposing gun port they went through the thinner wood with enough force to dismount the enemy cannon, evinced by the loud clanging and the screams which overbore the boom of blasted powder, though smoke made it impossible to see what bloody turmoil had been inflicted.

No one was considering those things on the *Semele* gun deck; they were too busy reloading. The recoil had taken the guns back to where the muzzles could be got at and new charges, wads and balls were being rammed home, new quills being fitted to the touch holes and broken to allow the firing powder to dribble through.

The gun captains were ready, and before the French realised what had just befallen them, before they had taken in their smashed guns, the broken scantlings and the bodies that littered the red-painted deck, they took a second, even more deadly broadside, which was sent through the already shattered sides.

'Depress your cannon,' came the order from Beresford in the infinitesimal lull, as more shot was loaded.

It was not easy to hear that command, given the roar of the guns, despite their covered ears, made men deaf. But it was obeyed, even as the third round was being rammed home, the wedges at the pommel bases being hammered in hard so that the muzzles pointed downwards as far as was possible, then the cannon were run up to fire.

Now the great balls tore through already shattered wood to smash into the gun deck planking on the French ship – thick boards on which to walk, but too flimsy to retard heavy shot. That it devastated them and went on to hull the ship below the waterline was only one part of the damage; the splinters created did terrible execution to the enemy gunners as, like swords and spears, they flew in a dozen directions to kill and maim.

'Reload.'

'What does Berry-boy think we're about?' gasped Rufus as he hauled on the relieving tackle.

'Sunday in the park,' Charlie replied, his voice equally hoarse.

If he was good-humoured, that evaporated as the cannon next to theirs was struck on the muzzle, the clang of contact ten times noisier than the blast of powder and balls. The men working the gun were blown away in a bloody mass of flesh and bone, the cannon, its relieving tackles shredding, rearing up like a proud stallion to topple over as the ropes parted under the massive strain.

'Secure that damned cannon!' Beresford shouted.

That was a priority; a loose cannon on a deck heaving on the swell was deadly to all. Ropes were slung by those who knew the drill and hung on to for dear life by those who did not. It was Charlie Taverner who got a whip round the muzzle, Rufus the more nimble who, with dancing steps, secured the pommel end, both men lashing off to the first fixed point that came to hand, carried out under the frightened gaze of an officer who would have been maimed in both legs had they not succeeded.

'I'll stand you a drink in Pompey, lads, for that,' Beresford cried.

'And will be held to it, Your Honour,' Charlie called cheerfully, moving back to his own cannon, which had been run out and fired with reduced numbers.

The quarterdeck was now like a charnel house, with bodies everywhere and bloodstains where the fallen had been removed. Still Devenow stood by his captain, unflinching, this while Gherson cowered as best he could behind anything that would afford him protection. In the end, both captain and bully-boy took their wounds at the same time, Barclay a ball in the soft part of his thigh, Devenow spinning away as, seeking to protect his master, another took his shoulder.

'Gherson, to me and hold me up,' Barclay yelled, before pointing to the now kneeling Devenow and calling to the great cabin servants, 'and get my man below!'

When his clerk did not obey he screamed at him that he would have him shot this instant if he cowered any more. To watch Gherson crabbing across to his employer would have been enough to make those facing death with equanimity – and Ralph Barclay was one of them – cringe, if they had not been too busy.

The quarterdeck of *Vengeur* was devoid of human occupation now. The wheel had shattered and the mizzenmast had gone by the board, hanging over the side and by its weight dragging both engaged ships out of a French line that had become jumbled rather than formed in any true order.

Montagne had fallen away south to a point where it could raise flag and act as a rally for the shattered French fleet, and the gun deck of *Vengeur*, pounded by broadside after depressed broadside, was being reduced to matchwood; it was also obvious that she had been badly hulled – she was taking on water as she began to settle.

'In the name of Christ,' called Barclay, actually leaning on Gherson's crouched back. 'Somebody get aboard that damned ship with axes and cut us free.'

'Stand by to board,' shouted Lieutenant Beresford, third at the opening of the action, premier now.

When the order was relayed, men left their guns below to become fiercely armed boarders, taking from the tubs the swords and axes they needed, rushing to the upper deck and running in screaming mobs to the side, there to leap over the hammock nettings and splintered bulwarks on to the enemy deck to continue the slaughter.

That the tricolour was cut away within minutes came as no surprise, though with continued fighting it was moot who had sliced the line, a Frenchman or a Briton. But it was clear to Ralph Barclay that the enemy ship was getting lower in the water by a foot at a time, evidence of serious damage below.

'Sir, you are bleeding copiously,' said Lieutenant Beresford. 'I must insist you go to the surgeon.'

'Insist, sir!'

'As is my duty, Captain. It will not aid us if you bleed to death.'

'Take possession of *Vengeur*, Mr Beresford,' Barclay said, finally, 'and save her if you can.'

Then the captain of HMS *Semele* passed out.

On the deck of *Vengeur du Peuple* the crew were surrendering or running below to seek safety, leaving Charlie Taverner and Rufus Dommet amongst others, chests heaving, rejoicing in victory.

'Christ, Rufus,' Charlie gasped, 'we'd want Pearce and O'Hagan here for this, would we not?'

Unbeknown to John Pearce, the fickle gods were in a foul mood as far as he was concerned; a man he had never heard of, Admiral Sir Berkley Sumner, had received his reply from Sir Phillip Stephens, finding himself astounded that not only was he again denied appointment, but that the Admiralty was not intending to take immediate and strong action against some poltroon and probable fraudster sullying the good name of the service.

There and then he decided it was necessary for him to act: he would go personally to Lymington and beard this damned impostor, taking with him his horsewhip as well, and he would be damn sure to let their lordships know of what he had done to protect the good name of the King's Navy, which would also make them aware that he was not past being of use.

Alderman Denby Carruthers had no trouble at all in finding out the whereabouts of a Lieutenant John Pearce, the information came back to him within a couple of days. Druce, his brother-in-law, used the same St James's gentleman's club as Henry Dundas, so it was not difficult to glean that the fellow was on active service having sailed from Buckler's Hard, a place to which he would return quite soon, certainly within the month, with the obvious caveat that nothing was certain when it came to time, survival, ships and the sea.

The only thing that perplexed the alderman, apart, that is, from the continuing strange behaviour of his wife and the increasing unreliability of his clerk Lavery, was that the Tollands, bad-tempered Jahleel and the seemingly more sensible Franklin, when told of this, immediately put any notion of their forthcoming partnership on hold; they were, it seems, off to the New Forest to find their man.

To a fellow dedicated to the making of money, if you excepted the need to revenge himself on Cornelius Gherson and deal with the ongoing problem of Codge and his blackmail, it seemed absurd to delay the accrual of profit in the pursuit of a personal vendetta. There again, he knew nothing of this Lieutenant Pearce or the cause of the feud.

CHAPTER TWENTY-THREE

John Pearce and Michael O'Hagan, in the company of their hosts, had spent two whole days looking at the various French outworks that formed an arc round the coastal region, each replete with a tented company of infantry, a pair of cannon, stabling for horses close to some building of note, a manor house or a large still-intact church, which, judging by the flying tricolours, acted as the local headquarters.

From each rose the smoke of numerous fires, to pine-scent the air, but not much in the way of activity, creating the impression that the generals of the revolutionary army had decided upon containment rather than aggressive suppression of the remains of revolt; Pearce had already been informed that the main task of the men occupying these encampments was in feeding themselves.

This being an activity which bore down heavily on the local farmers and peasants – the major landowners had all fled or were in hiding – it thus cemented their support for the revolt, because when they were paid at all for what was taken, and that was rare, it was at best with promissory notes or the worthless revolutionary assignats that served as currency in France.

The sweep of this extensive reconnaissance had been from south to north, starting out at near first light and lasting the length of each day. Pearce was, finally, bleary-eyed and weary, examining, as he had been for two hours, a more substantial redoubt backed up by proper barracks. There was also an open field on which, to the sound of trumpets and shouting, he had observed men drilling, as well as cavalry horses being put through their paces.

This was an army camp containing men in their several hundreds, possibly even thousands, and the reason for its size and importance lay far to the rear in the city of Nantes. France's premier port sat well inland on the broad River Loire which, being navigable to small sailing boats and barges, was the gateway to the interior.

For the two days they had been so engaged in this reconnaissance he had listened to every one of his hosts expound the same theory, and that continued as they made their ways back to the marshland hideaway: the capture of Nantes, with their aid, would be a worthy objective for any major incursion by the forces of Great Britain, though they were less forthcoming about their failure the previous year to achieve that very thing.

Puisaye and his ilk were sure that a token force of ships and soldiers could secure the well-guarded and powerful forts at the Loire estuary, which would open the river up to the Royal Navy – not the capital warships, which drew too much water, but certainly to powerful frigates. An army could then be safely landed to advance on Nantes itself, and with local aid succeed where the Vendée rebellion had failed.

'Achieve that, Lieutenant, and the Revolution will crumble.'

Willing to admit to himself he was no military expert either on land or at sea, John Pearce knew oversimplification when he heard it. What was suggested required a huge force of warships and hundreds of transports to sail down the Channel and get past the main French naval base at Brest without interference.

That being unlikely, they would then have to enter one of the most unreliable stretches of water in the world, the Bay of Biscay, while fighting, and land sufficient troops to take, in conjunction with the navy, the estuary forts, before proceeding up the tideway – both on foot and afloat, he surmised – while fighting a desperate enemy all the way, to invest a major city which had, he had got them to admit, stout walls.

'I know what I propose appears arduous, but it is not impossible.'

'Monsieur,' Pearce responded, determined to pour a douche of cold water on this enthusiasm, 'given the importance of Nantes, and the many wars Britain has fought with France, surely my government has considered this before?'

'And discarded any such plan as doomed to failure,' Puisaye responded, almost with glee.

'Yes.'

'There is one crucial difference, Lieutenant,' the count

cried, finger raised, eyes flashing once more as he leant out of his saddle to make his point. 'They will be able to land unopposed, for if we own little, we do hold a coast of many beaches. Once ashore and with our aid, they will help us trigger an uprising that will drown the ungodly in their own blood.'

After two days of travel, three for Pearce and Michael, everyone was weary and perhaps it was that which led to a degree of complacency. If Pearce had thought about it – and he had not, as had become habit of late – and put himself in the shoes of those these rebels were fighting, he would have reasoned that an active commander who knew what awaited him in the swamps and marshes might contrive a few tricks of his own.

That they had an old Indian fighter with them probably saved them from certain death; he was a man who knew which birds should be in the sky and which animals should be disturbed by passing horsemen and it was the lack of those signs which first alerted them to possible danger. His signal to halt, added to the look with which he peered ahead as they approached a deep stretch of woodland they intended to enter, must have told those waiting that to continue doing so was useless.

The musket fire was thankfully at near extreme range and none of those firing them seemed to be the kind of marksmen who kept their own barrels and made their own balls to fit. Nevertheless they got the prelate, perhaps because his canonical staff, raised to catch the sunlight, acted as a good target.

He took two musket balls, which had Pearce cursing

himself for a terrible thought, thinking he was a typically greedy priest even in death, that as he spurred his pony into a canter, shouting to Michael to do likewise. The Irishman was not listening; he had seen the muzzle flashes and lowered his own musket to reply, with Pearce, looking over his shoulder, trying to mentally calculate the reloading process taking place with those who had sprung the ambush.

O'Hagan fired and very sensibly flung himself to the ground, keeping hold of his bridle and beginning to run, dragging his frightened animal along with him but heading toward the gunfire, not away. Pearce, having hauled on his own reins, fired his pistol in the general direction of the enemy for no other purpose than to keep a head or two down, this while all around him the party of which he was a member scattered and split.

Puisaye, no fool, was riding hard for a fold in the ground to their right, gesturing that he should be followed, unaware that his opponent had worked that out as the place of refuge. The four men who stood and fired should have waited, for if they had, every man they sought to kill would have fallen victim, but excitement got the better of them and they stood to loose off a volley when those heading towards them had time to veer away and spoil their aim.

Pearce was shouting and gesturing that they should go back the way they came as the only safe course of action, only obliged because there was no alternative. Crouched over their withers, the party raced for the last set of trees from which they had exited, there to reform and seek to sort out an avenue of escape, passing as they did so the crumpled body of the bishop, staring glassy-eyed at the heaven he was so sure he was bound for.

They were out of range before they reached safety, in the trees, all telling each other the same thing, to get behind some cover, dismount and reload their weapons in a cacophony of unnecessary advice. Pearce was kneeling, reloading his pistol, which done allowed him to look for Michael, only then realising, after several unanswered shouts, he was not present.

'Do not worry, Lieutenant,' Puisaye gasped. 'We can go round this. They do not know the terrain as we do.'

'How did they know which way we would be coming?' Pearce asked, searching the land ahead for a sign of Michael.

'A coincidence, no more.'

'Not that someone has perhaps betrayed you?'

'If they have,' Puisaye snapped, 'they will burn in hell.'

'Like your bishop out there, perhaps?' That got a sour look, as if it was not only unbecoming, but also impious to speak so of the dead.

'We must move.'

'Not without I know what has happened to my friend.'

'Servant?' Puisaye said, confused, which got him the same kind of glare as he had just handed out.

'We cannot stay here, Lieutenant, this is the territory of the enemy and if we are held up we will be trapped. Please believe me that is not a situation you would wish to happen to you. Death is certain and it will be painful.'

The man in loose buckskins was beside Puisaye now, whispering in his ear, yet his narrow eyes, surrounded by many wrinkles, were on Pearce as if he did not trust him to overhear, he supposing that once the man had fought in the great forest of America against Britannia, there was no way of being at peace with anyone who represented them.

The flash of lighter colour above the long grass caught Pearce's eye, as two blue-coated men with muskets inched out of the treeline ahead, muskets at the ready, at which point Michael stood up from the hummock which had kept him hidden, hands raised.

'It would be best he had died,' Puisaye said, when Pearce drew his attention.

'Monsieur,' Pearce said, making a point of looking at the French Indian fighter's long musket, a weapon of some repute that had proved deadly in the hand of the colonials who had kicked out King George's armies. 'Are those men in range for you?'

The fellow looked at Puisaye, and Pearce saw the back of his head move as he nodded, which got a sharp response. The fellow moved to the very edge of the wood, kneeling and aiming carefully, his nose twitching as if he was actually smelling the wind. Then he waited, with Pearce having to contain deep frustration as he took time to pull on the trigger. The two French soldiers were close to Michael now and they were shouting, he with his hands still raised.

The crack of the single shot sent what birds had settled flapping and screeching into the air again, and in a blink one of the men approaching Michael spun away, having taken the ball. Out of the corner of his eye Pearce saw the shooter was moving with speedy grace to reload, not flustered, but with the ease of long practice, powder poured, ball out and in the muzzle, the rammer flicking twice, the powder horn now in the teeth ready to prime the cap.

More important, the second French soldier had become like a statue, his eyes, even at a distance, so clearly opening in shock, while his mate writhed at his feet. The clout Michael gave him sent him about ten feet and then the Irishman was running. The man in command, the officer who had sprung the trap, emerged from the trees to shout that his men should shoot at the fleeing Michael, who was dodging from side to side and stumbling as much as moving forward.

The long rifle was up again, aimed with repeated care, and when the trigger was slowly squeezed it was at that haranguing officer. Where it hit him no one could tell but the shooter, but the man stood still as if surprised for several seconds, then slowly crumpled to the ground. No one was shooting at Michael O'Hagan now and the second soldier who had come to arrest him was heading for his own trees at a rush.

'I think we might be able to move forward soon,' Pearce said softly.

That proved to be the case, those before them melting away without anyone to lead them. They collected the prelate's body for burial and as a bonus found Michael's pony grazing happily in another clearing, which was a double relief since the bishop's horse was gone and he was a burden to carry. The frontier fellow seemed mollified when he found out the man he had saved was Irish, not English, and their stilted exchange allowed Pearce to consider what he was going to do next.

He was not so vain as to think his appreciation would be enough to persuade Pitt and Dundas to send an expedition to the Vendée, nor was he sure that such a policy would be wise. Puisaye and his friends had taken care to show him what they wanted him to see, but that ambush had underlined that they were not wholly in control of what they claimed. In the end the solution seemed obvious.

'Monsieur,' he said to the Count de Puisaye, 'someone must return with me to England and seek to make your case.'

Expecting him to demur, the alacrity with which he agreed had Pearce wondering if that had been his hope all along; for a man of refinement, which he was, being locked up in a swamp could not be a life of choice, and given there was nothing more to see and the *Larcher* was waiting, it was agreed they would depart at first light. The next problem for Pearce was Amélie Labordière.

'I will beg if you wish me to, Jean?'

Much as he sought for a reason to say no, he could not think of one that would not make him feel like a scrub. He had a ship, she had a need and his only reservation was what would become of her when she landed in England, for she would be penniless. He had no choice but to say yes, though he did wonder as they made their ways to Noirmoutier to find HMS *Larcher* where he had left her, safely anchored in the bay.

They weighed as soon as the passengers were aboard, with John Pearce wondering what Emily Barclay would say when he turned up in England with an ex-mistress for whom he knew he was going to feel responsible. That was not a feeling that diminished much over the next few days of sailing, in heavy weather that made both his French passengers, who occupied his cabin, sick. Such distress at least saved him from anything other than minimal contact with Amélie, who in truth he feared to be alone with.

He had concerns over money, a future to construct in which he and Emily could live as a couple, no real career unless he bowed to the constraints of naval service and still three friends – his fellow Pelicans Michael, Charlie and Rufus – to whom he felt a debt.

Nor did his worries ease when he sighted the Lizard at last and Dorling set a course for the Solent and Buckler's Hard, having heard from a passing coastal merchantman of Howe's great victory on the first of June, which was being hailed from any vessel that sighted another, the capture of several line-of-battle ships, the damage to many more and the sinking of the 74-gun *Vengeur du Peuple*.

That promised a happy return to a country ecstatic in celebration, for nothing cheered Britannia like a proper naval victory. Perhaps, for all his unease, John Pearce would benefit from that euphoria and find waiting for him a woman not only happy that he was home again, but so full of love and understanding that she would accept Amélie Labordière as a charge on her charity as well as his.

Never one to be downhearted for too long, John Pearce worked hard to convince himself that would be the case, and such was his nature that by the time HMS *Larcher* cleared the Needles he was sure that what he was heading for was, if not unbounded happiness, something very close to that estate.

AUTHOR'S NOTE

For those readers who know about the Battle of the Glorious First of June, you will recognise that my fictitious 74-gun warship, HMS *Semele,* replicates very closely the actions of HMS *Brunswick* in both engaging and sinking *Vengeur du Peuple.*

So close was that action that the real captain involved, John Harvey, was killed along with forty-five of his crew, over a hundred being wounded. In using that and placing Ralph Barclay in place of Harvey, I have no intention of diminishing that gallant officer's behaviour or any action that he took over the three days of contact with the French fleet.

If you enjoyed *Enemies at Every Turn*,
look out for the next book in
the John Pearce series . . .

To discover more great fiction and to
place an order visit our website at
www.allisonandbusby.com
or call us on
020 7580 1080